The DECEPTION

FILTHY RICH AMERICANS | BOOK THREE

NIKKI SLOANE

Cyclops Edition

ISBN 978-1-949409-05-5

For Nick

PROLOGUE

As the glass elevator carried us up, Boston spread out before me in a tangled, weaving mess. The city hadn't been planned, and the narrow roads were laid atop horse trails from the seventeenth century. Snarling lines of concrete were wedged between skyscrapers. Traffic was a nightmare.

I felt a similar kind of chaos as my gaze focused on him.

He wore a black suit and a black tie dotted with silver specks. To everyone else, he'd look powerful and confident, but I saw through it, down to the uncertainty that lingered behind his blue eyes. It was unnerving to see him like this. I'd known him my whole life and only witnessed it a few times.

Breath seized in my lungs as his hand curled around mine and wove our fingers together. We were alone in the executive elevator, but the glass walls left me feeling exposed. Like anyone could see us. I wasn't supposed to be here.

The pad of his thumb brushed absentmindedly over the set of rings on my left hand, and it forced the words from my mouth, coming out like I'd discovered a great secret. "You're nervous."

He delivered a cool, irritated look. "Of course not. Why would you say that?"

I glanced down at our joined hands and back to him, wordlessly presenting his behavior as evidence. Currently, I didn't work at Hale Banking and Holding, and even if I did, displays of affection had no place here at the office, out where anyone could see.

He raised an eyebrow. "I wanted an excuse to touch you before the meeting."

It was a lie, but I didn't call him out on it because he had good reason to be nervous. He was about to walk into the most important board meeting of his life. A decision had to be made, and it would settle once and for all what had been in the works for years.

I didn't know which Hale was going to come out on top.

He didn't either, judging by his unsteady tone. "He doesn't have the votes."

There was too much anxiety in me to offer a response. It was like I'd swallowed broken glass and the shards jangled together in my stomach with each shallow breath I took. Everything had led up to this moment. Once the elevator stopped and the doors opened, things were going to get much harder.

My gaze flicked to the panel of buttons, and my nerves made my finger itch to reach out and press one—any floor below the one that was already illuminated.

He must have sensed my trepidation because his grip on me tightened. If he'd meant to reassure me, he failed. My pulse climbed higher with each floor we passed, and my heart ground to a halt the same moment the elevator did. He dropped my hand and stepped away from me, putting a professional amount of distance between us.

"Thank you for coming with me," he said in the quiet before the doors peeled back with a mechanical whine.

Like I had a choice.

I sucked in a deep breath, both wanting and dreading the next part.

He gestured through the now open doors. "After you."

My knees wobbled beneath my skirt, but I held my head up and fixed an indifferent expression on my face as I stepped into the hallway. I was Marist Hale on the outside, the perfect goddess, ready to rule alongside the other Olympians. And inside, I was the monster Medusa, preparing to take my victims.

I'd only made it a few steps before my husband turned a corner and spotted me in the hallway.

"Marist?" Royce's questioning look shifted from me to the man at my side.

As my husband's gaze crawled upward, his eyes widened, and the distance between us filled with ice. Darkness overtook his expression, and he turned to stone.

Gone was the unease that had plagued Macalister in the elevator moments ago. In the hallway, he was as comfortable as a general heading into a battle with twice as many men as his opponent. Bright, cruel victory flashed in his eyes.

I was the secret weapon he'd just deployed against his son, and a sinister smile spread across his lips.

ONE

Eight Months Ago

My heart thudded erratically in my chest like it had been placed inside a box and kicked down the grand staircase I was hanging on to. My fingers dug into the carpeted step, desperate not to fall, even as gravity seemed determined to pull me away.

Only it wasn't gravity. The unstoppable force working to rip me from the stairs was solid and cold and named Macalister Hale.

The Minotaur.

I feebly tried to push his hands away, but whatever Alice had done left me crippled and powerless.

"No," I whisper-sobbed when icy hands slid under my body and began to collect me. He blurred again into an indistinguishable shape as he sat on the steps and pulled my shoulders across his lap.

I did not want to die in Macalister's arms, and certainly not moments after mistakenly telling him I loved him.

But I couldn't convey anything, couldn't organize my

thoughts. They sifted through the holes Alice's drug had created in my mind, disappearing forever. The only thing I could hold on to was my fear. Not that I was dying, even though I was certain I was, but that I'd never truly know how Royce felt about me.

Had his declaration of love just been for show? A lie told as he played his role as the prince of Cape Hill?

"Marist." When a cool fingertip gently brushed a lock of hair back out of my eyes, it added to my horrible disorientation. Macalister's voice was uneven. Nervous. "What's wrong? What's happened?"

The light from the chandelier in the entryway was growing darker with every slow blink, and the hideous halos around it stretched longer. I was running out of time, and my brain was shutting down.

"Hera," I croaked.

The body beneath me tensed.

Zeus's wife Hera was beautiful, but she didn't have any redeeming qualities. She was jealous and vengeful and cruel toward her husband's lovers. Even if Macalister didn't understand my deeper meaning, he'd still know who I was talking about. The Hale family had dressed tonight for the masquerade party in a Greek mythology theme, and Alice had gone as Hera. The queen of the gods of Mount Olympus.

He would understand, though. He'd insisted on reading nearly every book on mythology I owned.

"What did Alice do to you?" His voice was quiet horror, but it still boomed down the stairs.

"Poison," I whispered. "Dying."

A pained grunt slipped from my lips as Macalister stood, shooting to his feet and carrying me up with him. The ache in my stomach was sharper and more violent, and I had no choice but to cling to the fabric of his tuxedo jacket. His first step down the stairs made my nausea increase ten-fold.

"*What the fuck?*"

It came from far away, across the room in a very angry, very male voice.

I tried to see him, but it was a hazy blot of white on black at the entryway. Instead, I had to picture Royce staring up at us. Me draped in his father's arms, the train of my green Medusa dress dragging over the red carpeted stairs as I was swiftly carried down them. His father descended the staircase like I weighed nothing.

Macalister ignored his son's furious tone, and once he'd reached the main floor, his shoes clapped out a loud, biting rhythm. It was a song of urgency as he stormed toward the door, and his voice was nearly as quick as his feet. "Is your driver still out front?"

"What?" Irritation simmered in Royce's words. "Put her down."

Macalister wouldn't be deterred, not even when his son stepped in the way, blocking the exit. It brought him to a jerking halt, and he spat it at Royce. "*Move.*"

It was clear there would be dire consequences if he didn't obey, but Royce didn't understand something was wrong with me. All he saw was his fiancée cradled in his adversary's arms, and tonight he was Ares, the god of war. "Fuck you. Get your hands off her."

"I'm taking her to the hospital, because she's dying. Get out of my way."

I was close enough now I could mostly make him out, and Macalister's statement went through him like a bolt of Zeus's lightning. It froze Royce in place, which meant he was still blocking the exit. "What?"

Macalister's grip was iron, but still I worried I was going to fall as I took one hand off and reached out for my fiancé. "Royce," I whispered.

The second my fingertips found the smooth skin over his cheekbone, it spurred him into action, and we were moving again. It was darker, and wind ruffled through my hair, signaling we were outside, but it was nearly impossible to keep my eyes open. I was sluggish, and everything took too much energy to do.

Thinking.

Breathing.

My heart to continue beating.

Down the steps we flew, my body jostling in Macalister's arms. The sound of a car door opening rang out, followed by warm hands on my shoulders. Royce's. Both men worked together to load me into the back seat of the town car until I was stretched across their laps.

For once, getting the two Hales to become a team was easy. All I had to do was die.

A door slammed shut, sealing us in the dark, cramped space.

"Port Cove hospital," Royce yelled at the driver. "As fast as you fucking can."

The force of the car peeling out drove me against the two pairs of legs I was lying on top of. At least the bulk of my body was resting on the center of the seat. Royce's arms circled around my shoulders as my legs draped over his father's.

"What happened?" It wasn't clear who my fiancé's question was directed at.

"She said she was poisoned. Call the hospital and explain we're on our way."

There was something cold resting on my ankle, and at that moment I realized what it was. Macalister's hand. He hadn't stopped touching me since he'd found me on the stairs, like he was afraid if the connection were severed, he'd lose me forever.

I was shifted gingerly in Royce's embrace as he pulled out his phone, but then his father was speaking, making a call of his own.

"Nigel," Macalister said, "have Sutton or one of his men meet you at the house. Alice is not to leave the premises. In fact, I'd prefer she stay in her room until I return. No one speaks with her until I have."

There was no conversation. He'd issued his orders and expected his assistant to execute them without question, the phone call ending as abruptly as it had begun. The cold hand wrapped around my ankle felt like a manacle, but I was too weak to do anything about it.

Shock and disbelief weighed down Royce's words. "Alice . . . did this?"

"Yes."

Macalister could have said I'd accused her. That it hadn't

been proven yet, but his resolute tone left no room for doubt. He didn't just take my word—he absolutely believed his wife was capable of murder. If I'd had any energy left, I would have shivered.

The car careened through a corner, and tires wailed against the asphalt.

Royce was still on the phone with the emergency room when I jerked with new panic. Turmoil bubbled in my stomach, and I struggled to escape his arms, only to have him drop the phone and clamp down his hold. My only option now was to turn my head away from him as my stomach erupted.

I made a horrible retching sound while the drugged tea and champagne from earlier tonight spilled from my mouth, narrowly avoiding his legs. Royce let out a sound of surprise, but he didn't let go of me.

"Oh, Jesus, Marist," he whispered. He stroked a hand over my hair, helping to hold it out of the way. "It's going to be all right."

I might have believed him if he wasn't trembling when he said it, but I took comfort anyway. It was strangely satisfying to feel him coming unglued. He was a great actor, but this moment was too real, too unscripted to be pretend. Maybe he loved me or maybe he didn't, but at least he cared about me.

That was undeniable.

The upside to throwing up was it temporarily cut through my nausea. I used the back of my hand to wipe my lips and swallowed the acidic taste from my mouth as best I could, then focused.

"She gave me tea," I said. Was there still any left in the

teapot in the kitchen? Maybe they could test it and figure out what she'd used to drug me. I tried to think back, but time bled together, and I wasn't sure how much longer I'd be lucid or conscious. I peered up at the prince I'd once hated and now loved, seeing flashes of his chaotic eyes as the highway lights streaked past. "Royce." My throat was burned raw, but I pushed through. "Tell me you love me. Again."

The cold hand on my ankle tensed, reminding me we weren't alone, but I didn't care. The night of the initiation, Macalister had told me during our waltz his son wasn't capable of love.

Maybe it was true, but I wanted him to at least believe he'd been wrong.

And I wanted to *prove* him wrong.

I didn't get to hear if he responded. Perhaps with a little more time I could have, but it slipped through my grasp. It poured faster than the red sand had through the hourglass in the flickering candlelight of the dining room months ago. When the sand ran out now, everything slowed to a stop, including my heart.

The hallucinations were the worst part. One moment I'd be convinced everything was real, and in the next, reality would evaporate. I couldn't trust anything. For a while, I was sure the drugs flowing into my veins from the IV weren't saving me, they were just prolonging the inevitable, and Royce had to stop me when I tried to unhook myself.

It had been hours since that dark moment, and the delusions were finally tapering off.

Once again, Macalister and Royce were in total agreement about my care, and as soon as I was stabilized, my transfer to Mass General was cleared. I wasn't sure which of the Hale men the staff at Port Cove Hospital were happier to be rid of. Macalister's tone was the sharp sting of ice, but Royce was fire and fury, and no answer the medical team gave either of the men was ever good enough.

The helicopter flight to Boston's premiere hospital was terrifying. I was sure at any moment the rotating blades overhead were going to stop turning and we'd fall from the sky. At least it'd be fitting that the first time I rode on the Hale's helicopter, I'd bring it down.

It seemed everything I touched in this new world came undone.

The seats had the HBHC logo embroidered in the leather, and I sat slumped in the back bench, my throbbing head resting on Royce's shoulder. Across from us in the rear-facing captain chairs sat Macalister and his personal physician, who'd come along to monitor me during the short flight. However, he'd been on the phone since we boarded, on hold with the lab to hear the results of the toxicology report.

As his private helicopter cut through the night, Macalister's gaze never wavered from me. I was the opposite. My focus flitted away. I was barely able to look at him or the emotions teeming in his eyes. It was *unnerving*.

He stared at me with both concern and heavy longing.

And he glared with outright jealousy at the man at my

side. Macalister didn't bother to hide that he wished to be the one I was leaning on. He wanted to trade places with his son.

The thought made me shiver.

Royce's lips pressed against my forehead the moment before he whispered, "Still cold?"

He didn't wait for my answer. His arm pulled me tighter against him, and I was grateful. Not only for his warmth, but for the display. It reminded his father who I belonged to.

Not you.

He may have been the one to find me collapsed on the stairs, but he hadn't rescued me. He was just the first one home, two minutes ahead of the son he refused to share a car with after they'd left the impromptu board meeting. Macalister wasn't the hero. He was indirectly responsible for how I'd ended up on the staircase.

I was cold, though.

My beautiful green dress had been left behind at the hospital, so all I had on was a thin hospital gown beneath Royce's tuxedo jacket, and a throw blanket pulled from one of the cabin compartments.

I'd been hot earlier, but being confined in this small space meant Macalister's ice could get to me faster. It grew worse when he undid his seatbelt and tugged off his own tuxedo jacket.

"No, that's—" I said, but it didn't matter.

The patriarch of the Hale family was on his feet, stooping so his head wouldn't hit the ceiling, and draped his open jacket over me. Had he done it so he didn't have to see Royce's arm around me? Or was it simply a power move? I wouldn't accept the gesture as an attempt to be nice. It had an agenda. Everything Macalister did was calculated.

"Yes, I'm here," the doctor said into his phone.

As he listened to the person on the other end of the line, I evaluated the man seated across from Royce. The doctor was exactly what I would have expected. Older and seasoned looking, with smart eyes and a serious demeanor.

"Has the patient's care team at Mass General been informed already?" He paused. "Very good. Thanks for letting me know." The doctor tapped his phone screen and lowered it into his lap. "We have a positive result for glycoside. Further testing will tell us which type." He spoke directly to Macalister, as if he needed to have the information, and not me. "I haven't been out to the house recently, but your gardens are extensive. Do you have any foxglove or lily of the valley flowers growing in them? Lily of the valley is white, bell-shaped—"

"I know what they look like," I said. "The florist wants to use them in our wedding." My stomach twisted horribly. They were the flowers Alice had picked out. A vision of her in her Hera mask sliced through my mind before my gaze flicked unavoidably to Macalister. "And Alice grows them in the garden closest to the house."

My tone was full of accusation, but there was no reaction in his steely blue eyes.

The doctor focused on me. "They're safe to handle but can be quite toxic if ingested. Anything made from its leaves will give you a high dose of convallatoxin, which is what caused your cardiac arrhythmia, but we've got that under control now. With the toxin identified, your doctors can get it flushed out of your system and you could be recovered as quickly as a few days."

"Mr. Hale," the pilot's disembodied voice came through the cabin speaker, "we'll be landing in ninety seconds."

The doctor slipped his phone into his slacks and subtly tightened the belt across his lap as the helicopter began its quick descent. "Although death is extremely rare from lily of the valley poisoning, you're a lucky woman, Marist."

If I wasn't so miserable, I might have laughed. I'd been poisoned by my future stepmother-in-law, and with Macalister's relentless gaze on me, I felt anything but lucky.

I'd barely been settled into the enormous private suite before Macalister's sharp order punched through the air, disrupting the quiet. "Clear the room."

The nurse, who'd been writing her name on the dry-erase board, froze mid-scribble. "I'm sorry?"

It carried the same weight as if he'd told her to fuck off. "*Out.*"

She stiffened, capped her marker, and set it on the rest before hustling from the room.

He turned his sneering expression toward his son, who sat in the chair closest to my bedside. "That includes you, Royce."

The sun had begun to rise outside, painfully reminding me we'd been up all night. I was as exhausted as Philippides after he'd run the fabled twenty-six miles from Marathon to

Athens to declare victory. My fiancé likely felt the same, judging by his heavy, red-rimmed eyes. His bowtie was undone, as were the top buttons of his white dress shirt, and his hair was ruffled from hands he'd raked through it countless times.

It did nothing to diminish his attractiveness.

As he rose deliberately to his feet, his exhaustion faded, and Ares came out, preparing for battle. He clasped a hand on my bedrail, not for support, but to assume a defiant stance. It communicated he wasn't going anywhere, and my gaze couldn't help but trace his long fingers or the muscles twisting along his forearm and disappearing beneath his rolled-back sleeve.

Jesus. He should have been an artist instead of a banker, because he had such beautiful hands.

"If anyone's leaving," Royce's tone hinted he was barely restraining his fury, "it's you."

Macalister lifted his chin like Royce had taken a swing at him and just missed landing the blow. His eyes were shrewd. "Marist and I need to discuss a personal matter."

He spoke so professionally, but my heart thudded inside my body, searching for ways to escape. The personal matter had to be what I'd mistakenly said on the stairs. I despised how weak I sounded, but I was frayed to the point of breaking. "No. Royce stays, and we have nothing to discuss."

How things had changed. When I'd first moved into the Hale house, Royce had been the enemy, and I had eagerly withheld information as he'd done to me. I'd cut him out and gone to Macalister alone. But nearly dying had given me a new perspective, and I knew who the real enemy was now.

I drew in a deep breath. "What I said when you found me—"

"I'm not interested in that at this time." Macalister waved his hand, brushing my statement aside. "The more pressing issue is Alice."

Words failed me, but the tendons in Royce's arm flexed and his knuckles went pale as he squeezed the railing. "You're fucking worried about *her*? After what she did?"

Macalister's stone-cold gaze swept from me to his son. "To say I'm disappointed in her would be a grave understatement, but no, the only concern I hold for her is how her actions will reflect on the Hale name."

Now it was Royce's turn to be speechless.

In an instant, I understood with terrible clarity what Macalister desired. Status held the utmost value to him, and he'd do everything in his considerable power to stay scandal-free. My gaze dropped to the blanket stretched across my lap. "You can't have a Hale go to prison."

Royce's tone was begrudging. "Like that would even happen."

"No," Macalister agreed, "I'm confident our lawyers would prevent that." His focus shifted back to me. "But it cannot get that far. Do you understand how disastrous the optics would be? My wife arrested for poisoning my future daughter-in-law. The media would be all over us, in every facet of our lives. Imagine how low the stock will drop when the story comes out. We'd have to put everything on hold, and table the takeover attempt of Ascension we voted to make."

Royce stiffened.

My body went cold as I asked the question I already knew the answer to. "What are you saying?"

"You agreed to protect both the Hale name and my company, Marist." Macalister grasped the edges of his tuxedo jacket and straightened it to hang properly on his broad shoulders. "I'm aware it's not an easy thing you're required to do, but you will do it regardless, because you are a part of this family now."

Not legally yet, but it didn't matter. I was bound to them both financially and with my word.

"When the time comes," he continued, "you'll explain that you made a mistake. A misidentified plant with unfortunate side effects. You didn't speak to Alice last night. She wasn't involved in any way."

All the breath left my body. "You want me to lie."

His tone was absolute, a direct order from the king. "To save the reputation of *our* family, yes. You will."

Well, I was a fucking Hale now, wasn't I?

TWO

ANGER ROLLED OFF ROYCE IN THICK WAVES. "NO. NO WAY DOES Alice get off scot-fucking-free."

"Of course not," Macalister snapped. "I will handle it with an appropriate response, but it needs to be done with . . . discretion."

"Discretion." Royce repeated the word like it made him ill. "She tried to kill Marist."

"Alice is many things, but she's not stupid. I don't believe that was her intent."

"Oh, really?" Royce snarled. "What the fuck was she trying to do, then?"

The words dropped heavily from Macalister's lips, and it was the closest to guilt I'd ever seen him come. "She wanted my attention."

The air in the room went still. Truth was such a rare thing between the Hales, it stretched the moment taut to the point it was unbearable.

"I'm not that good of a liar," I said.

My statement rankled him. "I have confidence in you."

Macalister's condescending tone gave me enough fire in my belly to burn through my exhaustion. "I'm supposed to tell people I'm stupid and made a dumb mistake—one bad enough to send me to the hospital. You expect me to sacrifice my reputation to save yours?"

Hostility skulked in his eyes. "The family's reputation—"

"Please. We all know what this is really about." I shifted uncomfortably on the bed, doing my best to sit up and not look weak. Had Alice realized the full extent of what she'd done? She'd handed me tremendous power over her husband, and I was about to wield it. "All that favor you've been building with Lambert won't mean a thing if the truth comes out. You can kiss your seat on the Fed goodbye."

Because no president would nominate someone attached to that kind of scandal. Macalister wouldn't survive his confirmation hearing.

He looked at me now like he used to. I was insignificant, a speck of lint daring to mar his perfectly tailored suit. "You will do this for me, Marist."

"Yes, I will," I wasn't sure if it was the drugs pumping in my system that made my heart race, or just the situation, "assuming we can reach an agreement."

Surprise made Royce's head snap my direction. I'd caught him off-guard, but he came up to speed instantly, and excitement flooded his eyes. He understood what I was about to do.

This was how I would escape Macalister's obsession.

A few long strides brought the man to my bedside, which would now serve as our negotiating table, and ugly resignation smeared across his face. He didn't want to bargain for anything and liked even less how much leverage I held over him, but he had no choice. There was no alternative.

"An agreement concerning what?" He sounded disinterested, but I saw through the pretense. He knew exactly what I was going to ask for . . .

And he *dreaded* it.

I licked my dry lips before pressing them together and set my hand on top of Royce's. My diamond engagement ring gleamed in the early sunlight, and I blinked slowly before lifting my gaze back to my opponent. My voice was steady. "You'll give me everything you promised me if I'd won that game and escaped the maze."

Beneath my hand, Royce's tensed a second time. Like me, he didn't want to remember that night in the hedge maze where I'd gambled everything and lost. He'd told me his father didn't play a game unless he was sure he was going to win, and I'd learned that lesson the hard way.

I should have known he was going to cheat. It was win at all costs, after all.

My eyebrows tugged together as I focused on the start of the game, where Macalister had laid out the rules. "You remember what you said?"

His expression turned sour. "Of course, I do."

"Then repeat it, so the terms are clear."

He let out a sigh of frustration, closed his eyes, and pinched the bridge of his nose. He looked like a spoiled brat, perpetually unsatisfied, even when he had nearly everything he wanted. "I will allow you to make your own choices."

I expected him to continue, but . . . he didn't.

Anger swelled inside me. "That wasn't all of it."

"Your car will be returned to you." He paused so long, I opened my mouth to protest further, and it pushed him to continue. "If you wish, you can live elsewhere until the wedding."

It was clear he wasn't going to say the most important part, so I did it for him. "And you're done trying to come between me and Royce. No more threats of taking away his board seat, no more games—chess or otherwise. Everything between us is settled and done. It's over."

It's over, and you lost, I wanted to say but didn't.

The muscle running along his jaw flexed as he ground his teeth together, restraining whatever he really wanted to say. The control he held over himself was razor thin, and I didn't want to see it snap. Last time it had, I'd wound up flattened against a bookcase in the library, and I didn't want to think about what would have happened if Alice hadn't caught him in the act.

His eyes were storm clouds looming over a turbulent ocean. "I believe I said I wouldn't stand in the way."

Even though my head ached, I shook it. "That's not good enough. This has to stop, Macalister."

His gaze darted to Royce. "You'll give us a minute."

Instinctively, I squeezed Royce's hand to keep him from moving, but he was already on the same page as me. Defiance coated his words. "I'm not going anywhere."

"He stays," I added, backing him up. If Macalister was going to plead with me, he could do it in front of his son.

A distance grew, first in his cold eyes, and then in his physical retreat. Macalister's posture was stiff yet challenging. Like he anticipated a fight he wasn't all that confident he could win and needed space to make his charge. "If that's what you want, then I will try. However, you gave me quite a different impression when I found you on the stairs."

Heat seared across my cheeks as the blood rushed to my face. "I thought you were Royce."

The corner of his mouth lifted, but it was too tactical to be called a smile. "Did you? We aren't often mistaken for each other."

It was true. Royce favored his father, but they weren't spitting images. Macalister was taller and narrower, with darker hair and lighter eyes. Even the way they carried themselves was different. Macalister moved with calculated efficiency, whereas Royce had ease and swagger.

"I'd been drugged," I said.

The question came from Royce in a tight voice. "What's he talking about?"

Arrogance washed through his father's expression. "I find it interesting that, as you lay there, believing you were dying, you chose not to say that. Time was of the essence, and you used it to tell me you loved me."

I nearly came up off the bed, hissing it at him. "Because I was hallucinating, and *I thought you were him.*"

His lips widened into an evil grin. Macalister didn't believe me. For as smart as he could be, deep down he was still human, and he'd twisted the situation until it fit the narrative he desperately desired.

And worse, I'd allowed him to play me. We were negotiating, and now I was on the defensive. My focus swiveled from my opponent to the boy who'd ceased moving. Did he believe me, or had he allowed his father to plant a seed of doubt in his mind? Even now, Macalister was trying to disrupt us.

"I'm in love with Royce," I declared loudly so both men would hear. "My loyalty is to him. If you want me to lie to save both you and your wife, then you'll agree to my terms."

It took him forever to say anything. Finally, "If I were to—"

"Ascension," I said abruptly.

Both men looked like I'd just driven over them with my Porsche.

Macalister's suspicious gaze angled toward his son. "What about it?"

Was I leaving money on the table? For years, Royce had quietly accrued stock in the competing bank for what I assumed was a plan to take control. And once he'd taken over Ascension, he would use it to go after HBHC.

But Macalister had somehow learned of Royce's plan and was making his own move to acquire the competitor. A defensive play to shut down everything Royce had spent years setting up.

"Agree that HBHC won't buy it," I said.

The shock on Royce's face drained away and he went . . . blank. His expression was too guarded for me to be able to read anything in it. I didn't understand at all. Was he worried if he showed an emotion, he'd give too much away to his father? I had the strange feeling he was unhappy about what

I'd said, but it was likely he was overcompensating. Surely, he wanted this. It had been his goal.

Right?

Honestly, I didn't know. He'd never let me in, never answered my questions. Even if he hadn't danced around them and given me an answer, I wasn't sure what to trust. For years, he'd spun lies, and the truth had only become murkier as I fell under his spell.

Macalister was far easier to understand. His jaw set and his eyes narrowed. My demand had truly offended him. "That is not up for negotiation. Let me make one thing crystal clear, Marist. I will not have business decisions dictated to me by you, or anyone else. Is that understood?"

"The board already voted in favor of it, Marist." Royce's voice was odd and distant.

"Overwhelmingly, I might add." Macalister lifted his chin, exaggerating the way he looked down on me. "Royce was the only dissenting vote."

I squeezed my fiancé's hand, wishing I could understand. Did he want me to try to fight for this, or was he subtly telling me it was already too late? I stared into his blue eyes, desperate for answers, but found none.

From across the room, a soft knock rang out on the suite door.

"We're out of time," Macalister said quickly. "I agree to your initial terms. Do we have a deal?"

I sucked in a breath and swallowed it. "Yes."

We didn't shake hands. He simply stood across the room and gave half of a nod, confirming the deal was closed. He didn't seem thrilled, but the pleased look that crossed his face made my stomach bottom out. I was tired and vulnerable, and in my weakened state, I'd made a mistake.

I should have bargained for more.

The door swung open, but it wasn't medical staff that came in—it was my parents. With all that had changed between us, it was shocking how it all was inconsequential now. My heart ached at the sight of them, and I bit down on my bottom lip to stop its trembling.

"Oh, Marist," my mom gasped as she flew toward me, her arms outstretched. Royce stepped back to make space, and I welcomed her hug greedily. She was soft, and warm, and my mom. As hard as it was to accept how fixated she was on money and status, I knew deep down she loved me more. My father, my sister, and I were more important than anything else.

My father stood beside her, his hand on her shoulder and concern on his face while she continued to squeeze me tightly.

"What happened?" She smoothed a hand over the back of my head in comforting, repeating strokes.

It was unfair that the first time I'd have to tell the lie, it would be to the people I most didn't want to.

"Uh . . ." I started.

And then suddenly Royce was there, doing what he'd been spent his lifetime perfecting . . .

He lied.

He explained how one of the staff members had turned me on to a homemade tea with leaves grown in the herb garden. Only last night, I'd misidentified the plant—easy to do, he added. They grew right beside each other. The lie rolled out of him with such ease, I nearly believed him.

My parents bought it completely.

"How awful. Thank God you're all right." My mother had grabbed my hand and refused to let go. "I'm sorry we weren't here sooner. I still had my phone on silent from the gala, and your father's was charging downstairs." She used her other hand to latch onto Royce's arm. "Thank you for sending your brother to get us."

From my bed, I peered up at him. "You sent Vance to my parents' house?"

To anyone else, his smile would seem warm, but I saw through to the unease masked beneath. "No one could get hold of them, and . . . I thought they should be here."

It was a slug to my heart. He'd been worried I was going to die before my parents even knew I'd gone to the hospital.

Tears stung my eyes, but I blinked them away before whispering, "Thank you."

And I'd thank Vance the first chance I got.

"From now on," my father said, "you only drink tea that comes from the store."

"Agreed," said the man lingering by the window.

At Macalister's deep voice, my mother froze. He'd been off to the side, and she'd been distracted by the sight of me and Royce when she'd come into the room, so she'd failed to notice him. Like an outsider, he was the only one not gathered at my bedside.

Panic swamped her face as she looked down and realized

what she was wearing. After Vance had woken them up, my parents had obviously thrown on whatever clothes were fastest and then raced to Boston. For my mother, it had been yoga pants and an Etonsons University sweatshirt. No makeup. Her hair was down and flattened from a half-night's sleep.

She'd never been so unkempt in front of my father's boss and the king of Cape Hill before, and he held even more power over us now.

"Macalister." She squeezed out a strained smile as she tucked her hair behind an ear. "I didn't see you there." Her gaze swept across the room, searching for who else she may have missed. "Is Alice here too?"

"No."

When he didn't elaborate, she exchanged a quick, puzzled look with my father. "Oh." She struggled visibly with how to proceed. "Have you been here long?"

She winced at her question, probably realizing the answer was obvious. He wore the same tuxedo she'd seen him in at the gala last night, so it was clear he hadn't had time to change.

Something was buried in his voice. Was that . . . pride? Macalister didn't smile, but it gave me the same uneasy feeling I had when he did. "I was the one who found Marist after she'd collapsed."

"Oh," was all my mother could say.

Her gaze flitted back to me in the bed, and I watched her throat bob in a hard swallow. If she was nervous about Macalister seeing her in sweats, she was downright terrified he was seeing me in a shapeless hospital gown. I could only imagine what my face looked like. The only makeup I wore was whatever was left over from yesterday, and probably beneath my eyes instead of the eyelids above them.

"Well, we're glad you were there to help her," she choked out.

She was likely recalling the terrible moment my sister Emily had thrown up all over Macalister's hand. He was basically the last person she would have chosen to see me like that.

For once, Macalister Hale said exactly what he meant. "I'm glad I was there too."

I fought the urge to suck in a deep breath.

The suite was like a high-end hotel, but it was still a hospital, complete with beeping machines and nursing staff that cycled through at all hours, making meaningful sleep impossible.

When the doctor informed me I needed to stay overnight, I tried to talk Royce into heading home and getting a decent night of sleep, but he wouldn't hear it. At some point when I'd been napping, he'd had clothes delivered, and then showered in the suite's full bathroom and changed.

Now, as the sunlight was fading outside, I rolled over in the bed and peered at him through the railing.

He sat on the tan couch, one arm slung along the back of it, wearing a maroon sweater over dark jeans, and his gaze locked on to the phone he held in his lap. His dark eyebrows were pulled together as he was deep in concentration. Whatever he was reading, it had his full attention.

I'd never been jealous of a phone until this moment.

I wanted his intense stare pinned on me, the one that used to make me uncomfortable, but now I craved. My voice was raspy from exhaustion, and breathless from the sight of how handsome he was. "Hey."

Royce's head lifted, and, when his gaze found mine, he pushed to his feet. "Hey, you're awake. How're you feeling?"

"Still weird," I said glumly. At least the lights had finally lost their halos and my head didn't hurt as much. But between the fatigue and the medicine I'd been given to regulate my heart, I felt disconnected from my body. "Did my parents leave?"

"They went to get something to eat and check in on your sister."

Because Emily was on bedrest, and probably not allowed to travel to Boston. I inhaled slowly. "And your father?"

His shoulders lifted in an equally deep breath. "He went home to deal with . . . things there."

It was like he couldn't bring himself to say her name, and I was grateful. "So, we're alone."

"We are."

The light coming through the window warmed, and the air in the room thickened.

"Come here," I whispered.

A faint smile teased his lips as he strode toward me, a gorgeous man who I hoped felt at least a fraction of the way I did about him.

"I know I'm a mess right now," I said, "but if you don't kiss me, I'll feel like I'm dying all over again."

"Fuck, Marist." His hand dove beneath my head, gingerly scooping me up into his kiss that obliterated everything else. His mouth was hot, a branding iron against my lips, marking me as his. His other hand cupped my cheek, holding me in place while he laid siege.

The Greek myth of Helen of Troy had been told a thousand different ways. In some versions, the most beautiful mortal in the world was stolen away from her loving husband, the king of Sparta, by an evil prince and dragged unwillingly to Troy. In others, she was seduced and ran away with her new lover.

The only constant in the myth was that it led to the Trojan War. Two great empires went to battle over the love of one woman.

Was that what this kiss was? Royce was king Menelaus, launching a thousand ships to rescue me from his opponent, the one who felt he was entitled to whatever he wanted, including me? Was Royce willing to sacrifice everything and go to war for me?

I sighed against the soft, deliberate brush of his lips over mine, each pass deepening our connection.

"Did you mean it?" I said breathlessly between kisses. "When you said you loved me?"

His mouth slowed and separated from mine, and with each inch of space he put between us, the farther my heart sank. He kept my face cupped in his hands but pulled back enough so I could see every fleck of uncertainty in his eyes.

We'd promised when we were alone, we wouldn't lie to each other. We'd said we'd always get to be the people we truly were when it was just the two of us. But I could see the struggle inside him. He didn't want to hurt me, but he also didn't want to lie.

As I waited for his answer, my breath came and went so quickly, I grew lightheaded.

His words were quiet and measured. "I don't know."

In theory, it was a better answer than a solid *no*, but somehow it felt worse. Like a sugar-coated *no*, only instead of tasting sweet, it was acidic.

"It's not a complicated question," I said, blinking back the tears that leapt into my eyes. I didn't want to push him, but I'd been through too much the last few days, not to mention hell last night, and couldn't stop myself. I needed him, and I would recklessly go after what I wanted.

Royce's gaze drifted down to settle on my lips, and his thumb brushed softly over my cheekbone. "The way I feel about you is hard to put into words."

I swallowed thickly. "Try."

His eyes turned back to meet mine. "Everything I've ever really cared about has been taken from me."

He hesitated and fell silent. This wasn't a 'poor little rich boy' act. He was talking about so much more than just possessions. He was talking about opportunities. Choices.

And his mother.

"So, after a time," he finally continued, "I learned it was better not to get attached to anything. It's easier then when he takes it away." He leaned in, setting the top of his forehead against mine. "You made that fucking impossible. I wanted to be cold, an unfeeling stone." His voice went low and thick. "But you, Medusa? You have the opposite effect on me."

He pressed his lips to mine, dropping a short, abrupt kiss on my mouth, too fast for me to react. Or maybe it was his words that made me slow.

"I'm never going to get that image out of my head," he said. "When he was on the stairs and had you in his arms, and I thought that was it. Like everything else, my father had succeeded in taking you away, and something in me—I don't know—broke."

I clasped my hand around his wrist, giving us yet another place where we were connected, wanting to show him his fear wasn't true. I'd never been or would be Macalister's.

"Before, I wanted to destroy him," he admitted. "Not *just* him, but everything he has too. Take away his money, and his power, and his company—"

I finished the thought for him. "Everything he cares about."

"Yes. And in that moment, where I thought you were his, it meant I'd have to go after you too, and I . . ." He searched for the right words. "I told you I wanted to take over my family's company so badly, I wasn't capable of caring about anything else. But, Marist, last night showed me I was fucking wrong."

I was short of breath, but he was too, like this confession was taking everything out of him. It was how I knew it was true. He lied with ease. Only the truth was difficult for him.

"The way I feel about you wasn't part of the plan. I've spent so long like this, not allowing myself to care, I wasn't sure I was even capable anymore. Honestly, in the beginning, it didn't matter who got hurt, just as long as it wasn't me, and I got what I wanted."

He'd told me this the night of our first date. "Because it's win at all costs."

"Yeah. I mean, it was." His relentless stare held me tight. "Until you changed the game on me. All I've ever wanted was to run HBHC. Every decision I've made has been toward that outcome, all until you came along with your green hair and your mythology book, and that little gasp you made when I had you pushed against that bookcase. I heard that goddamn moan in my head for weeks after that night."

Heat rushed through me and clenched my body so tightly I couldn't speak. I couldn't move.

"I want HBHC," he said, "but now I'm wondering if I want you even *more*."

He'd kept me walled off for so long, it felt like he'd just thrown open every floodgate, and it swept me away. "I think I need to lie down."

"You're already lying down." A smirk flashed on his lips before he turned serious again. "I think I can get to the place where I can say it back, when we're alone and you tell me you love me, but I'm not there yet." Determination flickered in his eyes. "I don't want to say those words until I know they're absolutely true."

I stared at him. "I know I'm on drugs, but are you too? I thought Royce Hale didn't talk about his feelings."

His smile was pained. "He does after he thought his fiancée might die and he didn't tell her any of the shit he should have." When he released me and rested his hands on the bedrail, my skin mourned the loss of his touch. His hands were spread wide, making his shoulders high and tight, while his head stayed tipped down toward me. "If you don't want to say it anymore until I do, I get it."

I ached for him and his banker's heart. He thought of love like a transaction, like a currency. A thing that shouldn't be given away without receiving something in return.

I softened my voice. "I'm not going to withhold how I feel just because you aren't ready to say it back. I love you, Royce. If it helps, I tried really hard not to."

He'd been so desperate to hear those words from me, and they landed with such an impact. The smile that broke on his lips caused a flutter in my chest.

"It does help. Thanks," he teased.

I lifted an eyebrow. "You didn't always make it easy either."

The glow in his eyes faded as he sobered. "No. I know I didn't."

Among other things, he'd sold me to his father for one hundred thousand shares.

Royce straightened and took in a deep breath. "I owe you an explanation, but it's a much longer conversation than I think we should have tonight. Can we wait until both of us have gotten more than an hour's worth of sleep?"

My pulse jumped. "You're going to tell me what you're planning?"

"Yes, Marist." Conviction spread across his handsome face. "I'll tell you everything."

It came out breathlessly excited. “Okay.”

As he leaned back in to give me a final kiss, I hated Alice a little less. Sure, she’d poisoned me and left me for dead, but she’d also set off a chain of events that had given me almost everything I wanted.

I was out from under Macalister’s grip. My choices were my own again, and he’d been forced to retreat.

And Royce was finally letting me in, both on his feelings and his plan.

All that was left now was to take his heart and make it mine. He wasn’t sure if he loved me? I was going to make that happen. As his lips captured mine, it sealed his fate.

Look out, Royce. I’m coming for you.

THREE

IT TOOK TWO EXCRUCIATINGLY LONG DAYS BEFORE I WAS released from the hospital, and I wondered if the doctors worked with an overabundance of caution due to the ring on my finger. No one wanted to be the one to send a future Hale home too early and incur the family's wrath if something went wrong.

But the toxins from the lily of the valley were finally gone from my system, my heartrate had returned to normal, and it seemed unlikely any complications were going to occur. I wasn't excited about returning to the Hale house, but my desire to get out of the hospital suite and back to class was much stronger and overrode everything else.

We didn't talk about Alice, other than Royce's comment that she'd been banished from the house. Macalister had ordered her to move into the stables, which had been converted into a guest house a few years back.

He'd stayed true to our agreement. I hadn't seen Royce's father since we'd struck our deal. Perhaps Alice had gotten her wish, and she had all his attention now.

Leaving the hospital was an ordeal. I'd been brought clothes to wear by a stylist, along with a whole hair and makeup team to conceal the dark circles under my eyes and my sallow skin. When they were done, I looked every bit the part I'd been playing for the last five months. Outwardly, the fake Instagram version of Marist Northcott was ready to take the stage and reemerge into society. No one would see the grayish lines leftover from the IV that had been taped to my skin because they'd been scrubbed away.

Like the last three days never happened.

But they had. I was closer than ever with Royce as a result.

All the prep work to make me camera-ready had been overkill. Royce's security team brought us down to the parking garage, loaded us into the back of a Land Rover, and we slipped out onto the streets of Boston before anyone noticed.

When the story broke that billionaire Royce Hale's fiancée was hospitalized, the media had flocked to Mass General, hoping to score a picture of the concerned groom as he came and went from my bedside. The rumors were rampant, with accidental overdose leading the pack.

But the only media outlet that succeeded was Sophia Alby, and it was because we'd orchestrated the whole thing. We'd let her snap a close-up picture of our hands clasped on my bedside, the *Wall Street Journal* draped in his lap and the hospital bracelet dangling around my wrist. The image couldn't have been more on-brand if we'd tried.

A single Instagram post from her, complete with hashtags about true love and fairytale romance, and the public fell more in love with us. It also worked to calm their curiosity. Allergic reaction was the official party line, and my DMs flooded with well-wishes and support.

Not that I knew any of them, or that they knew any version of me.

I leaned back in my seat and watched the buildings blur by in the cold October rain while Royce finished his call. He'd gone into the office this morning to put out a fire and sit in on a "can't-miss" meeting, but he was officially mine for the rest of the afternoon.

Excitement bubbled inside me as we headed toward Cape Hill. Macalister would be at the office for a few more hours, and even if Alice was on the property . . . she wasn't allowed in the house. With Vance being in his first year of law school, he was a virtual ghost. I only saw evidence he'd been at the house, but never the man himself.

It meant that, outside the staff, Royce and I would be the only people home.

Would he tell me everything now? We'd rarely been alone at the hospital—never long enough to have the conversation he'd promised. It felt like he would. There was a tension between us. It wasn't unpleasant—it was anticipation.

In addition to the rain, it was a foggy afternoon, and as we drove up the circle drive toward the Hale mansion, the impressive house didn't come into view until we'd pulled up to the front steps. Would I ever get used to living here?

And . . . did I want to stay?

I'd won back my freedom, which meant I could escape. There was zero risk of accidentally running into Alice or Macalister in a hall or the kitchen if I wasn't living under their roof.

But it meant I'd be farther away from both my school and my fiancé, and back with my parents, who'd probably try to squeeze me for money every chance they got. Not to mention, it'd only be temporary. My wedding date to Royce had been set at the beginning of June. I could move out, but I'd have to be back in six months.

It barely seemed worth the effort.

I promised myself I wasn't going to make my decision tonight. Six months might feel like a lifetime if Macalister didn't stick to his word and stay out of my relationship with his son.

"You okay with the stairs?" Royce asked, hesitating with his hand on the car door as we prepared to duck out into the rain.

Earlier, the long walk from my hospital room to the elevator bank had left me surprisingly winded. He was worried about me, but I gave him a sweet smile. "I'm fine, I promise. But thank you."

Last time I'd been chauffeured and arrived at this house in the rain, it'd been his graduation party, and I was struck by how much things had changed since then. He'd been the manipulative prince of Cape Hill and I'd been a *nobody*. Just the weird Northcott sister who'd reluctantly tagged along.

This time when I scurried up the steps in the cold drizzle, Royce put a protective hand on my elbow and hurried alongside me.

The house always felt cavernous, but it was much worse today. The tall ceilings stretched up for miles, and when my gaze landed on the grand staircase, I shivered. I still remembered how the fibers of the red carpeted steps felt against my skin. My stomach twisted with an aftershock of disorientation. I'd been so sure I was going to die there, either from the drugs or a fall.

Royce's hand crept around mine and squeezed. "Are you hungry? Should I tell Carla to make us something?"

"No, thanks."

I couldn't stop staring at the staircase and forced my gaze upward. Something was . . . different. I blinked in confusion as I looked at the landing and the empty wood paneled wall. "Where's the picture?"

"The family portrait?" He tried to disguise the unease in his voice. "My dad got rid of it."

Like a cliché, the large painting had been of the Hale family. Alice angled and seated in a formal chair and Macalister behind her, his sons flanking him on either side. It was regal and pompous as hell.

Now it was gone.

I couldn't shake the feeling Macalister had removed it in a fit of rage. The image of him yanking down the canvas and ripping it apart, tearing Alice from the rest of the family, played in my mind. He couldn't remove her legally. Divorce was failure, and Macalister didn't do defeat. So, destroying the portrait and banishing her from his life would be the closest he could come.

"I need to change," Royce said, glancing down at his suit. He tugged on my hand, pulled me toward the stairs, and kept his tone casual. "Come on."

When we passed by the library, a coiled circle of black fur on the back of the chair lifted its head and appraised us with apple green eyes. Lucifer was in his favorite spot, and he liked it more than his master, apparently, because even though Royce was now home, the cat looked at us with indifference before putting his head back down and returning to sleep.

He was so fickle, just like his owner.

We'd been together for months, but I'd only been in Royce's room a handful of times. Was he a naturally tidy person, or was the staff quick to make up his room after he left the house? It always looked perfect, like a set for a glamorous magazine shoot—

Well, there was that one time when it hadn't.

The night I'd agreed to play his father's game in the maze, Royce had come back to his room and ransacked the place. Vance had called it a temper tantrum, but there wasn't any evidence of it now. The white linens on the king-sized bed were crisp. The silver silk curtains which hung over the enormous floor to ceiling windows were flawless. The charcoal gray couch looked brand-new. Maybe it was.

I stood awkwardly in the center of his bedroom as Royce toed off his shoes and shrugged out of his suit coat before tossing it onto one of the pale gray chairs opposite the couch. His gaze locked onto me as his fingers loosened his tie and undid the top button of his collar.

"Have a seat." Amusement edged into his voice. "Stay awhile."

"Where?" I asked.

I was out of sorts here in this place that was *his* and not *ours*. Should I sit on the couch? The bed? It wasn't helping that he was currently undressing either. He untucked and unbuttoned his shirt, opening it to reveal a tight white undershirt that clung to his chest and trim waist.

He angled his head and shot me a look like I was being silly. "Wherever you want."

His cuffs were unbuttoned, one side then the other, then off came the dress shirt. His practiced, methodical movements made me want to bite my lip. He wasn't even shirtless yet. Why was this doing things to me? Why did my body clench with anticipation? And how in the world did he look even better halfway out of his suit?

"Will this be our room?" I asked. "I mean, when we're married. Or will we be keeping separate rooms like your father and . . ."

I struggled to say her name, but it was clear I didn't need to. He paused, and the intensity ratcheted up in his eyes. "It's whatever you want."

I pressed my lips together, unsure. I'd always assumed when I was married, I'd share a bed with my spouse, the way most people did. The way my parents did.

Rather than make the decision, I sent it back to him. "What do you want?"

He turned his head and cast his gaze toward the bed, which suddenly seemed both inviting and scary at the same time. Something suspiciously like hope colored his voice. "We should try it."

"Okay," I breathed.

Before I could say anything else, he reached behind his back, grabbed a fistful of his t-shirt, and pulled it over his head, revealing the sculpture of his chest and powerful arms. Thoughts vaporized from my brain at the sight. Subtly notched muscles ran down his stomach and disappeared beneath the waistband of his underwear, which rode a half inch higher than his suit pants.

I was irritated with myself. I wasn't supposed to be one of those girls who fell apart around Royce, but it happened anyway. My gaze traced every inch of him, from the silver watch on one wrist to the pronounced line his collarbones drew across his defined chest.

"I should warn you," he said as he turned and walked away, wordlessly encouraging me to follow him. "I don't know how that's going to go."

His socked feet carried him into the bathroom and deeper still into his enormous walk-in closet, the suits organized by color on one side, his casual clothes on the other, and the back was a wall of shoes and accessories. I stood at the entryway, leaning against the doorframe as he peeled off his socks and tossed them into a hamper.

"What do you mean?" I asked.

His intense eyes didn't give me a clue of what was going on behind them. "I've never had a girl in my bed."

Surprise coasted down through me. "Like, for sleeping?"

"For anything." He worked to unlatch the belt at his waist, but his gaze remained on me. I was captured prey he didn't want to escape, but that was silly. Didn't he know I wasn't going anywhere? His face contorted with an emotion

I wasn't used to seeing from him. Was he . . . shy? "I didn't bring anyone back to my room. This is supposed to be my space, where I can be *me*."

My pulse sped. "You brought me here after we went out the first time."

A smile hinted in his eyes. "You'd already agreed to be my wife."

A thrill shot through me. He'd been my first in so many things. I was excited to be his too, at least in some way. I swallowed thickly as his fly was undone and his pants fell around his ankles, leaving him clad only in a pair of underwear. The tight gray trunks hugged him and left little to the imagination.

My thighs tightened. "So, what you're saying is . . . I'll get to see this show you're putting on right now every night."

My statement caught him off-guard, and Royce's smile went wide. He stepped out of his pants, leaving them in a heap on the floor, and strode toward me. "Oh, you like this?"

I wanted to be as confident as he was, standing in front of me with barely anything on. I lifted my chin and puffed up my chest. "I do."

It was shocking to me how much power he held over me even now, when he was nearly naked and I was fully clothed. He threaded a hand through my hair, his goal of getting dressed forgotten. His lips slanted across mine in a scorching kiss that made my toes curl inside my Stuart Weitzman heels.

I sank into his kiss, both figuratively and literally, because as he deepened it, I was bent backward over his arm. His mouth roved against my mouth, licking and tasting, and my knees softened. God, would I ever get used to the way he possessed me? It all still felt so new and surreal. I'd spent years hating him, not to mention thinking he was going to marry my sister. I couldn't believe I'd ended up in Royce's closet, in love with him and letting him kiss the hell out of me.

But his kiss came abruptly to an end, like a thought had just occurred to him. "You're distracting me. We have shit to talk about."

"We do." I skimmed my palms along his back, sliding them over his warm, smooth skin. "Tell me about Ascension."

He extracted himself from my hold, bent, and retrieved the suit pants from the floor, talking as he hung them up. "Their growth in brokerage and credit accounts is incredible. A shareholder's wet dream."

"That's why you want to buy them?"

"No."

He let that cryptic answer settle on me as he grabbed a pair of jeans off a shelf and pulled them on, one leg at a time.

"But you've been buying stock in Ascension for years. You own almost five percent."

"Yup."

Was he purposefully trying to be a vague asshole? "That company's not as big as HBHC, but they're a competitor. Why do that? You buy Ascension, and then use them to try to take over HBHC?"

Because Royce on his own didn't have enough money to buy out the shareholders of his family's bank. But if he owned Ascension, he could gain interest from others to partner with on a takeover attempt. I only got a flash of his sly look before he tugged on a t-shirt, disappointingly covering his bare chest. His expression said one thing—that I hadn't guessed right.

"I don't understand," I said. "That's the only reason that makes sense to me."

"That I'm planning a takeover?"

I nodded.

Royce put his hands on his waist and stared at me with unflinching eyes. "And that's exactly what I want him to think."

Maybe the hospital stay had made me slow, because I couldn't connect the dots. "You . . . don't want to buy Ascension?"

"No. He needs to do it."

"Why?" What did he have to gain from his father buying it? In my confusion, I hadn't noticed his advance, and I let out a squeak of surprise as he scooped me up into his arms. "What are you doing?"

"I want to see what you look like in my bed."

As he carried me through the bathroom and out into the bedroom, I wondered if this was calculated distraction. Perhaps he didn't want to tell me his master plan after all, or he wanted to do it in stages.

"You want to have sex? Fine." I gave him a determined look. "But you're going to keep talking, Royce."

He set me down on the bed, but as he backed up, his expression was odd. "That's not what I meant. We can't have sex."

My back went straight as I sat up, tucking my legs

beneath me. "What? Why not?"

"I don't know, Marist." He tossed up a hand. "Maybe because you just got out of the hospital? Or because you barely made it down the hall to my room without needing to stop for a rest?"

It was true, I wasn't recovered, but like last time he'd done it, when he took away the option of sex . . . I instantly began to crave it.

"I'm fine," I said with exasperation. "If it helps, I'll let you do the majority of the work. I'll just lay there and take it."

He chuckled. "Sounds awesome, can't wait." He sat beside me on the bed, the mattress dipping and causing me to fall into him. "As much fun as it would be to say I fucked you so hard, it sent you to the hospital, you know that's the last thing I want, right?" He sobered. "It's one night. Neither of us is a stranger to waiting."

Because we'd both waited a year for each other after he'd cornered me in the library and demanded he be my first. But—*fuck*—we'd gotten engaged months ago, and yet we'd only had sex three times.

Irritation simmered in my core. "I'm tired of waiting. I almost died, and . . ." I knew it was a ridiculous thing to say, but I was greedy and wild. Desperate to reconnect with him in the way that felt honest and true. "I've never even given a blowjob."

He pressed his lips together, and amusement warmed his expression. "Just a heads up, I haven't either."

I narrowed my eyes at him. "Hey, remember when you told me you were going to fuck me non-stop once I had a ring on my finger? When, exactly, is that going to start?"

"Marist." He sighed softly as he traced a fingertip over my cheek, brushing my hair back. "You think I don't want to? You have no idea how badly I want you. But what I don't want is to be the asshole who tries to get inside you five minutes after you've come home from the fucking hospital."

I wasn't sure I could persuade him with words alone. I'd have to show him I was physically okay, beyond ready. When I smoothed my palm up his thigh, he caught my hand and stopped me before I reached my final destination.

"Please?" I aimed for the sultriest plea I could manage. "Let me go down on you. I promise to stop if it gets to be too much for me."

His hand tensed on mine, and his voice dipped low. "Jesus. Are you actually begging to suck me off right now?"

I slipped off the bed, dropping to my knees, and as I turned to face him, the electricity between us crackled. He twisted with torment and need. Lust was a beautiful emotion on his face. It made his full lips part and his eyes hood, and all the wicked thoughts I had swelled until I was too tight. The only way to keep myself from bursting was to act on them.

It came from him quiet and with awe. "You're something else, Medusa."

My insides quivered with excitement and nervousness as I closed in on another first, raking my fingers up the inseam of his jeans. But while my mouth would be occupied, his wouldn't be, and I still didn't understand. "Tell me why you want your father to buy Ascension."

Royce put his hands on the bed behind him and leaned

back on his straightened arms, opening his legs wider to make more room for me.

"On paper," he said, "they're a smart buy. It's only a matter of time before Ascension's growth in private banking and mortgages starts to rival our numbers." His heavy gaze was cast down on me, watching as I stroked my fingers over his fly and traced the outline of his thickening cock beneath it. The words were weighted with double meaning. "They're aggressive. *Hungry.*"

A smile eked out of me, in spite of the anxiety I felt. I didn't really know what I was doing. I'd talked him into this blowjob, but what if I were terrible at it?

"Ascension pushes its people to perform," he continued, distracting me from my worry. "They pit their executives and departments against each other and incentivize deals. I'm told it's ruthless, and almost as brutal as it can be at HBHC. So, it's right up my dad's alley."

His chest rose with a deep breath as I popped the snap at the top of his jeans and inched down his zipper.

"But if that's true, why'd you vote against it?"

"Because Ascension looks so good, it's *too* good."

I paused. "What do you mean?"

"Executives get bonuses when they meet or exceed their quarterly numbers. Each year the quota goes up and gets more unrealistic. And yet every year their top performers manage to pull it off."

Suspicion rolled through me. "What do you think they're doing?"

"They're forging signatures and opening dummy

accounts to inflate numbers. They'll tack on additional products without the client's approval. We're talking about tens of thousands of accounts, probably more. Corporate looks the other way because the only thing that matters is keeping the stock price up."

Whoa. What he was saying was serious bank fraud. I sat back on my heels. "You know this? How?"

He blinked. "Tate Isaacs works for them."

"Holy shit," I breathed. Tate was the closest thing Royce had to a best friend.

"If my dad took the time to really look at Ascension, there's a chance he might notice it smells off. But I know him. He won't. He thinks I want Ascension, so he's way too focused on taking it away from me. All that matters is winning. On the surface, Ascension looks amazing. He'll fight to get control, and once the deal's done, he'll welcome it under the umbrella of HBHC."

Everything went still. Time suspended as he looked at me. His smile was cruel and yet undeniably sexy.

"Ascension is a bomb I can activate with one call to the SEC," he whispered, "and when I do, it's going to blow up in his face."

Royce was wrong. Ascension wasn't a bomb.

It was a Trojan Horse.

FOUR

After a ten-year siege against the city of Troy, the Greeks constructed a huge wooden horse, only to abandon it and set off to sail their army home. The Trojans hauled the horse inside their gates, claiming it as a war trophy, unaware of the danger hidden inside.

That night, after the city was asleep, thirty of Greece's finest warriors slipped out from inside, including King Menelaus, and opened the gates. The Greek army hadn't sailed away—they burst out of hiding and stormed the city.

Troy finally fell, and Helen was reunited with her husband.

The most famous of the Greek myths endured. A Trojan Horse was anything your foe invited inside that brought about their own destruction.

Royce's blue eyes were fixed on me as I knelt between his spread knees, my hands on his thighs and his pants undone.

"Acquiring anything right now when our stock is down is risky enough, but when the board realizes what a terrible deal my father made? I'll call for a vote of no confidence and strip him of his seat."

The puzzle pieces snapped into place. "That's why you voted against it, even though you want the deal to go through."

A smile curled on his lips. "The board will see me as the smarter, reasonable Hale."

I nodded. "The one who's a better fit to be in control."

"My father's strength is also his biggest weakness, and he'll commit the cardinal sin of business. He doesn't care about the deal, or if it's any good, he just wants to win."

I knew firsthand it was true. Not just with the chess game or the night in the maze, but the whole way Macalister acted toward me. He didn't care if seducing me was a good idea. He only wanted to beat his son.

A dark laugh threatened to escape from me as I resumed my plan of getting my mouth on Royce. I curled my fingers around his underwear-covered dick, massaging him through the soft fabric.

Macalister had certainly failed, hadn't he? It was pointless he'd even tried to make me his. I'd belonged to Royce the second I looked up from the book I was reading in the Hale library last year and discovered his provocative eyes staring at me.

I captured my bottom lip between my teeth as I slipped my fingers under his waistband and inched his underwear past his hipbones. I worked the elastic down just until he was exposed. He was thick and hard, laying across his thigh, and when I leaned in, he twitched.

Once again, his words were full of subtext. "Do you like my plan?"

"I do," I whispered.

And then I sucked in a breath and ran the tip of my tongue up the length of him in one tentative lick.

It made his whole body shudder and his voice tight. "Oh—fuck—I think your plan is better."

I giggled, both at his humorous statement and my nerves. His head dipped back when I did it again—this pass slower and more exploratory. His skin was so soft, warm and velvety smooth against my tongue.

My unsure caresses must have sent the message to him that I was looking for direction, because he adjusted and leaned back on one hand, freeing the other to cup the side of my face. His tender touch disarmed and guided me to take him inside my mouth.

A deep, appreciative sigh rained from above as I widened my lips and slid down, taking more of him in. All the way until my mouth was full and I could take no more. I wrapped a fist around the base of him, holding his dick steady while also stopping him from going any deeper.

"Oh, God, yes," he groaned.

Pleasure ripped through me in a hot flash, landing as a pulse in the center between my legs. It felt different than when he touched me, but just as good. It stimulated my mind, rather than my body.

His fingers were buried in my hair and rested on the nape of my neck, and he used his touch to urge me to hold still. It was so he could slowly retract his hips, easing himself out of my mouth.

The head of his dick just cleared my lips before he began his advance. The push of him inside me in this new place was erotic. *Hot*. And when he let out another satisfied sigh, power coursed through my veins.

Before, I hadn't understood the appeal of the act. The enjoyment seemed one-sided.

But, oh, there was pleasure here.

It burned in my body with each labored breath Royce fought for and every stroke as he worked himself in and out of my pursed mouth. I enjoyed finding new ways to draw out his sounds of contentment. He groaned when I swirled my tongue. He throbbed when I sucked. A gasp poured from him when I tightened my fist and tried to keep still, letting him control the tempo.

Although he was doing the majority of the work, it didn't matter. I quickly went out of breath, even as all I had to do was kneel on the carpet beside the bed and let him fuck my mouth. An ache swelled inside me, hot and needy, and I shifted in my position so I could press my knees together and clench against the sensation.

Royce picked up the pace, sawing his hard cock in and out until it was slippery with my saliva and soreness crept along the muscles of my jaw. As his satisfaction began to build, his careful control slipped. The hand on the back of my head was firm and dominating. It urged me to rock with him and move faster.

Desperate, urgent, mindless sounds drifted from him. Sighs and groans soaked in pleasure. It made me squeeze my thighs harder against the ache. Was I . . . going to come? Just from listening to him? The power he gave me was like being high, and I wanted more.

"Yeah." His quiet encouragement was sandwiched between deep gulps of air. "Fuck, yeah."

I pushed my hair back out of my face, which had become damp with sweat. My heart beat wildly, pounding in my chest, and I swirled my tongue over him to mimic its frantic pace. His hips bucked and his cock throbbed, but he didn't slow down.

My gaze flicked up to connect with his. He was my beautiful Ares, the god of war, and I was happy to be conquered by him.

"You're gonna make me come. Is that what you want, Marist?" His tone was sinful. "You want me to fill up your virgin mouth?"

I moaned my approval, and it made him wild.

The bed creaked quietly from his strong thrusts. His hips weren't even on the mattress anymore, giving him more room to piston himself in and out of my mouth. I tried to match his intensity, sliding my tight fist furiously along the part of him I couldn't fit past my lips.

It unleashed a moan from him that could have doubled as a sound of pain, but it was obviously pleasure. His body jerked, and his controlling hand on my head locked down, holding me still as he erupted.

Hot, thick liquid filled my mouth in spurts, and his chaotic gasps of satisfaction came in waves. He shuddered like thunder was rolling through him before he sank down onto his back. When my throat bobbed in a thick swallow, it dragged a final, deep groan from him.

The taste of him lingered in the back of my throat. It

wasn't like the girls made it seem in porn, but with his reaction, I didn't mind it. When he stopped throbbing, I pulled away, sat back on the legs folded beneath me, and wiped my hand across my kiss-swollen, damp lips.

"*Fuck*," he uttered into the stillness that had settled around us. It deepened the contrast between the quiet now and the sounds of sex that had filled the room just moments before.

It was a battlefield after the cannons had gone quiet, and he lay on the bed as if I'd slain him.

Then, his chest rose with a heavy breath, followed by another, and his hands went to his hips, jerking the sides of his jeans and underwear up to cover himself. He moved swiftly, doing up his fly, and once finished, he bolted upright. His hands scooped under my arms, and he dragged me into his lap so I was sitting on him, one leg on either side.

It surprised me when his mouth claimed mine, so soon after what we'd done, but he didn't seem to care, and I was greedy for his kiss. It was intense and full of unexpected, real passion. In the aftermath of his orgasm, I wondered if he was even capable of lying.

"Was it everything you'd hoped it'd be?" he teased but then turned serious. "Because it was for me. That felt fucking amazing."

A smile burned across my lips and heated my face. "I'm glad you let me talk you into it."

One more short kiss was all I got before his arms banded around my back and he was moving—turning us until I was flopped down on my back on the bed, him crawling over me. He kept himself supported on his hands and knees, so I wasn't crushed beneath him, but he was close enough our bodies were connected.

I arched my back, pressing harder against him. I wanted to feel his weight on me. His skin touching mine. But he shifted to the side so one hip rested beside mine on the bed and coursed a hand over my leg, up under my skirt. It was so he could grip the back of my thigh and lift, draping my leg up over his waist.

"Oh," I whispered, turning toward him and grabbing fistfuls of his t-shirt, stretching it carelessly in my hands as his fingertips brushed over the crotch of my panties.

His words rasped as he asked the question, which I didn't have to answer. It was apparent. "Turned you on, huh?"

I closed my eyes and buried my forehead in his chest, so I couldn't see his evil smile, but I pictured it in my head.

"Next time, I'll make you take off your soaked panties. But tonight," he pulled the fabric to the side and out of his way, "this will do."

There wasn't time to catch my breath before his finger pushed inside me. There wasn't time to think, not about anything but him. It was how he was in life.

He invaded.

The stretch to accommodate him felt good. So, freaking, good. His thumb flicked across my clit while his long finger pulsed in and out at an unhurried pace. It was torturous, yet filled me with bliss.

One finger gradually became two, and I was hopelessly out of breath. Whimpers and soft sounds of need dripped from my lips. I wasn't going to last long like this. I'd already been close when I'd been going down on him.

He moved faster and harder, reaching a spot deep inside me that caused my legs to tremble and my pulse to roar.

"Look at me," he demanded.

Part of me didn't want to. I knew it would be my undoing, and I wanted to live here in this moment just a little longer, balancing right at the edge before he took me over. But when he asked for it, I immediately complied, and—oh—his eyes. They were such a beautiful blue, deep like the water just beyond the cape.

His gaze was a weapon. It was an arrow, slipping past any defense I could mount, driving straight and true into my heart.

I came with a cry, my gaze locked on his. All the physical pleasure I felt was reflected in his eyes. Like me, he enjoyed giving just as much as receiving. Maybe more. The sensations wracked my body, washing me in heat and ecstasy, and as soon as the orgasm released me from its clutches, I gasped for air.

It took me a lifetime to recover. "It's a good thing," I panted, "you talked me out of sex."

Concern washed down his expression. "You okay?"

"Yeah," I said. "Yes. It just, like, took a lot out of me. In a good way."

I'd done a terrible job convincing him because worry continued to twist on his face. It was strange and wonderful, and if I'd been told six months ago it was possible he could care about someone else, I wouldn't have believed it.

My palm made its home on his chest, hoping someday soon the heart beneath it would be mine.

"Seriously, I'm okay," I said softly. "I'm better than okay," I amended.

There wasn't anywhere else I'd have rather been than right here, in his bed and in his arms.

Royce took the plate from me and set it on the silver tray resting on the top of his dresser. He'd had someone from the staff bring dinner to his room, and we'd eaten in his bed, talking about all the things we should have months ago.

It was an eye-opening experience. He was a fan of the classics, he said. Tupac, Jay Z, Biggie, and the Beastie Boys. He thought the movie *Pulp Fiction* was overrated. And he was curious if I was interested in booking a private yacht for our honeymoon so we could tour the French Riviera.

"Or," he leaned back against the dresser and crossed his arms over his chest, "we can just stay on the boat the whole time. I don't know if we'll leave the cabin. I plan to spend a lot of time fucking the new Mrs. Hale."

His smile made a blush heat my face, but at the same time, his words caused cold trepidation to grow in my stomach, and I pulled the comforter tighter across my body. I'd been so focused on the initiation, and then the wedding planning, I hadn't thought much of what came after. I decided to deflect.

"What if I don't want to take your last name?"

I imagined the question had the same effect it would if I'd told him his bank account was empty. He stared at me, seated in his big, white bed, and utter disbelief streaked across his face. "Excuse me, what?"

I had every intention of taking the Hale surname, but he didn't need to know that. I blinked innocently. "If I give up my name, what do I get in return?"

His tone was wry. "A percentage of my enormous fortune."

"Besides that." I tilted my head and gave him a look to make sure he knew I wasn't serious. Although, I sort of was. We'd taken a big step today, but I hoped by the time we exchanged vows, he'd be ready to share all of himself. "What will you give me," I teased, "of *value*?"

He straightened and strolled toward me, finally understanding. Excitement and mock outrage painted his expression. "Are you blackmailing me, Marist Northcott—soon to be Hale?"

"Of course not." I spoke it syrupy sweet. "I'm trying to enter into negotiations with you."

He went to sit beside me, but we were interrupted. The quick rap of knuckles against wood wasn't much of a warning. We only had time to turn and look at the door before it swung open, and the temperature plummeted.

Macalister's suit was as dark as a black hole. He swept into the room with furious eyes, and when he discovered me resting in Royce's bed, a scowl hinted at his lips.

"I came to check on Marist," he announced, "and see if she was settled."

His gaze zeroed in on me, and I wanted to shrink beneath

the covers. I hadn't seen him since we'd struck our deal, and somehow that absence made this moment more awkward. It verged on terrifying.

"I'm fine," I said.

"Good. I'm pleased you've decided to stay with us."

The way he said *us* made it sound like he actually meant *me*. I frowned. "I haven't decided anything yet."

Royce didn't say a word, but the subtle shift in his posture gave away his displeasure. I was sending mixed signals, wasn't I? Saying I wasn't sure I was going to stay while I was nestled in his bed?

And I was the first girl he'd allowed here.

I put my hands down on the mattress and used them to push up, attempting to sit straighter in the bed. "It makes more sense for me to keep living here."

"It does," Royce said quickly.

"But I won't stay . . . if someone gives me a reason to leave."

Perhaps Macalister would think I was talking about *her*, and I was . . . but I also very much meant the warning for him.

He gave a short nod. "There's no risk of that happening. I've been quite clear with everyone, including the staff, about the boundaries."

I had no idea what that meant but didn't want him to elaborate. His presence in the room shattered the warmth and closeness Royce and I had built, so I wanted him gone as quickly as possible.

"You came to check on Marist," Royce said flatly, "which you've done. Is there something else you need?"

He sounded like he wanted his father gone more

than I did.

Macalister's hands hung loosely at his sides, but I didn't miss the way he curled his fingers, balling a hand into a fist of tension. "Yes." He leveled his penetrating gaze at me. "Alice has asked I pass on her apology to you." He spoke it like the language was unfamiliar to him. "She is quite sorry."

Royce's mouth dropped open. "Are you fucking serious?"

"No." Instinctively, my hand came up, signaling to stop. "I don't want to talk about it. I'm not ready."

Surprise and irritation mixed on Macalister's face, like he was upset I wasn't willing to accept this grand gesture he'd been forced to make on her behalf. "She confirmed her intent wasn't to kill you."

Royce's tone dripped with sarcasm. "Well, that's great." His shoulders were tense, his posture adversarial. "Her fake apology means nothing. The only person it matters to is you. I guarantee she isn't saying it because she feels bad. She's only apologizing because you demanded it."

An apology meant admitting you were wrong, and that mistake gave him power over her. She'd told me before she and Royce were Macalister's greatest failures. They didn't submit to him like everyone else did.

Now she had to.

Macalister pretended his son didn't exist and kept his focus locked on me. "You're a reasonable person. You understand sooner or later you will have to deal with the situation so we can all move past it."

Move past it? My blood simmered hotly in my body. "Sooner or later, huh? I choose later, then." I drew in a deep breath, filling my voice with as much power and finality as possible. "If there's nothing else—goodnight, Macalister."

Oh, he didn't like the way I'd spoken to him one bit and hated how he couldn't do anything about it even more. He was a burning glacier, raging fire trapped under thick ice. He cast a final look at me before he went, and it was so dark, it opened a void inside my stomach and threatened to swallow me whole. But I kept my face neutral, holding firm as he strode to the door and pulled it closed behind him with an angry thump.

My first night in Royce's bed didn't lend itself toward decent, restful sleep. I was a light sleeper, but he wasn't, and although his snores were relatively soft, I tossed and turned, unable to get comfortable or keep my mind quiet.

It amazed me how quickly he drifted off after turning off the light, totally relaxed to share a bed with someone else, even when he'd said he'd never done it before. If anything, I should have been the one more familiar with it. Emily and I had been close growing up, and I'd often snuck into her room and climbed into her bed. We'd stayed up late to whisper about cute boys and gossip.

There'd always been plenty of both to come by in Cape Hill.

But tonight, there was no whispered gossip with Royce. We didn't cuddle. He stuck to his side of the enormous bed and me to mine, and after a quick goodnight kiss, he'd snapped off the light and gone right to sleep.

I turned away from him and mashed my pillow beneath my head.

Earlier, when I'd changed and prepared for bed in my room, I'd discovered the chess set Macalister had given me—where the pieces were from the Greek myths—had been set up on my coffee table. A white pawn was placed forward two squares, as if Macalister were playing the white side of the board now and had made his opening move.

Instead, I put the piece back on its home space in the starting position.

I'd told him no more games, and I'd meant it, no matter how beautiful the chess pieces were or that I'd begrudgingly come to enjoy the strategy of it. What was he thinking, anyway? That I'd invite him into my room to play?

Fuck that.

The only time we'd used this set, the pieces had been flung across the room, and his mouth had smothered mine while he'd pushed me against the bookcase.

It irritated me how he was already trying to bend the rules when we'd only made the deal two days ago, although I wasn't that surprised. He liked to push. He was happiest when the people around him weren't.

And I was still upset from earlier, when he hadn't listened when I'd told him I didn't want to talk about it. What Royce had said was likely right. His stepmother wasn't interested in my forgiveness, only pleasing her husband.

I rolled back over to face my fiancé, doing it noisily to try to wake him, but it didn't work. His face was peaceful, and although he looked gorgeous like that, resentment itched across my skin. I was exhausted, but he made sleeping impossible. The least he could do was wake up and keep me company.

My mind kept going back to the chess set.

It was foolish, but I was becoming desperate. Maybe I'd be able to sleep if the set was gone, out of my room. I tossed back the covers and climbed out of bed. Royce didn't even stir as I padded on bare feet to the door and slipped out.

The hallway was dark; the only source of light came from the arched window at the end. The moonlight cast panes of silver over the rich red carpet, which looked like a swath of blood flowing to fill every corner. It was incessantly cold in the house, and I shivered in my cotton tank top and shorts.

When a black shadow stepped into my path, my lungs seized. It was a full second before my heart came back to life.

"Lucifer," I scolded the cat in a whisper. "You scared me."

He was unconcerned. He brushed against my leg and *meowed* softly, happy to see another soul awake at this hour, and he didn't care who it was. I let out my tight breath, reached down, and scratched him behind his ears. His deep purr was . . . satisfying.

The only pets I'd had growing up were fish, and they hadn't really been mine. For a while, Emily had wanted to be a marine biologist, so my parents had bought her a huge saltwater tank, complete with living coral and tropical fish, and hired a man who came twice a week to do all the things needed to keep everything alive.

My sister had let me name some of the shrimp and one

of the purple-yellow fish. He'd been Poseidon, of course. The shrimp were Oceanids—sea nymphs in Greek mythology. The tank had been gorgeous, but as I thought back on it, all I could see was the frivolous money behind it. By the time it was set up, Emily had begun to move on to the next thing. My parents didn't care. They loved us fiercely and gave my sister and me anything we wanted.

But if they had exercised a little restraint, it was possible I wouldn't have been wandering the halls of the Hale mansion right now at two in the morning.

I scowled at myself. That wasn't fair to blame them for my situation. No one had forced me. No one had made me agree to the life I now lived except me.

Lucifer followed me optimistically as I went into my bedroom, hoping for more attention, but my focus had already moved to the chessboard. I pushed the pieces to the center of the board and carefully picked it up. He meowed quietly while I carried it down the hall and into the library.

As I stepped inside, my gaze flew to the imposing figure looming at the window. The board tilted in my hands, pieces slid off the side, and clattered noisily to the floor.

My heart lurched to a stop.

FIVE

THE CHESS PIECES CRASHED LIKE STONES AGAINST THE hardwood, some with a loud bang and others with barely a ping, but the noise was enough to startle Lucifer and send the cat running.

Macalister turned at the sound, and pale moonlight cast across his face. It made him look even less human. Like he was a statue of unmovable granite. Helping that idea was the fact he wasn't wearing a shirt. Only a pair of loose black lounge pants that hugged his hips.

Not that he was ever the type of man to 'lounge.'

It was the most casual and undressed I'd ever seen him, and I found it terrifying.

Beneath the dusting of dark hair on his chest, his muscles were toned, and his waist was trim. It didn't look like the typical body of a fifty-one-year-old man, but one much younger. He obviously worked hard to maintain his physique. I'd been told he exercised religiously with weights, ate a strict diet and jogged on the treadmill most evenings after dinner, catching up on emails and watching the opening of the Japanese stock markets.

And he sometimes ran on the treadmill in the middle of the night because, unlike his son who was dead asleep down the hall, Macalister suffered from insomnia.

"Marist." He looked as surprised to see me as I was him, but that was where our similarity stopped. He gazed at me as an unexpected gift, and I viewed him like I was the prey caught in his trap.

I didn't want him to see the fear he caused in me, so I used a harsh tone. "You scared the shit out of me."

He didn't apologize. He simply watched me as I bent down and began to collect the scattered chess pieces. Hopefully, he didn't see the nervous tremble working its way up my spine. It was impossible not to feel the danger that still lingered in the library. The memory of what had happened just three days ago clung to the air like sickly-sweet perfume. It hadn't had enough time to air out.

"Did you come to play?" he asked.

"No." I set one of the rooks—a Greek column—down on the board with too much force. "I wanted this out of my room."

"You don't like it?" It was impossible to tell if he was hurt or angry or offended.

"No, it's just—" I put my hands on my knees, sat back on my heels, and gave him a hard look. "I don't like the memory that goes with it."

He nodded with understanding. "Ah. That was a difficult night for you."

Of course, he thought I meant the part where I'd been drugged by his jealous wife, and not where he'd demanded I come to his room wearing only my masquerade mask.

You will give me anything I ask for, he'd demanded.

He crouched down in front of me, bringing our gazes level. "It was difficult for me as well."

I opened my mouth to spew my angry vitriol at him, but he wasn't done speaking.

"Are you aware I was the one who found Julia after her accident?" His expression was calm, but it was like beautiful ice over a river, hiding the dangerous current roaring beneath it. "I held her in my arms as the life slipped out of her." The blue of his eyes deepened as he lowered the shield he typically held over himself. "I didn't think I'd ever have to experience that again, but then I found you on the stairs."

His statement filled me with both sadness and dread. No one should have to live through what he had. Watching the woman he'd clearly loved—and the mother of his children—fade away right before his eyes.

But to equate me with his first wife . . . was *horrifying*.

I scrambled to steer him away from the comparison. "I wasn't talking about that. I meant what happened after you lost our chess match."

His gaze turned down to the floor, and he picked up the upended Zeus, setting the king back on the board. "The craftsmanship on this set is excellent, don't you think?"

My jaw hurt from how hard I had it clenched. Wasn't he going to acknowledge what I'd said?

The answer was no. I snatched up the figure closest to me, and the sharp edge bit into my fingers. The words came out before I realized the double-meaning. "Hera's broken."

"Yes," he said.

There was a treacherous current flowing through the room, and it grew stronger when his gaze pinned me in place. He held me hostage as he studied me, his focus gliding down from my eyes, coasting over my lips, and slipping down the line of my throat. I felt every flick of his eyes as they worked me over, taking in the hurried, uneven breath I drew in and the peaks my nipples made through my white tank top in the cold room.

My voice faltered when I wanted it to sound confident. "You promised."

He scowled. "I haven't done anything."

But the way he was looking at me was a clear violation, and we both knew it. He tore his gaze away, picked up the board, and set it on the desk. The moonlight rippled across his bare, strong back.

"I'll have it fixed or replaced," he said, arranging the pieces in the proper place. And then he moved a white pawn forward two spaces, the same opening from earlier.

I shot to my feet. "No. I'm not playing with you."

He turned, giving me the full intensity of his expression, and my mouth went dry. "And I am done playing with you, Marist. You told me you loved me. You can lie and say you thought it was him, but we both know better. What you confessed was the truth. You were dying and had nothing left to lose."

Fire smoldered in my bones and locked up my body. "No," I seethed. "I don't love you, Macalister. I can't, because *I hate you.*"

The smile that spread across his face was slow and wicked. "You're young. You don't understand the way you feel about me, and that's all right. I can be patient. In time, you'll say it again."

My eyes went so wide, it was painful. "You're fucking delusional."

His eyebrow arrowed up in irritation, although I wasn't sure if it was the language I'd used, or the concept, or both. "Hate and love are nearly the same emotion—a powerfully strong reaction." His tone was sharp and cutting. "Every one of the myths you enjoy is fueled by one or the other. How quickly does Persephone's hate turn to love for Hades?"

Did he see himself as Hades? The desire to run filled every inch of my body, and I turned, practically sprinting toward the door.

"Marist," he called after me, slowing my escape. "There've been exactly two other women in my lifetime who've said they hated me." He was all intense eyes, gleaming in the low light of the room. "You should know, I married both of them."

I ran from the library, not stopping until I was in my own room and I'd turned the bolt on the lock to my door.

As if it could keep out the horrible things Macalister had said.

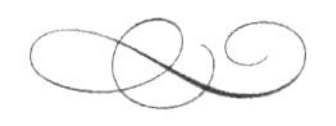

I sent a text to Royce in the morning on my way to class.

Me: Sorry I left last night. Couldn't sleep and didn't want to wake you.

Royce: It's okay.

But was it? That was the only reply I got all morning, and I spent a good portion of my day overanalyzing it. Had he woken up, discovered an empty bed, and felt bad? Or had he been relieved? I chewed at my nails during the lecture on corporate finance.

I'd missed several hours of class on Monday and Tuesday, but my professors were understanding. I was given reading assignments and notes from teaching assistants, and as soon as I returned home, I went to my room and delved in—determined to get caught up.

So determined, in fact, that it was after eight o'clock when I checked the time on my phone. Royce was typically home by seven, and we usually ate dinner together when we didn't have a social obligation. Had he returned from the office and decided not to bother me? Or was he avoiding me?

His bedroom door was left open so Lucifer could come and go, but I could see the light wasn't on.

Me: Are you still at the office?

Royce: Sorry. Working late.

Bubbles appeared as he continued to type.

Royce: Working on Ascension with my dad. Will be home late.

Disappointment I wouldn't see him was slightly offset by the fact I wouldn't have to see Macalister either.

As I ate dinner, I devised a plan. I didn't have much experience in the art of seduction, but the only way to get better at it was to practice. It was just another form of manipulation, and I was a bit eager to try that kind out on the man who excelled at it.

He'd been my first in nearly everything.

So he could be the first to make love to me too.

And I'd make it impossible for him to avoid me. Armed with my course of action, I went into his room, all the way into his closet. The dress shirt he'd worn yesterday was still in the basket to be laundered, so I dug it out.

I stripped off the clothes I'd been wearing, dropping them in a heap on his closet floor, everything except the lacy panties I wore, then pulled on the white shirt that was too big for me.

It smelled like him. Woodsy and masculine.

The shirt hem barely covered my ass, and I only did up the bottom few buttons, leaving the top open so it was clear what I was and wasn't wearing beneath it. The final piece was the green tie he'd worn the night he'd appeared in the library. I looped it around my neck and tied it loosely so the knot hung between my breasts.

Then I climbed into his big bed and waited.

Anticipation crawled up my spine. It made me hyper-aware of my body and the way the silk of his tie and the soft bedding felt against my skin. It had me imagining all the different scenarios that could play out when he got home and discovered me in his bed. Would he drop everything and crawl on top of me? Would he be upset I'd come in here without his permission?

Would he *punish* me for it?

A sexy shiver glanced through my shoulders.

Without making a conscious decision, my fingertips crept down the front of my panties, moving to alleviate the ache. Royce had spent a lot of nights in this bed thinking about me while he touched himself, and I liked how I was now doing the same.

I swallowed thickly as my fingers glided over my clit, bringing warmth and satisfaction. My eyes fluttered closed, and I relaxed back against the pillows, settling in to enjoy myself. Not too much, though. Hopefully, he would arrive soon and finish me off.

A sigh slipped from my lips. As I rubbed faster, the sensation caused me to arch my back. I wanted to writhe with pleasure. Give myself over to it and find release, but I controlled myself. The teasing was delicious and awful.

Time passed, although I wasn't sure how long. I wasn't aware of anything other than the heat building inside my body and the craving for him. When I got too close, I pulled my hand away and pressed it to the mattress, gulping down air. My heart raced, sweat dampened my temples, and—

New, different awareness rolled through me. A tingle activated an alarm, and my eyes popped open to discover Royce's blue eyes fixed on me. His expression dripped with sex and lust and want. He looked at me like I was the sexiest thing he'd ever seen.

Warmth flooded my face. He'd seen me touch myself before, but that was when we'd been in the shower and during sex. This was different. I wasn't embarrassed, but I was surprisingly shy. Vulnerable and exposed and showing him something no one else had seen.

I was showing him the effect he had over me. Did he realize how much power he held?

His penetrative stare was a heat lamp, both exposing and lighting me up, and two words fell from his mouth in a dark command that could have easily been a growl. "Don't stop."

Oh, Jesus.

Fire ripped through me, and goosebumps burst all along my legs. I had my knees drawn up and my feet on the bed, causing his shirt to gape wide, the edges caught on my breasts. It made the tie hang between them like a long necklace. I held his gaze through my parted legs as my fingers oh-so-slowly dipped back beneath the lace. Electricity swirled between us while I followed his order. His jaw set, and I wondered if he'd done it to hold back a groan.

But I only complied long enough to watch the satisfaction twist on his face. We'd spent too much time thinking about each other while satisfying ourselves. Desire thickened my voice. "Make love to me."

His answer was immediate. "No."

I froze. What did he mean, no? Breath caught in my lungs.

It released when his hands went to the tie he wore and jerked the knot free. It was thrown to the floor, and then he went to work, shedding the suit jacket, and his nimble fingers sped down the buttons of his shirt.

"That's not what I want," he said. "Not what I think about when I picture you in my bed." A dark look burned in his eyes. It was dangerous and thrilling. "I'm not going to be delicate or gentle. That was yesterday. Tonight, I'm going to be hard and rough and *exactly* how I've imagined it, where you're shaking and moaning, and I get to find out if I can make you scream. That's how you want it, don't you?"

"Yes," I breathed. There was no other answer.

He smirked as he tugged off his shoes, undid his pants, and kicked them off. I started to undo the tie I wore, but he shook his head. "Oh, no, Marist. You put that on for me, so it fucking stays on."

I touched the tip of my tongue to the roof of my mouth, keeping a moan from leaking out.

He was a blur as he climbed onto the bed and crawled up my body, and when his hot mouth closed over mine, I didn't have a chance at keeping my moan at bay. His hands . . . his *fucking* hands went everywhere. He wasn't exploring, he was triumphant. Ares reveling in the spoils of war.

His palm was warm against my thigh, and he curled it behind my knee, pulling my leg up until it was hooked around his waist. Pleasure slipped through me as his erection pressed against my center, right where I was aching.

Once his hands were inside the shirt I wore, he began to make good on his promise. Royce's touch was rough and urgent. He pinched and gripped me so hard, it stole my breath. And as I'd done the last time we'd been together, I matched his intensity. My arms were around his shoulders, and I moved them to score my nails down his back.

He sank his teeth into my neck, biting hard enough it made me cry out, and I knew it would leave a mark. He heard my hiss of pain, but he didn't apologize or ease up, and thank God. I'd thought I wanted him to make love because I wanted passion, but there was so much of it here it ran through his mean hands and dripped from his cruel kiss.

I fucking loved it.

"Were you thinking about me?" He pawed at the open collar of the shirt and buried his face inside, nosing the tie out of his way. "When you were touching yourself in my bed?"

"Yes."

"You better have been." He sucked hard at me, releasing my nipple from his lips with a soft *pop*. His hips thrust forward, stabbing himself at the seam of my legs, and my eyes threatened to roll back in my head. We weren't even having sex yet, and it still felt so good.

He jammed a hand in his underwear, stretching it down just enough to free himself, hooked a finger in the side of my panties to shove them out of his way, and lined his cock up so he could push inside me with one rough thrust.

"*Fuck*," he cursed into the side of my neck.

My body throbbed and ached around his invasion, a weirdly enjoyable pain. There hadn't been much foreplay between us, but I'd been more than ready, and the slide of him inside me set me alight. The craving for him shifted as tinder on a fire, making me burn hotter still.

He settled his weight into the cradle of my hips and began to move, pumping while he still had his hand holding my underwear aside.

"He thinks I'm a child. I'm forever that ten-year-old he can't control." Royce's voice was dark and bitter. "But I can be fucking patient, can't I, Marist?" His thrust was hard, punishing. "No matter how much it killed me, no matter how badly I wanted you, I *waited*."

My head spun. While I liked hearing it, I had to fight the recoil at the mention of his father. I wanted this moment to just be between us. Determination ringed Royce's eyes as he drove into me. The sharp slap of our bodies was followed by my unstoppable moan.

"You know what that was like?" His question was mindless. "How hard it was to watch him go after you, and know if I did anything to try to stop it, it'd only make it worse?"

"Royce," I panted as he writhed on top of me. The pleasure was building so much it grew difficult to speak.

Abruptly, he reared back, and as he pulled out of me, he raked his hands down my hips, dragging my panties along with them. They tangled with my feet as he hastily yanked them off and cast them aside.

"Mine," he growled.

There was darkness in him tonight, and he became a blend of Ares and Hades as he threw himself back on top of me. He made good on his threat. His way was careless and selfish. Pushed to the edge, he became ruthless. As if every aggression he'd held back had spilled out and there was no putting it back in the bottle. Being submissive to his father had taken its toll on him, and I was paying the price, but in this moment I didn't care. I fed off his intensity and waged an assault of my own.

"You think you're the only one who suffered?" I snarled. "I waited and then some."

When he kissed me, I bit his bottom lip hard enough he gave a grunt of discomfort, but inside me, his cock throbbed.

I had instigated tonight, but Royce had taken control, and he demanded I keep up with him. We were a partnership, after all.

"Mine," I echoed, claiming him right back.

His sound of satisfaction was sexy as hell. "I'm going to fuck you here in my bed every night. I don't care if you get sore or tired." Our joined bodies moved together, undulating on the bed so hard, the headboard began to thump steadily against the wall. "We've got too much time to make up for."

He was absolutely right.

We fucked until we were both sticky with sweat. At some point, he wriggled out of his underwear completely, so he was free to move his legs and get better leverage. And then he demanded I unbutton and open the shirt I was wearing so it wasn't between us. Only the green tie that hung around my neck as an unclaimed leash.

My hands gripped his hair, the dark tresses threaded through my fingers, as I held onto him. Exertion had left him short of breath, and he panted in the curve of my neck, filling the space with sweltering heat.

I wanted to come. Not just to experience the pleasure, but to lose myself in him. To give up all control and show him how he left me undone. He was close too. The cadence of his body had changed. Shorter, deliberate strokes and tense muscles made me think he wasn't giving freely anymore. He was holding himself back from his end so we could keep going.

And while it felt amazing, my body had hit a frustrating plateau. It left me dangling right on the cusp, tingling with anticipation but no end in sight. With him pressed so tightly on top of me, I couldn't wedge a hand between us and push myself over the edge.

"Make me come," I pleaded.

Fire flashed through his eyes, and for one fleeting moment, it was scary how much they looked like his father's. But his tone wasn't commanding, it was sinful. Wicked and teasing. "You don't get to tell me what to do."

He pushed up on his hands, shoving his knees beneath me while keeping us connected, and wrapped a fist around the knot of my tie. It was so he could draw me up with him as he sat up. It made me feel like I was his puppet and he was my master. The silk dug into my skin, and the muscle of his strong bicep flexed as he yanked me up into his arms.

Royce was sitting back on his heels and I was straddling his lap, the open shirt hanging loosely around my sides, and the collar beginning to slip down off my shoulders.

The change in position made my eyes widen, and pleasure bolt through me in a white-hot flash. I was fitted so tightly against him, it put pressure against my clit in a new way, and his hand at my hip urged me to grind against him.

"Oh, fuck," I groaned. My head tipped forward, my forehead landing against the hard flat of his shoulder.

But it didn't deter him. His exacting hand pushed and pulled and guided, making pinpricks of heat travel along my legs. I gasped and clung to him, the shirt hanging at my elbows while I rode him at a frantic pace.

"Yeah," he encouraged in a strained voice. "Get there."

It tumbled from my lips, followed by uncontrollable moans. "Oh, my God."

An instinctive force took over. It swept through my body as the devastating orgasm crashed into me. It made me move and writhe to wring every last drop of pleasure from him, like a dance I hadn't learned the steps to but knew anyway.

I'd been so lost in my own bliss, I'd barely recognized he'd reached his climax at the same time until we were both coming down. My shuddering body was encased in his arms, his heaving chest beating against mine as we cooled and recovered.

His soft request broke the stillness surrounding us. "Tell me you love me."

I lifted my head to peer down into his eyes and watched the guilt edge into them. It was a moment of weakness, and he was displeased with himself for asking when he'd said he wasn't going to anymore.

When his lips parted to say something, I pressed a finger to them. I matched his cocky tone from before. "You don't get to tell me what to do." I brushed the finger away so I could put my lips in its place, but not before I uttered, "But I love you anyway."

I made my second attempt to sleep in Royce's bed that night, but by two in the morning, I snuck out and stole away to the comfort of my own room. In the morning, he told me he didn't mind. All he wanted was for me to be comfortable. After a week of it, I stopped feeling guilty. We had time to figure it out, I told myself.

The cycle continued until we fell into a pattern.

Sex. Sleep. And then I'd slip out.

We were both busy. I had school and he had work—which kept him busier than ever—and we both had events to go to. Plus, there was wedding planning that needed to be done. It mostly fell on my shoulders. In the month since the dreadful night of the gala, I hadn't seen or heard from Macalister's wife. Not so much as an email.

I barely saw Macalister either. He was often gone on business trips overseas, and when he was home, he was hard at work on the Ascension deal. I foolishly hoped his obsession with me was waning, but I knew better. An uneasy feeling churned in my gut as if it were the calm before the storm.

He wouldn't give up, and it was win at all costs.

I wouldn't be able to avoid him or his wife for much longer, though. It was mid-November, and the upcoming holiday loomed overhead. I'd spent every Thanksgiving—along with everyone else in the high society of Cape Hill—in Aspen. It was as if the entire Massachusetts town relocated to Colorado for an extended weekend of skiing and drama.

We rode in the back of the town car to Logan Airport, Royce's hand resting comfortably on my thigh as he pressed his phone to his ear and listened in on a meeting that was wrapping up. He was always touching me now, even when cameras weren't around. As if I might disappear if the connection between us was broken.

The car pulled up to the sleek private jet, which was waiting for us with the door open, a gaping mouth threatening to devour us.

We hadn't talked about what was going to happen, but I knew. The other black Range Rover parked on the tarmac confirmed it. Royce and I weren't flying to Aspen alone. It made sense. The Hale jet was big enough for a dozen people.

Acid churned in my belly as the driver opened my door, which meant I was expected to get out, walk across the pavement, and climb the steps, then endure a four-hour flight locked in a confined space with Macalister.

Royce would be there too, though. We parted just long enough to get out of the car, pull our jackets closed in the blustery November wind, and then he took my hand, entwining our fingers.

"It's not that long of a flight," he muttered, like he was saying it for his own benefit and not mine. I didn't understand why he was so anxious about it until the doors of the other Range Rover opened and I caught the swath of blonde hair.

My knees locked, bringing me to a rigid stop.

SIX

I SHOULD HAVE ANTICIPATED THIS, BUT I WAS SO FOCUSED ON Macalister, I hadn't thought about her. Of course, *she* was required to make an appearance Thanksgiving weekend. The rest of the world believed everything was right with the Hale family and it wasn't splintered into a million pieces.

Seeing her forced her name to crash through my head like a wrecking ball.

Alice.

She stood statuesque on her high heels, wrapped in a perfectly cut dress coat of blue wool that looked made for her, and it probably had been. Her pale hair was down and sleek, the ends curling faintly under to give her lift. As usual, her makeup was flawless, but gone was any warmth. Like her husband, she mirrored his iciness.

When we locked eyes, there was no reaction from her. She didn't drop my gaze in shame or flash an evil smile. She was indifferent. Unapologetic. And it was exactly as I expected. Hera never felt guilt about the terrible things she did to Zeus's mistresses, even the ones who'd been unwilling or tried to run from him.

For a split second, I felt fear, but it dissolved in the acid in my stomach, leaving only anger. I wasn't going to give her that kind of power over me. She'd tried to kill me . . . and she'd failed. Maybe she *should* look at me with shame. I was one of her failures, and Macalister craved perfection.

Royce stopped at the same moment I did, and tension tightened his shoulders. He said it in a loud voice, projecting across the tarmac. "We agreed you'd be on the plane already when we got here."

Likely so Royce and I wouldn't have to see Alice.

Macalister didn't care for his son's tone. "Yes, but unfortunately, my business doesn't run on your timetable."

And with that exchange done, every pair of eyes swung toward me, gauging my reaction. I ground my teeth and sucked in a deep breath, then strode defiantly toward the steps. Beneath the layers of my coat and clothes, I thought about the Medusa tattoo buried in my skin.

Like her, I wasn't easy to defeat.

The interior of the plane was decorated in the same gold and cream color scheme as the helicopter had been. Plush, oversized chairs were arranged in pairs around a table on either side of the aisle, with more seating in the rear of the plane beyond an open partition that sectioned off the space. I made a beeline to it. At least this way, I could either keep my eyes on Alice and know where she was at all times, or Royce would close the door, and we wouldn't have to see her at all.

I ducked into the window seat in the back corner and busied myself with getting settled while impatiently waiting for Royce to join me. But he stood in the aisle, his hand resting on the back of his chair and his gaze fixed on the other passengers boarding the plane. I couldn't see them beyond the glossy wood panel, but I sensed their presence.

And Macalister's irritation. "You appear to be waiting for someone else."

Royce's expression was impossible to read when he was in profile. "We are."

It sounded as if Macalister had taken his seat. "Vance is flying with the Lamberts."

"I know. It's not Vance."

Out the window, a steel gray Aston Martin prowled into one of the spaces beside the airport hangar, parked, and the lights turned off. The man stepped out, wearing a navy suit, a camel colored coat, and a pair of aviator sunglasses. I didn't need to see his eyes to know how confident he felt as he pulled his suitcase from the trunk and marched toward the jet.

His arrogance rivaled Royce's, and it made sense. He'd become the king of Cape Hill Prep the year after Royce had graduated.

"Tate," Macalister said. "I wasn't aware you were joining us."

"Hope that's not a problem, sir. My family isn't flying out until tomorrow, and Royce said you had space."

"It's fine."

As Tate moved down the aisle toward Royce, he came into view. The sunglasses had been tucked away in a pocket, and he pulled off his overcoat.

"I say it every time we see each other," Macalister said

abruptly, causing Tate to freeze, "but when are you going to get serious and come join us at HBHC?"

As Tate finished pulling off his coat, a slow smile widened on his lips. "Ascension is good to me."

"Is that so? I would be better." Macalister had said *I*, and not *we*, as if he were the entirety of his massive company. His tone was barely disguised disgust. "Where do they have you now, loans?"

Tate turned back to face him directly. "Wealth management."

"We both know you're better than that."

"Thanks, but I like New York."

If he was nervous saying no to Macalister, it didn't read in his body language. Perhaps it was why Macalister seemed to respect him. Alice had told me Macalister was only interested in something when he had to chase it.

"You're putting off the inevitable." Macalister's voice sounded as close to friendly as he could manage, but the threat was laced inside. "Sooner or later, you'll be working for me."

Tate laughed it off. "If you say so, sir."

I exchanged a look with Royce. Did Tate know what was in the works? Had Royce shared any of his plan with his best friend? The shake of Royce's head was so subtle, I wasn't even sure if it was there, but a thrill coasted through me.

I was the only one he'd confided in.

Tate joined us in the back section of the plane and dropped down in the seat across from me. His dark-eyed gaze swept over me in appraisal. "Marist. Long time, no see."

It made me feel like an intruder, when it shouldn't have. He'd known Royce better than I had for years. Although, was that true? Royce had shared the real part of himself with me, and likely no one else. Time didn't automatically make you closer.

A dark voice in my head reminded me the same was true with Emily. We'd been best friends our whole lives, and yet she'd kept things from me.

"Hi, Tate. It's nice to see you again."

He smoothed his palm down his tie in a gesture that was meant to seem innocent, but I suspected he'd done it to draw attention to the way his fitted shirt emphasized his broad chest and hinted at toned abs.

Playfulness warmed his eyes as he caught me watching. "I bet it is."

I blinked and shot both him and my fiancé an unamused look. Royce had said nearly the same thing to me when we'd met in the library last year. "Did they teach you that line in school? Like, being cocky is the same thing as being charming? Because it isn't."

Tate grinned, his gaze darting between me and his best friend seated at my side, whose hand was laced with mine. "Sure seemed to work on you, though."

Heat warmed my face and probably tinged my cheeks pink. Oh, it had. I'd told myself I'd hated Royce's cockiness, but if I were honest, I found it undeniably appealing. I turned my gaze out the window as I heard the attendant retract the steps and close the cabin door.

It didn't take long before we were rolling down the

runway and the engines carried us up into the sky. Royce and Tate chatted about politics and business, discussing the latest mergers and shake-ups in New York, and who had been poached from one house to another. It was the closest to gossiping I'd heard my fiancé do.

There was an ease and confidence to them both as the private jet sped toward the luxury vacation homes awaiting us in Aspen, and I couldn't help but feel a tinge of irony for the man sitting across from me.

As the only black student in a sea of white at Cape Hill Prep, Tate could have been classified as an 'other.' But the only color that seemed to matter at our school was green, and the Isaacs had a lot of it. His parents were ultra-successful attorneys, and their son had been universally loved by all. He may have looked different than his friends, but he wasn't.

It was the weird, outspoken Marist Northcott who was the 'other' at Cape Hill Prep.

But today on this plane, I didn't feel like an 'other.' I'd seen behind the curtain of the Hales, whereas Tate was blissfully ignorant. What were Royce's motivations for inviting him along? Surely, he wasn't going to talk Ascension with his father in earshot. Maybe he'd done it to prevent Macalister from doing so. His father wouldn't discuss a takeover when one of the target company's employees was in the same room.

After the plane had leveled off, Macalister appeared at the doorway, and his cold gaze zeroed in on Royce's hand tangled with mine.

"Marist," he said, "after we've arrived, Alice and I would like a word"—his eyes flicked to Tate—"in private."

My mouth dropped open, but before I could say anything, Royce's hand squeezed mine. "Sorry, the three of us have plans."

Tate was in a rear-facing seat, which meant Macalister couldn't see the confusion drift through his expression. If we had plans with him, it was news to Tate, but he said nothing.

The information unraveled in my brain. *This* was why Royce had invited Tate. He'd anticipated an ambush by his father and brought his friend along to foil Macalister's plans. Alice couldn't deliver a personal apology while someone outside the family was around.

Royce had done it to save me, and I was grateful.

But Macalister wasn't going to give up easily. He turned his attention from his son to me and issued it like it was non-negotiable. "It will only take a few minutes."

I gave him a flat smile that didn't touch my eyes, hoping he would understand my meaning. "Of course. When I'm ready."

Satisfied, he turned and went back to his seat.

There was already a fire going in the fireplace when I followed Royce into the bedroom, and it wasn't the altitude that took my breath away—it was the view. Floor-to-ceiling windows showed off the Rocky Mountains in glorious splendor. We were surrounded by white peaks, which gave way to dense evergreens, some with ski runs channeling through them, and below the orange-yellow glow of Aspen in early evening.

"We're the highest house on this mountain," Royce said. "No one is allowed to build above us."

Even the balcony off the bedroom was surrounded with glass railings so as not to obstruct the view. "It's stunning." I turned to face him and found him staring at the king-sized bed. "What's wrong?"

He lifted his blue eyes to meet mine, and determination crystalized in them. "I'm not going to tell you where the guest bedrooms are. This is our room."

My heartbeat quickened. I strived for a teasing tone, but now he was the thing leaving me breathless. "I'm smart. I'll probably find them."

"No, you won't. I've decided we're not leaving Aspen until we have our sleeping arrangements sorted out."

I swallowed thickly as he made his steady approach. "Are you saying I'm not allowed to escape anymore?"

He slipped his arms around me, picked me up, and dumped me on my back on the soft bed. He loomed over me, his handsome face full of desire and something that looked dangerously like love. "No, you're not." His hands went to his belt and worked to undo it. "And right now, I'm going to give you a good reason to stay."

"Oh?" I purred.

"Yeah." He looked quite amused with himself. "A *big* one."

I laughed but made a production out of rolling my eyes, pretending his cocky statement had fallen flat. I didn't want him to see how much he affected me, even though he probably already knew. His deep eyes slipped right past any shields

I tried to put up.

He smoothed his hands up my leggings, reaching beneath the sweater dress I wore to start pulling them off. "But, seriously, I have an offer."

I feigned a serious face as I lifted my hips, making it easier for him to drag the leggings and my underwear off. "I'm listening."

He dropped the fabric to the floor and stepped between my parted legs, his hand working himself over. Just a few quick strokes, and he was impossibly hard. "You asked me to make love to you. I think I'm ready to try it."

The muscles low in my belly clenched. "Now?"

The corner of his mouth lifted in an impish grin. "No. Right now, I just want to get inside you. I'm so fucking horny I can barely see straight. You make me crazy."

"Same, Royce," I fake scolded. *So, fucking, same.*

He licked the pad of his thumb, which looked so indecent it should have been illegal, and pressed it to my clit, brushing tiny, slow circles. My toes curled into points behind his back.

"So, the deal is this. We make love? You have to stay in our bed."

My heart jerked to a stop then lurched forward with excitement. I liked his offer very much, and there was no need to counter.

"Deal?" he asked.

"Deal," I whispered.

His smile was a mixture of happiness and sin as he pushed himself inside me.

We went out to dinner, avoiding the rest of the Hale family we were sharing the enormous house with, and afterward, we met up with Tate and the rest of the people who floated in Royce's social circle at an outdoor bar. There was snow on the ground, but heaters attached to open patio umbrellas rained down warmth, along with the stone firepits blazing in the center of the groupings of chairs and couches. It was warm enough, most people had their coats off or at least unbuttoned.

String lights draped from umbrella to umbrella, a connected web that gave the space a magical feel.

Vance sat on one of the couches, Jillian Lambert curled up under his arm. I could tell her affection for him was genuine, but I had no idea if it were true for him. Like his older brother, Vance was a great liar. His father had proclaimed he date Lambert's daughter, and it was unclear if he had any feelings and was simply following orders.

And his thoughts on Alice were even murkier.

Had he cared for her as a lover? Or was she just a way for him to stick it to his father? Perhaps he was like Royce and believed he was incapable of caring about anything, unless he wanted to risk Macalister taking it away.

"How's law school?" I asked him as I sat down in the chair closest to the fire.

His gaze darted away from mine. I hadn't seen him in at least two weeks. Was it possible he'd been avoiding me?

He said it so quietly I almost didn't hear it over the

conversations and laughter happening around us at the bar. "It's . . . hard." He drained the beer he was drinking and pasted on a smile, nudging Jillian. "Hey, mind getting us another round?"

She sat up and gave him the evil eye, probably about to tell him she wasn't his servant—

"It took us fucking forever to get drinks when I ordered them. Royce and Tate are still waiting. The bartenders are only serving the hot girls tonight. It'll take you, like, two seconds."

Mollified, Jillian stood and collected their empty drinks.

She was barely gone before he straightened, leaning in to speak in a hushed voice. "I'm sorry."

I froze. "For?"

"I dunno. A lot of things. I wasn't thinking about anyone else that night." His eyebrows pulled together and his forehead wrinkled. "I didn't think Alice would care if I hooked up with Jillian. I mean, she didn't just sign off on it with my dad, she'd practically told me to do it." He sighed and ran a hand through his already unruly brown hair. "I would've sworn she didn't give two shits about me, and, well—I decided that night I was going to find out."

Meaning he'd wanted to get caught, just to see her reaction. My voice was dead. "What a terrific plan you came up with."

"Yeah, I know." He scrubbed the hand down the side of his face. "So, I'm sorry. I had no idea she was going to lose it like that."

"You and me both."

The sincere guilt he felt made me uncomfortable. Had he been callous with Alice's feelings? Absolutely. But they were both adults, one of them married, and I didn't blame him.

"Hey," I said softly, "you didn't make her do what she did." I glanced around to confirm no one was listening. "She made that choice on her own."

"I didn't help the situation."

"No," I agreed. "But afterward you did. Royce told me you went to my parents' house. You've been so busy I never got a chance to thank you."

"Well, don't." He gave a tight smile, trying to lighten the mood. "I got to see your sister, who—by the way—is still hot, even when she's pregnant as fuck."

"Aw," I said, overly sweet, "you're gross."

"What are we talking about?" Tate asked, lowering into a chair across from me. Royce appeared beside him, carrying both of our drinks.

"How hot Marist's sister is," Vance announced.

Tate's head bobbed in agreement then swiveled to glance around. "Where is she?"

I took the glass of wine from Royce as he sat beside me. "Emily couldn't make the trip. She's on bed rest."

Macalister had invited my family to Thanksgiving dinner tomorrow night, which meant they had to come, but my sister's doctor didn't want her to travel. Royce had installed staff at the house over the weekend, so she'd have round-the-clock care while my parents were away. I was worried she'd be lonely, but she assured me she was fine.

Tate looked confused. "Bed rest?"

He lived in New York these days, so he wasn't up to speed on his Cape Hill gossip. "She's eight months pregnant."

"No shit. Really?" When I nodded, he asked, "Who's the dad?"

Before I could give him the canned response, Royce leaned forward and his voice was grave. "It's you, Tate."

For a fraction of a second, Tate went still, and then an enormous smile burst onto his face. "Fuck you, man. I was never with her. Not all of us can land a Northcott girl, you know."

A million thoughts streamed through my mind in an instant. First, I didn't want it to be, but it was bizarrely flattering to be thought of as a status symbol. And second, we were seated in a room full of people we'd gone to high school with. None of them had ever made an attempt to 'land me.'

"Royce was the only one with the guts to try," I said plainly.

Tate's mouth hung open in surprise before curling back into a smile. "Well, now I'm pissed I missed my chance."

"I'm not," Royce said, giving me a glance out of the corner of his eye.

Tate viewed me like stock. I wasn't worth much until Royce wanted me, and then my value quadrupled overnight.

He shifted uncomfortably in his chair, slouching down. "I didn't know Sophia Alby was going to be here." Tate and Sophia hadn't been very nice to me in the past, but they hadn't run in the same circles. School was over, but he still understood the power she wielded. "Why are you waving her over here?" he demanded of me.

When Sophia's gaze landed on the man seated in my

group, her eyes lit up like a target had been acquired and she was prepared to strike.

It was petty, but kind of fun to watch him squirm. "Oh, I invited her."

It was late when Royce's driver brought us back up the mountain to the house. The headlights cut through the dark, lighting up the winding road and the frozen forest beyond.

On the inside, I was vibrating with chaotic, excited energy. Royce wanted me in his bed tonight.

He wanted to make love to me, and by his own admission, he'd never done that.

We'd cross into this new territory together, and I was ready to jump out of my skin. How would he start? What was going to happen? I wouldn't have called him a hopeless romantic by any means, but he was plenty capable of seduction. He understood romance. Would there be candles and flowers like there'd been when he'd proposed?

The answer was no.

Just the warm, flickering fire trapped behind glass in the fireplace and the soft lighting in the elegant bedroom. I liked this. It was cozy and intimate. He opened a bottle of white wine and poured us each a glass, then brought me over to the couch opposite the bed and against the enormous windows. Before I sat, I took in the view one more time. Moonlight turned the snow on the mountains silver, and Aspen continued to glow brightly below, nestled in the valley.

We settled beside each other on the couch and sipped our wine in silence. Desire curled in the air, twisting with anticipation, making it hard to find words.

"You look nervous," I said.

His blue eyes were electric. "You've always made me nervous."

He was the prince of Cape Hill, and at just twenty-five years old, he was one of the wealthiest men in the country. I couldn't make anyone nervous, and certainly not him. I laughed softly. "Ridiculous."

He raised a perturbed eyebrow. "You don't believe me?" He leaned over, set his glass of wine down on the side table with a thud, and fixed the full intensity of his stare on me. "You, Marist, are the only thing in this world I've ever wanted—that I wasn't sure I was going to get."

My lungs refused to work.

When we were alone, he wasn't supposed to lie. He'd told me he wanted it more than anything. "What about your father's company?"

"Oh, I *know* I'm going to get that."

He moved, sliding off the couch and onto his knees, working his way until he was kneeling between my legs. It was like the night of our first date, where I'd ordered him to put his hands on me and he'd obliged. Only it was possible I was more nervous and desperate for him tonight than I had been all those months ago.

Royce took my wine glass from me and set it aside then drew me away from the back of the couch, so he could kiss me slowly and deeply and thoroughly, until every inch of me clamored to melt into him.

Nearly every night over the last month, we'd had sex. There'd been a few times where he'd been away on business, or we'd come home from a social thing and been too exhausted to do more than kiss goodnight. But typically, our evenings were spent crawling and scratching, writhing and biting and tangling in the sheets until we both found our release.

He fucked like Ares and I like Medusa.

We'd learned most of the secret places on each other's bodies to drive the other wild. Where to kiss to draw a moan, where to touch to create shudders and gasps. So, it was silly to be nervous. We should have felt comfortable. What we were doing wasn't physically different than any other time.

And yet, as his lips brushed down the curve of my neck, trembles worked along my legs. This felt different. Every sensation was heightened, each sound was new, and gravity deepened. Like what we were about to do was going to change *everything*.

He was lovesick Hades, and I was Persephone, his once unwilling bride who now was all in.

His kiss and touch were sedate and deliberate as he peeled us out of our clothes. He was taking his time, and his unhurried hands were strange and exciting. Completely different from our desperate encounter when we'd struck our deal earlier tonight.

When there wasn't a stitch of clothing left on our bodies, he fitted me tight to his waist and let me feel the hard, heavy weight of his cock against my center. Our warm, bare skin pressed to each other, my breasts flattened to his chest, and I swallowed a deep breath. His eyes locked onto mine, and the power of his stare leveled me. How was it possible I'd existed the first twenty-one years of my life and not seen the person he truly was? He'd hidden it so well.

And he'd seen me exactly as I was—better than anyone else.

He looked so beautiful like this. The outer edges of his irises were ringed in a darker color, like they'd been drawn first, outlined in navy and then filled in with a steely blue watercolor. His high cheekbones had only a faint shadow of darkness because he'd shaved before we left for dinner. As his gaze slipped down over my face, his lush lips parted, and he took in a slow, deep breath.

Watching him stare at me while longing painted his face was erotic.

I cupped his head in my hands and pulled him into a feverish kiss, eager to be connected to him in all ways. He was too but had better patience than I did. His hands, which were resting on my knees, smoothed up my thighs and over my hips, around my waist and up my back. His lips were sealed to mine, and his kiss advanced, easing me back against the couch cushions.

Royce's warm mouth carved a trail down through the valley of my breasts, leaving cool, damp skin behind. The fire raging in the fireplace was hot, but it didn't compare to my naked fiancé on his knees in front of me, steadily working his way toward the center of my legs. His kisses marched across my fluttering belly, and as he moved lower, he settled back on his legs, making himself more comfortable.

Like he planned to use his tongue to tease and pleasure me for a long while.

Goosebumps lifted and pebbled on my skin in the wake of his roaming hands, and my breath went ragged as he peered up at me from between my thighs, his mouth hovering only an inch away. Was he waiting for permission?

Or for me to start begging?

I was a heartbeat away from pleading with him to put his mouth on me before he set his hands on the spots where my legs met my body and used his thumbs to peel me open. All the air went out of the room when he leaned in.

One painfully slow lick made bliss crackle through my body.

I was a live wire beneath him. Every careful flick of his tongue caused me to jolt and jerk, but his hands held me steady. And his eyes—his fucking eyes—never let me go either, even when I closed mine because the image was too much to bear.

It was incendiary.

Tiny whimpers fell from my lips, and the tremble in my legs grew more intense. Royce knew how to make me come when he had his mouth on me. He could do it quickly if he wanted, faster still if he eased a finger deep inside me, but tonight he wasn't going for speed or efficiency. He wanted to draw it out and build my orgasm up layer by lush layer.

I was restless, though. The sensations were more acute tonight, which meant the tingling anticipation was sharp and demanding. I craved release mindlessly, squirming against the cushions, and tried to get him to increase the stroke of his tongue. Speed or pressure or whatever the fuck he wanted to do—just as long as he gave me *more.*

The need inside me drove my hands into his dark brown hair. It forced labored breath in and out of my lungs. Could he feel how badly he made me quake? Each pass of his tongue injected pleasure and heat in me, gathering strength as I rolled toward my climax.

I bucked and moaned, but he didn't let up. One of his hands slid to the inside of my thigh and pressed my leg back, opening me further to his indecent kiss and making my lower leg drape over his back. It pulled a loud, satisfied groan from my chest, and I reached behind me to grip the edge of the couch. If he kept this up much longer, it was possible I was going to scream. Maybe that was what he was waiting for.

My eyes fluttered open, and I looked down at him over my heaving chest, my nipples hardened into points. He gazed at me through hooded eyes, and I—

In spite of the fire and what Royce was doing to me, a cold draft washed down my spine. Something wasn't right, but my mind was soaked in lust, and the fog made it difficult to pinpoint what had set me off.

Wait. The door.

Had Royce left it like that, or perhaps ajar, and the hinges had let it slowly swing away from the frame? Because the ornate door with its brass handle was currently open, revealing the empty hallway beyond.

Not empty, a warning voice in my mind whispered.

I peered through the doorway into the darkness, letting

my eyes adjust to the form lurking there. As my gaze met his, Macalister stepped out of the shadows.

SEVEN

MACALISTER'S SILENT ENTRANCE TORE ME OPEN, POURED HOT lead inside, and then dumped me into the harbor. I sank into the depths, the pressure of the ocean water making it impossible to move or scream.

There weren't words to describe his expression. He was angry, that much was clear, but a myriad of other emotions skulked in his eyes. Longing. Jealousy. Hurt.

Interest.

With his back to the door, Royce was unaware of the danger who had edged into our room and now stood towering just inside the doorway. He was too focused on what he was doing to understand I'd seized up because of an intruder and not his tongue caressing my clit.

When I opened my mouth to speak, he pushed his finger past my entrance and deep inside my body. The unexpected pleasure was so great, my mind fractured and my body bowed instinctively. I let go of his hair and latched my other hand behind me, my elbows pointed to the ceiling as I arched up, away from the couch.

My moan was louder than the sound of satisfaction Royce gave, and it wasn't likely Macalister heard a thing besides me, anyway. He braced one hand on the doorframe, and the other that hung at his side curled into a white-knuckled fist.

All the control he had on himself was clutched in those fingers like a hand gripping reins, and the tense way he held his body screamed of the powerful chaos trapped inside. It was desperate for escape, for release.

His glacial eyes pierced mine as a harpoon and dragged me in, even as I tried to resist. He wordlessly demanded to know how could I do this to him.

The longer he stood there and stared at me, the angrier I became.

The door had been shut, I now knew that. This was still his house, and he owned everything inside, so he didn't feel the need to knock. He'd come in here unannounced, perhaps to stop what he suspected was happening.

I'd told Macalister I was in love with Royce, but he wouldn't accept it. A dark, sinister voice made a suggestion.

Show him.

I was vaguely aware it was a fucking terrible, dangerous idea, but he'd pushed me repeatedly to my breaking point, and I cruelly wanted to return the favor. My hands ached from how hard I gripped the back of the couch, but I tipped my chin down to my chest and glared at him through my heavy-lidded eyes.

Watch, I dared.

As he'd pointed out back when I'd lost in the hedge maze, it was nothing he hadn't already seen. Macalister had stood beside the dining table the night of the initiation with an hourglass gripped in his hands while his son fucked me with both his mouth and his cock.

I turned my head to the side so I wouldn't have to look at Macalister and gasped it into my arm. "Oh, my God. Yes, Royce."

My fiancé's finger pushed and pulled inside me, moving faster to match the hurried pace of his tongue lashing at me. I gulped down air but grew lightheaded anyway. There was nowhere to look. Not at Royce, whose penetrative gaze made me want to explode, or at Macalister, who appeared both tormented and enraptured.

I knew it was wrong.

That I should send him away, or at least open my mouth and say something. This moment was supposed to be between Royce and me. But if I spoke up, it'd ruin everything. Royce would be rightfully furious, and he didn't handle his emotions well. What if he lost control and said something he regretted? What if he gave away what he was planning?

The greedy, selfish part of me didn't want this to be over. I was close to orgasm. Royce's mouth lapped at me, and when he added a second finger to join the first, my lips parted into an inaudible cry. Electricity danced over my bare skin. My breasts ached, and my nipples pinched tighter.

So, I kept my tongue leashed and let Macalister watch how his son pleased me. I allowed him to listen to my soft sobs of pleasure and the sound of Royce's fingers as they made me wetter still.

The wrongness of it was so overwhelming, it consumed

everything. It pinned me to my seat on the couch and in Royce's hands, naked and squirming as I gasped for breath. I tried to keep my gaze on the man kneeling on the floor, but Macalister's presence demanded attention and stole my focus.

The way his fingers tensed on the doorframe made me think he was imagining what he'd do with them if given the opportunity. How he would use them to coax out an orgasm. It was difficult to concentrate with my climax closing in, but I stared at him, trying to give him the darkest look of disapproval I had.

Without a sound, I made my battle cry.

Macalister made his with the corner of his mouth lifting in an evil smirk.

There was power in this room, and it had all been mine up until this moment. Like a fool, I hadn't realized we were playing a game, and as usual, Macalister was already two moves ahead. His hand came down off the doorframe and seemed to glide through the air in slow motion.

Holy shit. I watched with dread and sick fascination as he cupped himself through his slacks and began to massage his building erection.

My hands tunneled into Royce's hair, preventing him from turning and seeing the horrifying thing unfolding behind him. It was hypnotic the way Macalister's palm slid up and down, and how his fingers clenched and gripped. Dark, twisted satisfaction spread across his face.

He wasn't mad anymore. No, he was enjoying the view. His gaze trailed over me, lingering on my breasts, and followed the lines of my spread legs. I felt his scrutiny the same way I imagined his cold fingers would feel.

This had to be a bluff, I told myself. Macalister couldn't stand I'd been in control, and he'd done what he could to level the playing field. I held his gaze with defiance. He wasn't going to actually . . .

God, I was supposed to know better. It was win at all costs in this family.

I hopelessly chased my breath while watching his fingers methodically undo his fly, and my muscles coiled with anxiety. I choked on air as his zipper was pulled down, tooth by silent tooth. *No, no, no,* repeated in my head, but I didn't issue a whisper to stop it. I was drunk off desire.

The flurry of Royce's tongue seduced. His fingers touched the spot deep inside me that made my heart skip and stumble. I was right on the ledge, only a fingertip's grip away from falling into ecstasy.

My frantic gaze bounced between him and Macalister's hand as he buried it inside his undone pants and dug around. And then it began to move, sliding up and down in long strokes.

It was beyond fucked up. So perverse, even the Greek gods might have been proud.

Royce's fingers plunged inside me so fast the couch began to shake, and I forced my gaze down, wanting to see him and nothing else. I was a passenger who naïvely boarded a rollercoaster, but only once I was strapped in and the cars were climbing the hill did I realize what a mistake I'd made.

I needed off. I had to find a way to stop it, I had to—

Satisfaction erupted and burst from my core, spiraling

out along my limbs faster than lightning as I came. A shocked moan crashed through me while I flinched and contracted and let go of Royce's head. It felt like I was being jolted with a Taser, only instead of painful electricity, it was hot pleasure.

He sat back but left his fingers buried inside me, where he could feel every reactive pulse my body gripped him with. He watched me with wonderment and desire, and I forgot about the other man in the room. All I wanted was the one who'd waited a year to have me, even when he wasn't sure he'd get to.

The man I loved who was trying to dethrone a king.

"Royce." My voice cracked with emotion as I begged. "Make love to me."

For a moment, Hades stepped aside, and Ares took over. His expression said he'd go to war and march through hell, and Royce would spend every last dollar he had to keep me. Nothing would stand in his way.

I blinked, unleashing a tear I hadn't realized had collected in my eye, and Hades returned. He came to me, wiped the tear away, and pressed his mouth to mine. His arms caged around me, and I was Persephone, happy in her prison.

It was unclear when Macalister left, but by the time Royce lifted me up off the couch, his father had vanished. He must have shut the door behind him because it was closed again. A stone of guilt settled on my chest, crushing my heart. I shouldn't have allowed any of that to happen.

There wasn't time to dwell on it. Wooden beams decorated the ceiling, and their lines continued down the back wall, so they were the only thing breaking up the floor to ceiling windows, and Royce walked us toward it until my upper back was flat to the smooth wood.

He was already hard as he stood between my legs, but I clasped a hand around him and pumped my fist, trying to repay at least a fraction of the pleasure he'd given me. His palms were on the beam over my head and he looked down to watch my strokes, and although it severed the connection of our stare, it didn't break the spell between us. His chest rose and fell with his uneven breath, and he throbbed in my hand. He enjoyed the feeling, but I couldn't help but wonder if he was allowing it more for my benefit than his own, giving me an opportunity to reciprocate.

His eyes met mine and announced all he wanted was to follow the command I'd issued.

Make love to me.

A breathless sigh slipped from my mouth as his hands drifted around me, both behind my waist. One moved to splay across my back and the other slid down over my backside. Without thinking about it, I hiked my leg up to wrap around him, and his fingers trailed lower. They skated down through the crevice of my body between my cheeks, and he stifled the noise of surprise I made by planting his mouth over mine.

There was only the faint brush of his fingertips against my clit before he moved on and his palm slid against the underside of my thigh. I was balanced on the ball of one foot, but then he was lifting, and it left me with no choice but to wrap my legs and arms around him and hold on.

He stared at me like he might die if he didn't, and slowly

lowered me onto him, inch by impossibly good inch. On the outside, we were so still we were practically statues, but inside everything was going haywire. My pulse was an engine in overdrive. Nerves fluttered in my belly. A whine threatened to bubble out of me.

Once he was fully seated inside, my body tight around him, Royce began to move. His hips drew back and pressed forward, pushing the small of my back against the wall. It didn't take long for our gasps to sync. I banded my arms tighter around his neck and dropped my forehead against his shoulder, letting moans pour from me freely.

The position was taxing on him, but he didn't set me down. He struggled for breath, and it fluttered the loose ends of hair beside my neck, and his muscles quickly began to shake with fatigue. But he kept going. He wasn't able to tell me he loved me, and maybe it was foolish to believe he did, but he affirmed his feelings for me with each slow thrust and deep kiss.

The edges of the beam bit into my back, and he'd become so slippery with sweat it was hard for me to hold on to him, but I wanted it to last forever. I wished we could freeze time and exist the rest of our lives here where we were just ourselves, connected to each other.

"*Marist*," he uttered against the shell of my ear. The single word was loaded with so much emotion, it was nearly the same as the three words I hoped to hear from him someday.

The hands supporting me lowered until I could put my feet on the floor, and then I was turned in place, so my back was against Royce's toned chest. He used one hand to steady himself, and the other grasped my hip to guide him back inside me, and as soon as it was done, he folded our arms together over my chest, lacing his fingers on top of mine.

His mouth latched on to the sensitive spot just below my ear and sucked gently, and it made the muscles inside me clench on him. He groaned his satisfaction.

It could have been hours or minutes before the pleasure became too much and we neared our end. When he trailed his fingertips down my stomach and pressed them to my aching clit, it set me off. I slapped my hands against the beam in front of me and gasped through the onslaught of my orgasm, which was so strong my legs threatened to give out on me.

Once I had come, he let himself loose. He moved at a faster tempo. The hand on my hip squeezed until my flesh dented around his fingers. Behind me came the sounds of his approaching orgasm. The slew of tight, short breaths followed by a lengthy groan and shudder while his hips jerked to a stop.

It was quiet besides our heavy breaths and the soft hum of the gas fireplace.

"I love you," I whispered in the silence.

He captured my chin between his thumb and forefinger and turned my head into his needy kiss. It was so powerful, it was overwhelming, and he carried me to bed.

Where I curled beside him and slept the whole night through.

The dining room of the Hale's Aspen house was similar to the one in Cape Hill, only here it was warm and open and less formal. It still had high ceilings, a crystal chandelier, and a rectangular table big enough to seat twelve, but the back wall was a window, allowing for more light. It meant there were fewer shadows, both metaphorically and literally.

We'd assumed the same seating arrangement we'd used for our weekly family meals at the Hale house before Alice and her lily of the valley tea had shredded the dynamic. Macalister sat at the head of the table, his murderous wife to his right and his plotting eldest son to his left. While I wasn't directly across from her, she was only a few feet away, and I spent most of the dinner looking toward my parents seated beside me, or down at my dinner plate.

The Thanksgiving meal was prepared by a Michelin star chef, but the food tasted bland in my mouth. There was too much tension everywhere I looked. Macalister's gaze was always fixed on me whenever I made the mistake of looking his direction. Across from me, Vance was seated between his former and current lovers, although Jillian was oblivious to the undercurrent in the room.

My parents were for the most part too. They didn't speak much during dinner, probably worried about saying anything that could draw Macalister's attention or ire. I was glad they were here, but I wasn't sure why he'd invited them. Was it to remind them who held the purse strings and make them feel small?

Plates of mini pumpkin pies were set before us on our chargers, and Jillian cleared her throat. Her voice was hesitant. "So, my family has a tradition when the dessert is served, and I was wondering if we could do it tonight?"

It came from me before I could think better of it. "I'm sure. Macalister's a big fan of traditions."

A choked, strained laugh came from Royce that he tried to play off as a cough.

Hot irritation simmered in Macalister's question. "What is it?"

Jillian was visibly regretting her decision to speak up, but there was no going back now. "We go around the table and each say what we're thankful for." She tucked a lock of hair behind her ear and straightened her shoulders. "I'll go first. I'm thankful to the Hale family for inviting me to dinner." When she realized that wasn't enough, she tacked on more, but it wasn't the least bit convincing. "And . . . for being so welcoming to me."

I pressed my lips together to stop my mouth from running away.

She turned toward Vance expectantly, who gave her a blank look. When she didn't break, he reluctantly shifted in his seat. "Yeah, okay." He wiped a hand over his mouth while he struggled to come up with something. "I'm thankful Professor Robuchon didn't call on me in class on Monday because I didn't do any of the required reading."

Cold annoyance wafted down the table from Macalister, but Vance was indifferent.

Jillian scrunched her mouth to the side. It wasn't the answer she was hoping for, but she wasn't going to say so. When the table went quiet, she peered around. "Um . . .

anyone else?"

Awkward silence answered, and I scrambled to save her. "Sure, I'll—"

"I'm thankful for my husband," Alice announced, her chin lifted high as her gaze zeroed in on me, "who knows what we have is unique and special, and will always be my partner, no matter what happens." Her smile was devoid of emotion. "And, of course, this family too."

It was Alice's classy way of spitting in my path, marking her territory, which was totally unnecessary. I wanted nothing to do with her husband. Beneath the table, I dug my nails into my thigh, letting the pain distract me from losing my head.

"Then, I suppose I'm next," Macalister said. "I'm thankful for Marist."

If there had been a record playing, the needle would have dragged loudly across it. I could hear the *what the fuck* echoing through Royce's head, and see it visibly on Alice's face.

Macalister wasn't finished. "For her upcoming union with my son and uniting our families together as the mother of my children had always hoped for." He cast his inescapable gaze on me. "You've brought me great happiness by coming into our lives."

I nearly heaved the contents of my dinner all over my dessert, but Royce's hand found mine and held me together. His tone was casual, ignoring the bomb his father had just detonated, or how the fallout was currently washing over his stepmother. Color drained from her face and emptied into her neck, turning it a violent pink.

"I'm also thankful for Marist," my fiancé said.

He lifted our joined hands out from under the table and kissed my knuckles, his eyes twinkling. It was a silent message telling me not to let them get to me. To do as he did when others were around. Play a role.

I peeled my lips back in an uneven smile, digging deep inside myself to find the Instagram version and not the Medusa one who wanted to destroy her enemies. "I, uh . . . am thankful for Royce, especially everything he's done for Emily."

Royce's smile hung strangely, but I blinked, and it vanished. Or maybe I'd imagined it. Macalister looked at me curiously for a moment too, but then retreated into his normal, cold veneer.

I meant it, though. Being alone on Thanksgiving had to be hard, and Royce had done everything he could to help my sister. For a man who pretended he didn't care about anything, his actions sure said otherwise.

My parents must have felt obligated since everyone else had participated, and both ended up saying they were thankful for being invited and that Royce and I had found each other. The strange thing was, my mother had sounded genuine.

The words had barely left her lips before Alice pushed back from the table and excused herself.

"I hope she's feeling all right," my mother said. "She looked pale."

Macalister's tone had a note of finality to it that I doubt my mother picked up on. "She will be fine."

With Alice gone, it made the rest of the dinner tolerable—as long as I avoided Macalister. I felt his gaze boring into me, though, and I clenched my teeth. He was shameless, not bothering to be discreet. He was Zeus again, the king of the gods, and he was above reproach. He'd do whatever the fuck he wanted.

People were still pushing pie crust crumbs around on their plates and talking politics when I excused myself to the washroom. After I'd finished washing my hands, I rested them on the sink and stared at my reflection in the mirror.

My dark brown hair hung straight, halfway down to my elbows. I'd spent a long time blowing it out this morning, and even more time on my makeup the way Alice's makeup artists had shown me. I looked picture perfect in my black dotted Yves Saint Laurent dress.

But I barely recognized myself. There was a hard coldness creeping in at the edge of my eyes. The Hale influence, no doubt. The only good thing was the glow. I didn't love the style that had been forced on me, but being in love? That suited me.

I fluffed my dried hands through my hair, grabbed the doorknob, and pulled . . . only for Macalister to push his way inside and shut the door, closing us in together. His expression was all darkness and aggression.

I lowered my voice to an angry whisper. "What the hell do you—"

That was all I got out before one of his hands grabbed my waist and the other covered my mouth, pushing me roughly back against the wall.

EIGHT

I SUCKED IN A SHARP BREATH THROUGH MY NOSE, AND MY GAZE darted frantically around the small half-bath. I'd look anywhere but at the man who loomed over me. His palm was a muzzle of ice against my lips.

"You won't speak another word until I'm finished, Marist." His tone was absolute, and so dangerous it felt like I was standing on a tightrope over sharpened spikes. "Do you understand me?"

I gave a slow nod, making his hand on my face move along with my head. Either he didn't trust me, or he liked the control, because he left his hand right where it was.

"Tonight was unacceptable, but I'm not going to apologize for her. You will let her do that herself."

I tried to mumble a *no*, but when the word hit his palm, his fingers clamped down, preventing it from escaping, and heat flared in his frigid eyes.

"You need to be sensible about this. Alice is a part of this family, one you cannot avoid forever, and I won't stand another evening like the one we just had."

When I shifted my weight, trying to squirm away, he moved in and used the full breadth of his body to block me. Alarm stiffened through my muscles, but it seemed to soften his. His fingers loosened, and his palm slipped down until it gently ringed my throat. It meant he felt the enormously hard swallow I made.

His voice went low. "She can't move past this until you allow her to."

Vehemence coated each word. "I don't care."

"But I do, and unfortunately for you, that's all that matters." His eyes traced his hand wrapped around my neck, and I had the sinking feeling he liked the way it looked. "Tomorrow, when Royce goes out with everyone else for the slopes, you'll stay in and listen to Alice's full confession and apology. I've made it part of her penance."

"No," I hissed. "You don't get to tell me what to do. You don't have control over me anymore."

Amusement faintly lit his eyes. "Don't I?" His index finger lifted and pressed over my lips. "Open your mouth."

What?

I split in two at his order. My mind filled with fury, and my body with shameful heat. "Excuse me? No. We had a deal."

"You're correct, we did." He put extra emphasis on the past tense. "But it's null and void now. I won't say it again. *Open your mouth.*"

In my confusion, I did—only to protest, but it didn't matter. He used the opportunity to slide his long, cold finger past my lips, and my eyes went wide. My head was already back against the wall, and as I tried to turn away, the rest of his fingers pinched my face and held me still.

It was shocking to have any part of him inside me, even in the relatively safe place of my mouth. It didn't feel safe, though. His finger pulsed in and out in a deliberate stroke, and it was horribly sexual. Intimate.

It was impossible to speak and not to think about the sex act he was mimicking.

"You told me," he said, "you wanted us to be done, but as I suspected, you lied." His shoulders lifted in a deep breath. "If you really wanted that, you wouldn't have allowed last night to happen. Or, by the very least, you'd have told Royce about it, but you didn't, did you?"

The question was rhetorical. He already knew from the guilt flooding my eyes what my answer was.

Victory burned through his expression. "We'll be waiting for you in my room tomorrow after breakfast."

He left off the threat, but it was implied. If I didn't do as he said, there'd be consequences. At least one of them would involve him telling Royce how I'd let him watch us, and that he'd pleasured himself during.

God, I was a stupid mortal. Maybe I deserved to be tricked by the gods for being such a fucking idiot.

Macalister withdrew his wet finger and dragged it slowly down my chin. His gaze focused in on my lips like he was remembering all the times he'd forced his kiss on me and was considering doing it again now.

"I'm not going to your room," I blurted.

His voice was quiet, yet it filled every goddamn inch of the stifling room. "The lounge, then. The time has long since passed for you to stop avoiding what needs to happen."

My heart ground to a painful stop. What, specifically, was he talking about? Alice's apology, or the interest he claimed I still owed him from denying him his turn during the initiation?

The striations in the color of his eyes were tiny, menacing teeth. "We're so similar, after all. We know it's best to deal with problems as soon as they present themselves." He stepped back, giving me space to get out from beneath his shadow. "The closure will be good for all of us."

Anger gummed up my system, making everything slow and too disorganized to respond immediately. He gave me a final once-over, taking in the fire in my eyes and my hands pressed to the wallpaper at my back, and left the room wearing a satisfied look.

Royce pushed his head through the neck of a gray long-sleeved thermal shirt and eyed me still nestled amongst the covers of our bed. It was early, and he was lit by the soft morning light, even though the sun hadn't peeked out over the mountaintops yet.

I hadn't realized the full benefits of sleeping in the same bed with him until I'd done it. Morning sex. And now I got to watch him get dressed after his shower too, a sexy reverse striptease.

"You sure you don't want to come?" he asked. "I could teach you."

"I have zero interest in learning how to snowboard."

It wasn't a lie. I wasn't even a good skier and had given up years ago. The last five Thanksgiving holidays my family took in Aspen I'd spent it curled up by the fire in the lodge with my iPad, reading. Essentially, the perfect vacation.

Finished getting ready, he glanced down at the screen of his phone, checked the time, and looked displeased, although I couldn't tell if it was because he was late, or the current situation. He strolled to the bed and sat, jostling me into his arms.

Concern edged into his voice. "I don't want to leave you here alone with them."

Meaning his father and stepmother. I stared at the pattern on the duvet, not wanting to lie. "I doubt they'll stay in, and it's a big house."

While I had massive anxiety about my impending conversation with Mr. and Mrs. Hale, there was a kernel of truth to what Macalister had said. Alice wasn't going anywhere. As stepmother of the groom, she'd be a major figure at my wedding. Like a terrible coworker I was forced to work with, I had no choice.

I needed to confront her on what she'd done so we could both move on and get back to business selling the lie that the Hales were a perfectly happy family.

Royce looked unconvinced. It came from him as more of a statement than a question. "You'll call me if anything happens?"

You didn't the other night.

"Sure," I choked out.

His kiss was long and sensual, and he lingered like he was having second thoughts about leaving. But in the end, Tate and the promise of fresh powder won out, and my fiancé went, blissfully unaware of the guilt knocking around in my chest.

I wasn't an avoider like the rest of my family, but I dragged my feet. I took my time in the shower trying to scrub away the unclean feeling that clung to my skin. I spent five minutes brushing my teeth, still unable to get the persistent taste of Macalister out of my mouth. It took forever to select dark gray washed jeans and a black cashmere sweater to wear.

Breakfast was skipped, my stomach too unsettled.

When there was nothing else left to do, I made my way toward the lounge.

The room was at the top corner of the house, so instead of one glass wall, it had two, and another that was entirely made up of the stone fireplace, the requisite twelve-point buck head mounted above it. The roof was pitched and paneled in honey-colored wood slats, rising above the four brown leather chairs circled around a low table.

Macalister was seated in one of them, wearing black trousers and a tan sweater over a white collared shirt. Perfectly business casual, which was as dressed-down as he got. His focus was on the phone in his hand, probably reading emails because, as CEO, he didn't get holidays off.

Alice wore an oversized maroon sweater, black leggings, and a vacant expression as she was perched in the chair beside her husband and stared at the nothingness before her. Her back was ramrod straight, and although she always had excellent posture, there was something eerie about how she carried herself. Her hands rested palms up in her lap, and she was so still, it was as if she'd been placed that way.

Or directed.

Tension corded in my body like a rope twisting. Her husband had ordered her to wait for me like that as her—what was the word he'd used? *Penance.*

At my entrance, his attention rose from his phone screen, and I knew I had to act fast before he took control of the conversation.

"I'm not here," I said, "because you told me to come. I'm here because I want this done, and that's it. The deal we made is still valid."

A slow smile burned across his full lips as he stood, pocketed his phone, and let his gaze wander down the length of my body. It was uncomfortably hot beneath his heavy eyes. "You entered into it in bad faith. You continue to argue you want nothing to do with me, when we know that's not the case."

"It is!" I tensed my hands into fists at my sides. "I'm in love with Royce, and I'm marrying him, which means the only role you'll have in my life is as my father-in-law. One I preferably never see." I'd been off my game last night, but with time to prepare, I unleashed the pent-up things I'd meant to say then. "And if you touch me again, you're likely to lose a hand. Or at least a fucking finger."

He *laughed.* A genuine, deep-throated laugh, and hearing a sound of such enjoyment from him literally blew me back a step. The ground beneath my feet became unstable.

"All right, Marist." His condescending tone was the same

one I imagined he'd used when one of his sons had thrown a temper tantrum.

"I'm serious," I added.

His amusement spent, Macalister turned back into the god I was more familiar with. Zeus's expression was straightforward. "If you insist, we can renegotiate."

"What? No. There's nothing to—"

He raised a hand and silenced me. "I'll continue to uphold our agreement, even when you choose not to."

I stared at him, waiting for the other shoe to drop. When it didn't, "In exchange for?"

"You stay while I reprimand Alice and you listen to her full apology. You do not leave this room until it's done."

Sirens wailed in my head. *Too easy.* "That's it?"

His pale eyes were glittering enigmas. "I imagine it will make you uncomfortable."

I swallowed an enormous breath. On the surface, this didn't sound terrible, but I understood what I was up against. Negotiations were a game to Macalister, and he was always thinking two moves ahead. He didn't play unless he was confident he was going to win.

"No." I set my hands on my hips, letting my body language reinforce my defiance. "I'm not renegotiating. You hold up your end of our deal, or I'll tell everyone what she tried to do to me."

It was subtle, but Alice flinched, and it was the first movement she'd made since I'd come in. She'd been such a statue, I'd nearly forgotten she was there.

Macalister hardened and gave me a lethal look. "That

would be very unwise." He glanced at his wife, giving her a nonverbal reassurance, and then set his oppressive attention back on me. "I don't believe you've thought it through. It's been more than a month since that night, so there's no evidence to support your claim. It would be your word against ours, whereas we've never changed our story."

My pulse quickened as his words sank in, and he wasn't finished either.

"If you were to go down that foolish path, my legal team would spin you as greedy and desperate for attention, and that's the story that will become the truth. You'll be nothing but a tiny bump on my road to the Federal Reserve, Marist." He put one foot in front of the other, and as he approached, he grew ten feet taller. "It wouldn't stop there, though. I'll take everything away. To use your analogy, if you try to touch my business, you're likely to lose a hand. Or at least your *fucking* house."

It was so rare that Macalister swore, it gave his profanity the strength of a nuclear weapon. His bank owned my parents' house and all the debt they'd accumulated over the years. We had no money to fight back if he came after us. Everything I had was his.

Even my fiancé.

Macalister's words and his face full of domination squeezed me as a thousand ropes wrapped around my body and pulled taut.

Perhaps I looked like I was about to be sick, because he issued a low sigh of frustration and turned slightly human. It was shocking, but it was as if he didn't enjoy causing me discomfort. When I'd first moved into his house, he seemed to live for it. All those nights spent losing to him at chess . . . God, I couldn't go back to that.

Whatever terrible uncomfortable thing Macalister had planned, it wouldn't last forever. I'd rather deal with it now than give up control. Nothing could be worse than that. But on principle, I couldn't accept his first offer. I had to counter with something.

"One round of chess," I said. "If I win, I can leave whenever I want."

Oh, he liked this idea immensely, and I was counting on it. He was so sure of the outcome, he'd forgotten completely I'd won the last time we'd played. I wasn't confident I could do it again, but it was better than nothing, and one of the only games I could play with him and ensure it was fair.

Excitement etched his face. "If I win?"

"Then, I accept the terms of your renegotiation." I sipped in air, trying to remain calm. At least I was going in with my eyes open, prepared to lose. "But if we play, you agree not to tell Royce about any of this. Especially the other night."

"That moment was between us." His smile was downright evil before he turned to look at the bookshelf beside the wet bar. "I believe there's a set on the top shelf."

Meaning he expected me to fetch it.

My feet moved as if the rug were made of thick mud, but I went to the bookcase and pulled down the wooden box with a checkerboard pattern on top, making the pieces rattle inside. When I turned to face him, he pointed to the circular table at the center of the chairs.

There was an uneasy familiarity as we sat across from each other and set up the board, but things were markedly different, besides just the location. There was Alice seated between us, watching but not moving or speaking, like she'd fully become the robot I had sometimes wondered if she secretly was.

Macalister picked up a black and a white pawn and put his hands behind his back. His shoulders shifted as he moved the pieces around between hands, and when he was convinced I didn't know where the white pawn was, he nodded. "Choose."

I pointed to his right side.

He brought his arm forward, turned his palm upward, and uncurled his fingers to produce the black pawn. There'd be no first move advantage for me today, and I took the piece from him, turning the board so the black side was mine.

He made his opening move, followed by mine. As he considered his next one, he ran the pad of his thumb over his fingertips.

My chess games with him weren't just the pieces on the board, it was everything we did and said, and I wanted to distract. My gaze flicked the Alice. "Is she not allowed to talk? Or move?"

He made his move. "No, she's not."

I picked up my knight and set it down in its required L-shaped move. "Why?"

He slid his bishop diagonally a few spaces. "Because when I found you on the stairs, she made everything stop for me. I think she should experience what that's like."

I couldn't rein in the gasp. His words punched it clean from my lungs.

He lifted his piercing gaze from the board to meet mine, his words heavy with subtext. "It's your move."

I tried to swallow, but my mouth had gone completely dry. I sat up straighter in my chair and peered down at the board, but it was hard to concentrate. His words continued to ring in my ears. I'd wanted to distract him, but he'd just given me a master class.

My voice was meeker than I wanted it to be. "How long does she have to stay like that?"

He tilted his head to the side, considering, and once the decision was made, he directed the statement at his wife. "You may move any time Marist is touching a chess piece."

Alice's hopeful gaze turned to the board, and when I set my fingertips on my queen, she came to life. Her shoulders relaxed and a hand flew up to rub the tip of her nose, satisfying an itch she hadn't been allowed to scratch.

I moved my queen into play, and the second my fingers came off her, Alice solidified, returning to her statue state. Darkness inside me wanted to grin at what Macalister had done, how he'd given me control over her. I liked the taste of power.

We continued to play, and I enjoyed deciding how long I would let her have freedom. It made her so dependent on me, and it was a sweet role reversal.

"I've missed this," he said as he captured my bishop. It wasn't clear if he meant playing against me, or defeating me, because he was currently doing both.

"I haven't."

His lips twitched like they wanted to smile, but he wouldn't allow it. "You're right, you're not a very good liar."

My eyes burned at him, and I clenched my jaw. Did I miss the strategy of the game? Maybe a little. But not him as a partner. The only reason I didn't play it on my phone anymore was because I didn't like how fast the program made its move. There wasn't any body language to learn or read.

It was only a few more moves before we entered the endgame.

"Check," he said. "I appreciate what you were trying to do over here," he motioned toward the trap I'd laid in an attempt to capture his queen, "but I saw right through it."

The game was already lost, but the cruel thing about chess was you had to keep playing until the end.

"Checkmate." Macalister leaned back in his chair and put his arms on the armrests, satisfaction streaking through his expression. "Thank you for the game."

I stared glumly at the board, waiting for him to either begin or give Alice his approval to start, and although I wasn't looking at him, I sensed his irritation when I didn't respond the way he would have liked me to.

The leather of his chair creaked as he stood. "To reiterate the terms, if you leave before we're through, the deal's off."

I glared up at him. "I understand."

"Good."

He extended a hand toward his wife, which she took, and he pulled her to her feet. She stood beside him, waiting for his direction like she was a lowly soldier under his command.

And he looked back at her as a general who found her lacking.

"What you did," he said to her, "nearly cost me everything. My disappointment in you is . . . immeasurable."

Alice blinked, and her chest moved faster as her breathing quickened. Her throat bobbed in a nervous swallow. "I'm sorry."

As she grew more human, it was the opposite for him. He was cold and indifferent. "I don't believe you are."

"No, but I am." She glanced at me with watery eyes. "I'm sorry, Marist. I wasn't trying to kill you, I—"

He angrily snapped his fingers in front of her, drawing her attention back to him. "No, we haven't gotten to that part yet. Your first apology will be to me."

Her shoulders pulled back, and confusion splashed on her face. The thoughts running through her head were loud and clear. She thought she'd already apologized to him and she wasn't sure why she had to do it again.

I understood.

It was a power trip. Macalister wanted me to see her remorse.

Alice scratched a spot behind her neck as she thought about what to say, unsure of what exactly he was looking for. "I'm sorry. I wasn't thinking. I was careless and selfish and"—emotion gathered in her like a storm—"all I could see was her lipstick smeared all over your face and I wish it had been mine. I love you, Macalister. I've given you everything you ever asked for. Why isn't that enough?"

Tears slipped down her face, but she didn't move to wipe them away. I doubted she even knew she was crying.

"I gave you everything," she whispered, "while you give nothing."

He was immovable stone. "Not everything."

Was he talking about her submission? She'd told me she'd never surrendered full control to him.

She stiffened. "Well, now you have that too." She swiped at her face, quickly shooing the tears away like they'd never existed. "I'll do whatever you want."

He considered her declaration critically. "All right," he said finally. "In exchange for her silence, I promised Marist I would handle you appropriately."

The temperature in the room dropped a million degrees, and my body froze to the chair when he reached for his belt and made quick work unsnapping his buckle. My eyes had to mirror Alice's enormously wide ones as he grabbed one end of the black leather and pulled it free from his belt loops with a quiet *vrrrip*.

I couldn't move.

Couldn't think.

Nothing inside me—including my heart—worked right now, but Alice faired marginally better. She took an uneven step back. We watched in stunned silence as the belt was folded once to make a loop before he clenched it in his fist.

"Turn around and undo your pants," he ordered.

And then Macalister stared down at me, his voice as cold as a graveyard in the dead of winter.

"Tell me what number you think an appropriate response would be."

NINE

THERE WAS A SMALL ANTIQUE CLOCK ON THE MANTEL IN THE lounge, and its swinging pendulum had been quiet up until this moment. Now, every tick was a gunshot as I stared at the belt Macalister clutched. His makeshift whip he planned to use to flog his wife.

Alice had gone absolutely white and backed away from her husband but had not yet fled the room, although she looked like she was considering it. She'd given him her submission and told him she'd do whatever he wanted, but now she was much less sure.

My stomach filled with acid, and the sour taste quickly made its way into my mouth. He wanted to know what number an appropriate response was.

"Zero," I spat. "Zero is the appropriate amount." He had the audacity to look at me like I was the crazy one, and I couldn't believe I had to say it out loud. "I'm not going to watch you beat your wife."

A jolt shot down Macalister's back. "Jesus, I'll do no such thing." He looked offended at the accusation. "I'll deal with her the same way I handle any bad behavior that needed to be stopped—with punishment."

I pressed my hand to my chest to try to stop my heart from cracking. Had Macalister done this to his sons while growing up when they'd needed to be punished?

Oh, God.

Had he done this to Royce when he'd refused to get out of the limo at his mother's funeral?

"*No,*" I snarled. I balled my hands into fists so tightly, my fingernails were sure to leave crescent mark indentations on my palms.

His expression hung. "You don't think she deserves to be punished?"

"Not like this."

The clock continued its loud, persistent click. His eyes narrowed a degree, and his voice was incredulous. "After what she did, you find it acceptable she walks away free and clear?"

I was petty, and excellent at holding a grudge. "Well, no. But . . ." The belt remained in his hand, taunting me, right along with Alice's panic-stricken face. I could barely look at her because it made me feel the same fear she was experiencing. "Macalister, please." It bordered on begging from me. "Don't."

"You prefer I use a different method."

Visible relief flooded her face, and I nodded. "Yes," I said quickly. "Anything else."

He cast the belt aside, dropping it so easily onto the floor with a loud *thunk*, it sparked suspicion in me. Had he really intended to use it, or had this been a test for her? Or a bluff for me? His half-smile all but confirmed it.

"I find it fascinating that, after everything, you have compassion for her," he said.

I was still struggling to catch my breath and get my heartrate back down to a normal level. I wrinkled my forehead. "I don't, I just—"

His eyes were all-knowing, all-seeing. "Then why are you holding that rook?"

What was he talking about?

I looked down to discover the white castle piece clasped in one of my hands. I didn't respond, but we all knew why. He'd told her she couldn't move unless I was touching a piece, and subconsciously, when the belt had come out, I'd wanted her to run.

I hesitantly put the chess piece back on the board. All Macalister had to do was get me to see genuine fear in Alice's eyes and she was essentially forgiven. Maybe there was hope for me after all and I wasn't turning into a Hale. I still cared about people other than myself.

"Alice, come," he said in a harsh voice, like a master calling a disobedient dog.

When his belt had thudded to the hardwood, it had dispelled a significant amount of the tension in the room, but the undercurrent remained, and as she carefully approached him, it ramped back up. Whatever alternative form of punishment he'd crafted, he seemed ready to dish it out.

The last thing I'd expected him to do was kiss her.

Judging by her reaction, it was the same for her. When

his large hands seized her face and tilted it upward so he could lean down and capture her mouth, she let out a sound of surprise. It was followed instantly by an excited whimper that was quieted under his kiss.

Her perfect posture evaporated beneath his lips, and she arched up onto her toes. She kissed him with a desperation I knew all too well. It was the same way I'd kissed Royce in the hedge maze the night he'd sold me to his father. Alice kissed her husband like she hated his guts, but she'd also walk to the ends of the earth for him.

Her hands slid up his neck and cupped his jaw, and the kiss deepened. The way she responded to it and how she touched him . . . was this the first time in months they'd done it? They'd never been affectionate in front of me, but I had assumed behind closed doors they were, at least occasionally.

But maybe she'd only had Vance, playing the role of stand-in for her husband's duties.

The longer Macalister passionately kissed her, the more I began to wonder who, exactly, he was punishing. Her sigh of contentment announced he was giving her all the attention she'd craved, basically rewarding her. And I was the one who had to sit there and endure my future in-laws making out with each other.

Macalister awkwardly broke off the kiss, dragging his lips across her cheek. She swayed, looking adrift for a moment, his mouth temporarily drugging her, and she blinked her cloudy eyes at him.

"There. I gave you what you wanted." His tone was unexpectedly flat. "Your lipstick smeared on my face. Does it make you happy?" His upper lip curled into a cruel smile. "Because I was imagining you were Marist the whole time."

Oh, my God.

The blissful expression on her face froze, and I shirked back in my seat. This was just the beginning of it, I knew. It'd get much worse before he was done. The alternative method of punishment he'd selected was psychological warfare and—oh, shit—maybe I should have let him use the belt. It likely would have been less painful for both of us than what he had in store.

He grabbed her around the throat and pushed her roughly down to her knees. She nearly fell, putting a hand down to stop herself, and turned her surprised expression up at him, wordlessly asking what he was doing. The only answer he gave her was to step forward, putting the fly of his slacks right at her eye-level.

"Let's see if you can even get me hard, or if I'll have to imagine she's you."

Oh, my God!

There were a million tightly wound springs beneath my chest that all broke at the same time, leaving me a jangling, chaotic mess on the inside. They screamed at me to run, to fucking do something. But there was a reason I shouldn't, some part of me remembered on a basic level. I couldn't remember it specifically because my brain was barely processing, but the warning was enough to make me hesitate.

Alice's gaze darted to me, but he was prepared for that. "Would you like her to complete your task?"

Her focus snapped back to him like his words had

magnetized her. "No."

Determination overcame her as she accepted his challenge, and then her hands were crawling up over his legs. He stood still, his head tipped down to watch and his hands hanging relaxed at his sides as her palms worked their way toward the center of his pants.

My mouth was dry and full of dust, making it impossible to swallow. What the fuck was I supposed to do? Sit here and watch as she gave him a hand job? My body was a cage, locked tight with horror when her fingers focused in on what she'd been searching for and began to massage him through his slacks.

They were positioned sideways to me, so I could see one half of each of their faces, and behind them the view of the mountains surrounding us. We were on Mount Olympus now, the mortals below in Aspen. Zeus stood motionless as his jealous wife knelt on his expensive inlaid hardwood floor and tried to service him.

Her glossy pink fingernails scratched over his fly, and she cupped him, twisting her grip along his length, but there was no reaction from him. He stared at her with impatience etched across his face, and the atmosphere in the room began to shift as Alice fully committed to what he'd asked her to do. I was forgotten, all that mattered now was pleasing him.

But he wouldn't let her forget. While he had her full attention, she had none of his.

He turned his head and stared at me with a look that was scary as hell. It threatened dominance and control and promised wicked pleasure if I'd allow it. When our gazes connected, he inhaled a deep breath, and his wide shoulders rose. I was cornered, trapped by his intense stare, but I let loose a silent scream inside my head.

He didn't tell us what he was thinking about, or what awful fantasy with me he was conjuring up. But whatever it was, it was working. The crotch of his pants grew tight and it began to tent.

Alice's excited fingers curled on the top of his slacks and the button holding them closed, but his focus flew back to her. He seized her hand and twisted it away, his thumb pressing deep into her wrist to stop her. "Did you want something?"

The word was barely a breath from her. "Please?"

He considered it for a long moment, and time suspended. Then it launched forward when he released her, flinging her hand away. "Go on, then. Take it."

She attacked his zipper with renewed energy, eager to have him unrestricted in her hands. He crossed his arms, grabbed the sides of his sweater, and tore it up over his head in one swift move. It was balled up in his hands and thrown away with force before his glittering gaze swung back to me.

"I'm going to imagine this is your mouth, Marist."

He wasn't smiling, and he hadn't said it just to provoke a response from me or her—he was deadly serious. A ruthless, cutthroat businessman during a hostile takeover, and I was the target he was determined to acquire.

Move, Marist! Fucking move!

Suddenly free, I leapt to my feet so quickly I nearly toppled over. My gaze reeled around blindly, searching for the exit, and although I avoided the worst of it, out of the corner of my eye I saw her latch onto the sides of his pants and jerk them down.

I made it two steps toward the door before his dark taunt rang out. “Leaving so soon?”

My shoulders tightened to my ears, and I closed my eyes. Blocking the scene out gave me just enough of a reprieve for my brain to start working. If I left, things would go back to how they used to be, and I’d lose everything. Giving over control to Macalister would be handing him the passcode to the security system I’d built around Royce and myself. He’d get inside and break us down, and I couldn’t let that happen.

“Stay,” he commanded. “I want you to watch, like how you wanted me to.”

The shudder started with my shoulders but graduated to my full body as the image of him looming in the shadows, watching as Royce went down on me, sliced through my memory.

Was I really considering this? Staying in this room and witnessing this deeply intimate act I had no business or desire to see?

His voice was loaded with the sinful challenge. “Unless the sight of me with someone else is too difficult to bear.”

Holy fuck. I whirled around to face them, refusing to let even a molecule of the shock I felt show on my face. It wasn’t too difficult to bear. I couldn’t care less, and I’d fucking show him that.

And I reminded myself I’d partially seen this before. It had been dark in the woods, and Alice had been with Vance when I’d spied them together the night of the initiation, but a blowjob was a blowjob. It couldn't be all that different with another partner.

I kept my voice firm and my head up as I marched back to my chair. "I don't give a fuck who you're with, so long as that person isn't me."

Macalister's eyes shrank to slits. But the sides of his mouth lifted in a joyless smile, telling me he didn't believe me. Worse, he wanted to test the theory. His fingers worked to undo the buttons on his shirt, releasing them one by one.

As each one popped free, the tension inside me multiplied. It held my muscles stiff and made it difficult to sit, but I managed somehow, dropping into the leather chair with barely a sound. It unfortunately meant I couldn't avoid the scene before me any longer.

He had the legs of a runner. Powerful and toned, the tan from countless summers spent on his yacht fading to pale as it went up his thighs. The classic dress shirt had a longer front and tail than the sides, covering the indecent parts, but I got a flash of his buttocks as he worked to undo the last few buttons.

The shirt was pulled open, revealing the full bare swath of him from chest to knees, and he left the white shirt to hang on his shoulders. Alice already had both hands on him, obscuring part of his cock, but it was unmistakably and unavoidably *there*. Hard, and long, and thick, and turning my insides to glass. If I moved, I'd shatter.

He watched me intently and curiously as I took in the exposed sight of him. He was cold steel, but the room was scorching, and the needle on the thermostat continued to climb as she heaved both of her hands over him, pumping her fists on his angry cock.

Chess was over, but we were still playing a game, and as I shot him an uninterested look, I made it clear I considered it his move now.

He didn't want me to miss a thing, which was why he pushed the side of his open shirt out of the way and set the hand closer to me on his hip, displaying as much of him as possible. The other one drifted into the glossy strands of her blonde hair and urged her head toward him, signaling what he expected.

She parted her rose-colored lips and complied, her eyes fluttering closed as the head of him slid into her wide mouth.

I didn't like the way Macalister and I both sucked in a deep breath at the same moment. It was like I was involved, a part of this, when I was desperate not to be. It made me angry how my gaze kept wanting to slip from his and better watch what was happening at his waist. I absolutely hated the low, dull ache it created in my center when his eyes lidded with desire.

At least he looked mortal like this. He wasn't impervious to what she was doing to him.

Gravel edged into his words like the pleasure he felt was stuck in the base of his throat. "I've imagined you on your knees for me a thousand times."

Don't, I whispered to myself, but it was already too late. I saw myself in her place, my knees squeaking against the wood as I rocked on my legs, my mouth steadily sliding over him. A traitorous muscle deep between my thighs tightened, causing a horrifying spark of satisfaction.

His hips remained perfectly still, but his grip on her hair clenched, twisting the strands to the point of discomfort because her eyes burst open and peered up at him with surprise. And while she looked at him, he looked at me. His wife was nothing more than an instrument. A toy to appease him while he gazed at what he desired but had not yet had.

Was he aware she did the same thing with his son? Used Vance as a substitute for the husband who wouldn't even look at her anymore?

The table between us had a glossy finish, and it was safer to watch the fuzzy reflection in it as Alice bobbed her head and kept up with the demanding tempo her husband required. She had one hand wrapped around the base of him and the other cupping underneath, and saliva dripped over her shiny fingers.

The lens of the table allowed me to tell myself it wasn't real. Her head didn't rock side to side as she inched down and slowly took his cock all the way to the back of her throat. The soft sound of her cough broke the spell and drew my gaze back up.

The pleasure made his eyes smolder toward me. "I look forward to training you to do this." Macalister's tone was seductive. "Just like I did her."

Oh, fuck. I could picture it all so clearly in my head. He'd loved teaching me chess and enjoyed the role as my instructor. He'd probably try to make a game out of it. Benchmarks and rewards for improvement on my deep-throating lessons.

Thick sludge, hot like lava, moved through my veins.

"No," I said, both to him and the shameful response thrumming through my body.

As Alice retreated, her cheeks carved into hollows and her hand clamped down at the edge of her lips. She moved her fist in perfect time with the steady seesaw motion of her mouth, and I saw mostly the whites of her eyes as she stared up at her husband.

God, the way she looked. Couldn't he see how badly she longed for him? It was cruel. I'd wanted to see her punished, but this . . . it didn't satisfy. It only made me feel unease, like it was too much.

Enjoyment twisted on his face as our gazes were horribly locked together. The hand on the back of her head pushed with more urgency, and his hips succumbed to a craving to move that he'd held back until now. He thrust forward, stabbing in her mouth, and her cheek bulged as the head of his cock pressed into it.

It was a raw display of sex and power, and he was utterly in control of everything. Her pace. His pleasure. My emotions.

My face burned, and my pulse was in overdrive. I tried to control my breathing, but it came and went in ragged bursts. The physical response to the lewd scene playing out before me was that I grew embarrassingly damp between my legs, and it was like he knew. He licked his lips and gazed at me as the hungry Minotaur.

"I want you," he growled.

Three plain words, but they carried an enormous gravity coming from him, especially when there was a woman at his feet, surrendering over again to him with each stroke of her hand and swirl of her tongue.

Pinpricks of anger stabbed at my skin and injected fire into my bloodstream. "You can't have me."

"I already do, Marist." His grin was more like a sneer. "I haven't been inside you or tasted your pretty little cunt yet, but I own you. You're mine."

Alice pulled back off him and jerked to a stop. "What? You haven't . . ."

Her stunned eyes searched his when he glanced down, her hair still clenched in his fist.

"That's right. You weren't made aware." He was condescending. "She made Royce my proxy that night and gave him my time. So, the answer is no. I was denied my two minutes and wasn't allowed to touch her."

Her shocked gaze swung from him to me, and the room went still.

Her lips were swollen and glossy from what she'd been doing, and they parted like she wanted to say something, but nothing came out. Regret built in her, layer by painful layer, as she realized she'd tried to kill me based off her assumptions.

And those assumptions had been wrong.

TEN

MACALISTER'S AGGRESSIVE HAND JERKED ON ALICE'S HAIR, forcing her mouth back around him. She only hesitated for a second. Then he didn't need to give her as much guidance as he had before. She shifted on the floor, widening her knees a little, and made a moan of approval.

If anything, she looked fucking thrilled. As if she hadn't lost him to me after all. Like there was still hope she could get him back.

Love had made her delusional, but I saw him with clear eyes. The Minotaur didn't care about the people once they'd been consumed, and he'd used her all up.

I crossed my legs and ran a hand through my hair, affecting the demeanor of someone who didn't care that they were sitting ten feet away from a man with his dick halfway down his wife's throat. I was strong and unbreakable. The Minotaur couldn't eat Medusa. She was just as much of a monster as he was, if not more.

"I'm not yours, I'm Royce's." I leveled the darkest gaze I possessed at him. "Are you almost finished? I have shit to do."

It was the equivalent of entering the endgame, and he was pissed he didn't get to do it on his terms. "I'm sure." His blue eyes turned to storms, and electricity crackled in the clouds. "Will you use the vibrator I gave you while you do it? I still have the controls set on my phone."

The perfect rhythm Alice had been keeping abruptly fell apart, but he gripped the hair at the top of her head with his other hand, so he could push and pull her with both. A single bead of sweat rolled down over his defined chest, coursing a jerky path over his flat stomach.

"And I still remember what you sound like," his words were clipped, "when I brought you to orgasm with it."

The shudder his memory forced on me was strategic. It kept my tongue still long enough for him to squeeze out another comment.

"Next time I make you come," he said with a loud exhale, "I'll be inside you."

My mouth fell open. Not so much from what he'd said, but the way his body moved. Vibrations undulated through his arms as he fucked her mouth at breakneck speed, and darkness overwhelmed his expression. His chest was heaving with labored breath, mixed with groans that were soaked in pleasure, and it continued to build.

Oh, God. He was about to come, and I sat rooted to my chair, not wanting to watch but also dying to know what he looked like when he lost control.

Abruptly, he took one urgent step backward, and as soon as he was out of Alice's mouth, his hand was there to replace it. He kept hold of the hair on the top of her head so she couldn't go anywhere, but he issued the order anyway.

"Stay still."

He ran his palm over the swollen length of himself, twisting his grip that was so tight, his cock lost some of its color. It was hypnotic how he jerked in shallow, furious strokes. The tip of him was only an inch from her face, and she must have figured out his intent, because her eyes slammed shut.

Blood roared loudly in my ears, and my breath cut off as Macalister's shoulders tensed and he let out a loud, long grunt. As he came, he stared at me with his bottomless eyes and his face twisting with ecstasy.

She flinched with each streak of liquid that struck her, and he painted ribbons across her face while his body shook and shuddered. At last, his fist slowed and he issued a sigh, releasing his hold of her with a small backward shove. It made some of the semen drip down off her chin and onto her designer sweater.

It was such a shockingly vulgar and demeaning act, it was breathtaking.

He was almost done recovering when he spoke to her. "Now," he said, "tell Marist you're sorry."

I gasped with horror as she turned to look at me with her face covered in his semen and her shame. "I'm sorry," she whispered.

His tone was plain. "That time, I believed you."

He bent, grabbed the sides of his pants, and as he pulled them up, he assessed the result of his work across her cheeks and lips. His expression was cold and unfeeling as she peered up at her husband, desperate for him to say something. Anything.

"Go wash your face," he ordered. "You look pathetic."

There was no audible snap when she broke. She didn't cry out or even say a thing as she cleaved down the middle. Alice climbed gingerly to her feet, her knees no doubt tender, and looked utterly dead inside as she carried herself from the room, her vacant eyes connecting with nothing. She moved as if she were hollow, and she was.

The Minotaur had eaten her soul.

I was at a complete loss for words as he finished doing up his zipper and began to button his shirt.

My voice was disembodied. I didn't realize I was speaking until it was out. "You're . . . you're so *fucked up*."

His hands ceased moving. There was the subtle, resigned nod of his head. "You told me you love fucked up things, though." The uneven way he said it was disorienting. "It's your favorite part of mythology."

It was true. I wondered if something was wrong with me because I enjoyed such twisted stories, but I only liked them when they were trapped inside their medium and couldn't touch me. My life as a tragic, fucked up myth didn't have any appeal.

I couldn't stand to be in this room with him a moment longer, especially when what he'd done to her still lingered freshly in the air. I pushed to my feet and balled my hands into fists. "I hate you."

His reaction was shocking. Why did he look so stricken? "I don't care very much for myself right now either."

What?

He tucked his shirt into his pants and bent to retrieve the sweater he'd cast off. "But I did what needed to be done. Do you hate her?"

His humiliation of her was so horrible, all my anger flipped on its side and I only felt sorry for her now. "No. Only you."

"Good." He pulled on the sweater, tugging it into place. It was amazing how quickly he composed himself. "I can't control how you feel about other people's actions, but I can control my own, so I've absorbed the anger you had for her."

Meaning he'd purposefully been awful so I would see him as the villain of the story and not her.

His shoulders rolled back, and his posture straightened so he looked ten feet tall again. "You can believe you hate me, Marist, and that's fine. But, given enough time, I will change that."

"We're done here," I hissed.

"Yes, we are."

There was a finality to his statement that would have given me pause if I weren't so fucking eager to get away from him.

I had only made it down the hall before I collided with Alice as she stepped out of the guest bathroom. Her face was pale, as she'd scrubbed most of her makeup off, and her eyes were pink, but she wasn't currently crying.

My heart hurt for her. "Are you okay?"

"I'm fine." She bristled. "But this is your fault."

I froze. "Excuse me?"

"Hales only want what they can't have. Once the chase is over and they've won, they're on to the next thing." Her eyes were as hard as the diamond earring she wore. "If you'd just given Macalister what he wanted, this would have been over months ago."

She pushed past me like I was a spoiled child she didn't want to deal with, and as she strode down the hall, I felt less sorry for her.

I treated the horrible afternoon in the lounge with Macalister and Alice the same way I treated the initiation. It was something to never be spoken or thought about, because nothing good could come of it. At least my guilt over not telling Royce lessened each day.

After the Thanksgiving weekend was over, we returned to Cape Hill, and I moved into Royce's room. Or *our* room. Thankfully, Macalister continued to make himself scarce, or at least the impending offer for Ascension and the end-of-the-year reports kept him too busy.

Or perhaps he was avoiding me. Either way, I was glad.

The week before winter finals, I was in my Porsche, driving to Boston for my first wedding dress fitting with Donna Willow, when my phone rang. My mother's number flashed on the center console, and I clicked the button on my steering wheel.

"Are you running late?" I asked. She was supposed to meet me at the salon.

"No. I'm taking Emily to the emergency room." Her panicked voice cracked through the car speakers. "Baby isn't moving."

My sister had decided she didn't want to know the sex of her baby until birth. She wanted it to be a happy surprise, she'd said, so we all used the term of endearment. Her child wasn't a 'the,' they were Baby. I'd hated it at first, but it had grown on me, bringing a smile to my face. But now cold fingers slipped inside my body and squeezed my heart.

"Which hospital? Port Cove?" My hands trembled as I navigated onto the shoulder of the highway and put on my hazards. I'd turn around if her answer was yes.

"Mass General."

Okay, that was good. I wanted my sister in the best possible hands. "Right. I'll meet you there." I checked traffic and was able to pull back onto the road. "How is she doing?"

"She's scared, Marist. We all are."

I did my best to sound calm and even. "It's going to be okay."

"How can you know that?"

My bottom lip quivered, but I held it together as I echoed what my fiancé had said to me before. "Because Royce has more money than God, and he'll make it so."

It was a tense, stressful drive to the hospital, and when I called to tell him what was going on, I was shocked to learn Royce already knew. My mother had called him first, before me. I was her sister and best friend, and he was her—what? Soon to be brother-in-law?

I took a page out of my mother's passive aggressive playbook and got several digs in while we were placed in a room and waited for Emily's doctor to arrive.

"I understand you're hurt," my mother said, "but I was panicking and didn't know what to do. Emily's doctor was out of town, and . . ." She sighed. "The Hales have a lot more power to throw around than we do. So, yes. I called Royce first, but I did it because I knew he'd help get my daughter what she needed."

Her face softened as she stared at my sister, who looked uncomfortable and frightened as she lay in her hospital bed. They'd strapped a monitor to her belly, and she was fixated on the screen of the machine, even as we had no idea what it meant. Once it had started running, it was like everything else in the room ceased to exist.

My mother's hand was cold with fear when she grabbed mine and squeezed. "He's been so good to Emily." Her voice dropped low, only for me. "Has he been good to you?"

She peered at me and, with everything happening, it must have given her focus on what was truly important because she actually *saw* me. Her thoughtful eyes begged for my honesty.

"Because if he hasn't, you leave him. I'm serious, Marist. I know you worry about us, but you shouldn't. We'll be fine." Her grip tightened, like she wanted to put extra emphasis on what she was saying. "I'm sorry if I made you think otherwise, but I want you to know the only thing that's ever mattered to me is you girls and your happiness."

I already knew it was true, but it was good to hear it again and reinforce it. My parents had given my sister and me the best of everything, including their love. The most important thing had been free; I just wished they hadn't gone underwater to give us everything else.

But it was done. The only pathway was forward now.

"Yes, he's good to me." I squeezed her back. "I love him. Like, really. Somehow, it worked out."

Her smile was full of relief. "Good, thank God. I'm happy for you both." Her gaze left mine and drifted to her other daughter. "It makes things . . . easier."

"It does," I said.

My marriage would bring enormous privilege to my family, but she'd never know that falling in love with Royce or becoming a Hale had been anything but easy.

It wasn't long after that when Emily jolted in her bed and new concern streaked across her face. "I think my water just broke."

Everyone was up out of their chairs. She wasn't due for another three weeks.

It had been chilly in the hospital room like they always were, and so after Emily had changed into a gown and gotten into bed, the nurse had put a heavy blanket over her. Now, my sister cast it off and peered down at the soaked bed.

Crimson stained the sheets and blotted her legs. She was sitting in a puddle of blood, making my mother scream and dash toward Emily's bedside. I reached behind me, trying to find the chair I'd been sitting in, but the horrifying feeling was overwhelming.

I couldn't stand the sight of blood.

It made my limbs go weak. My stomach flipped, over and over in a dizzying sensation, speeding up until everything abruptly went black.

Emily nearly died.

The doctor didn't say it in those specific words, but his grave tone and somber expression as he delivered the post-op summary did. When he used phrases like detached placenta and extreme hemorrhaging, I focused more on the way he was saying it than what he was saying, because I worried I'd pass out again. There'd been so much blood, I didn't know how she or her daughter had survived.

I wasn't a religious person, but after I'd come to and Emily had been taken away for an emergency C-section, I prayed. I'd held on to my mother with one hand and an ice pack to my side with the other, begging for my sister and Baby to be okay.

When I'd fainted, I'd collided with the chair, catching it right in my ribs, and it ached with each deep breath I took. Nothing was broken, thankfully. Just an ugly red line that would likely turn blue-purple tomorrow. I was upset with myself. When I'd passed out, it caused even more chaos in the room and unnecessary stress for my mother.

But we Northcott women made it through.

And now my mother was a grandmother. Selene Marist Northcott was seven pounds, one ounce, with a full head of brown hair . . . and perfectly healthy. Once Emily had been moved to her suite, we spent hours fawning over the newest member of the Northcott family. We'd called my dad at the office and told him she was going in for a C-section, and by the time he'd rushed over, Selene had been born. The doctors had moved fast.

It was late when the nurse came by to take Selene to the nursery so my sister could get some much-needed rest. She hadn't been able to hold her baby much, and I knew that was hard for her.

"Em," I said, my voice filled with awe, "you made another person, and she's so amazing."

My sister was exhausted, but a smile lit up her face. "I do good work."

I laughed, and it felt so good after the day we'd had. "You do."

Our parents weren't here—my dad had taken my mother down to get some dinner, and it was nice being just the two of us. I tried to savor it. It'd likely be one of the last quiet times between us for a while.

But I didn't get to enjoy it. There was a knock on the door at the front of the suite, and Emily and I exchanged a look. I got up, walked through the small sitting area, and opened the door, only for my jaw to hit the ground.

"Who is it?" she asked.

"It's Brandon," Dr. Galliat answered back.

He stood in the hallway, wearing an expression of hesitation and carrying a large bouquet of flowers in a vase. I narrowed my gaze at him. I'd had him as a professor my sophomore year for Intro to Psychology, and he hadn't changed much since. He was still young and handsome, probably with the same dimples when he smiled that made all the girls take a second glance.

"Marist," he said, recognizing me. "Can I see her?"

"I don't know." I asked it louder, so she'd hear. "Can

he see you, or do you want me to tell him to come back another time?"

Emily didn't get a chance to answer. Dr. Galliat's expression shifted to panic and went over my shoulder to the woman in the bed who'd just given birth to his daughter—the one he'd wanted nothing to do with.

"Please." He was desperate. "Emily, please. I left her, okay? Can we just—?"

"Fine," she said.

As soon as I was out of his way, he strode toward her bed, dumping off the flowers on a side table. "How are you?"

She ignored his question and surveyed him from top to bottom. Maybe she checked to see if he was still wearing his wedding ring, but he wasn't. Like me, her eyes were also narrowed. "What are you doing here?"

"Your mother called me." A strange look filled his face. Guilt? Embarrassment? He closed his eyes and ran his finger over an eyebrow. "She was upset and had some choice words for me."

The corner of my mouth wanted to tug up into a smile at the idea of my mother going all tiger mom on him. If she blamed Dr. Galliat for nearly killing my sister, I understood. I felt that way a little too.

He sighed. "You don't owe me anything after the way I treated you, but, Emily, I made a mistake. I was scared, but I'm not anymore."

My sister had such a big heart, I could already see his words thawing the ice he'd put around it. It wasn't my business, but I couldn't help myself. My tone was pure condescension. "Good for you."

He wasn't fazed, and his focus remained locked on my sister. "I'm sure you're tired and you've been through hell, so I'll get right to the point. I want a second chance. Maybe you can grant that to me, and maybe you can't, but at least let me be a part of our daughter's life."

She pressed her lips together, but her chin began to quiver, and tears flooded her eyes. "I'm not going to keep her from you, but I don't know about anything else right now."

It wasn't a solid 'no,' and Dr. Galliat seemed to take it as a win. He let out a breath like some of the tension in his chest had eased. "You didn't answer me before. Are you okay?"

She lifted a shoulder in a shrug, but then winced when her body reminded her not to move. "I'm tired and—"

There was no knock on the door, because he'd unfortunately been in this hospital's suites before and understood how they afforded privacy. Royce came in, the tail of his tie hanging out of the pocket of his long overcoat, and an even bigger bouquet than the one Dr. Galliat had shown up with. My fiancé scanned the room, found me, and flashed a smile before moving deeper into the suite and depositing the flowers beside the other arrangement.

"Congratulations," he said to my sister. "Your mom pointed her out to me in the nursery. She's as beautiful as her mother."

Dr. Galliat's shoulders lifted and his chest broadened. It was a territorial posture, and he gazed at the younger man like he was a threat.

"Thank you," Emily said. She turned her gaze up to her

former—and I suspected soon to be current—lover. "Brandon. This is my sister's fiancé, Royce."

Dr. Galliat went rigid, and his voice was strained. "Royce Hale?"

"That's right. You are?"

Emily wasn't sure what label to use but decided to go with the truth. "This is Selene's father, Dr. Brandon Galliat."

Something flickered in Royce, like the name was familiar, but he couldn't place it. He held out his hand for a handshake. "Nice to meet you."

Dr. Galliat stared at the offered hand like it might bite him, and the mood in the room quickly became awkward when he didn't move. But finally, he broke and accepted a quick shake.

"Congrats," Royce said.

Dr. Galliat's eyes widened. "For what?"

Royce's head ticked to the side. "Your daughter?"

"Right. Thanks." He turned to Emily. "I should go and let you get some sleep."

She blinked, stunned. He'd just gotten here, dropped a bombshell, and now he was leaving? "Oh. Okay."

He was already moving toward the door. "I'll text you tomorrow and see how you're both doing, if that's all right."

"Sure," she said, sounding anything but.

"Okay, good." He paused at the doorway as if there was something else he wanted to say, but he didn't. He went out the door without another word. Like he couldn't get out of this room fast enough.

"That was weird," I said.

Royce looked indifferent. "Sometimes it happens."

"What happens?"

"The Hale name makes people uncomfortable." He stared at me with his enigmatic eyes. "You'll get used to it."

Would I? I doubted it.

ELEVEN

After the holidays were over, I'd hoped things would settle down, but they only grew more frantic. I entered my final semester of college with a plate full of wedding planning. Even with a team of event coordinators to handle things, there were still obligations I had to fulfill personally.

Like my bridal shower.

Since my sister had a newborn and was still recovering, another bridesmaid stepped in to help—Sophia Alby. Paired with Alice as a host, my two frenemies threw a lavish luncheon, complete with a fairytale theme and specially commissioned Swarovski crystal figurines as party favors. They were a glittering version of Cinderella's pumpkin carriage, and I wanted to laugh at Alice's shade.

She wasn't wrong. I was the poor girl, playing dress up and pretending to be someone else while I fell in love with the prince. But her plan to get under my skin backfired. The figurine said more about her than it did me. It was a paperweight in the digital world—its only use was for the background of Instagram pictures.

The weekend after my twenty-second birthday, Royce attempted to take me to the British Virgin Islands, only to discover when we arrived at the airport the jet was already gone. An emergency with the German branch had called Macalister away with just enough time to change the jet's flight plan, but apparently not enough to let us know about it.

It was Friday evening, which made it impossible to arrange anything spur of the moment, and with such a short trip anyway, we were forced to scrap our plans. Frustration rolled off Royce in thick waves.

"It's okay." I curled my hand around his arm and snuggled closer as we stood in the frosty airplane hangar. "I just want to be alone with you. I don't care where."

The irritation raging in his expression faded. "I know. Me too. But, fuck, Marist. I was promised you were going to wear a bikini."

I snorted. "I can still put it on. You just have to let me wear socks too, though, because your dad keeps the house freezing." My voice trailed off at the end. Why the fuck had I said that? With the mention of Macalister, Royce stiffened. I had to try again. "There's always our honeymoon."

He'd booked the yacht for the French Riviera like we'd talked about, and we'd leave for Nice the day after our wedding in June.

At least, if there wasn't an emergency for Macalister that required our yacht.

In March, HBHC presented its offer to Ascension with a 'bear hug' letter. It was called a bear hug because it was an overly warm and generous offer to the target company's shareholders. Ascension had been trading at forty-two dollars. HBHC's tender offer was fifty a share. The market went nuts. I could feel the frenzied air sweeping in from New York all the way up in Boston.

Everyone was abuzz with the announcement that Hale Banking and Holding was plotting a takeover. Wall Street sharks smelled blood in the water. Royce and I were up late the night the news broke, and we watched the scrolling banner on CNBC in bed together, our breath tight.

Maybe he already felt he'd passed the threshold, but for me, this was the moment where there was no turning back. The offer was out, done, and it was Ascension's move now. They could counter the proposal, or fight, or reject it, but each path had its own pitfalls. If they turned it down, they risked being sued by their shareholders.

And I was currently in bed with one of them. I didn't know how much stock, specifically, he owned, but if the company accepted HBHC's offer, he stood to make a fortune larger than most third-world economies.

Some of my classmates were talking about the offer the next morning, but to each other and not me. Since becoming Royce's fiancée, I suffered from a different type of ostracism. The other students in my Financial Crises class viewed me as one of the gods from Mount Olympus, and as mere mortals, believed they were forbidden to speak to me.

It was lonely, but familiar.

I stared blankly at the table at the front of the classroom, waiting for the lecture to begin. Where was the professor?

As if on cue, she breezed in, moved the strap from her bag over her head, and dropped it on the podium. "Sorry. This is last minute, so please bear with me." She took out her phone and tapped the screen. "We have a guest professor for today. Hold on while I pull up his bio."

She didn't give a name as she began reading, but it only took a few details before my stomach dropped. Harvard MBA. CEO of one of the biggest banks in the world. *Enjoys chess in his spare time.*

My professor's smile was wide. "We all know the impact of the subprime financial crisis of 2008, but this is a rare opportunity to get an inside look at how one bank found themselves in jeopardy and then responded. Let's give a big welcome to Macalister Hale." She gestured to the open doorway. "Mr. Hale?"

There were audible gasps when he strode into the room, looking powerful in his black suit and red tie. Some of the women clapped. Others were too busy gazing at him as if Gordon Gekko had magically come to life and decided the first thing he'd do was give a lecture at a women's college in Boston.

He'd just announced to the world he wanted Ascension. What was he doing here?

His surveyed the room critically as he moved to the podium at the center and noted the bag on it with a look of disdain.

"Oh," the professor said with a too-bright, enamored

smile. "That's mine."

She grabbed it by the strap and in her flustered state immediately dropped it, sending makeup and car keys scattering loudly across the hard floor. He didn't help her as she apologized and scooped the items up. He simply stared at her, and I could hear the thought running through his mind. *Be gone with you.*

When she finally stepped to the side and took her seat, he placed his hands on the podium and lifted his steely-eyed gaze to meet mine.

I'd barely seen him in the last few months, and when I had, all I could ever see was his face the moment he'd reached his orgasm. How his mouth had parted to drag in breath and how his eyes had gone hazy, but he didn't dare drop his focus from me.

The air in the classroom went thin, but Macalister and I were the only ones who seemed to be having difficulty breathing. He held my gaze for a lifetime and a single beat, and then his focus shifted away to the class in general.

"Thank you." His tone was cold and professional. "I'm happy to speak with you all this afternoon, and hope you find what I have to say informative."

For the next forty-five minutes, he recanted the tale of how he, as a newly-minted CEO in 2007, had struggled to lead the bank through the darkness of the housing bubble burst and come out the other side of the Great Recession with his family's company still intact.

Once I divorced my mind from the man I knew personally, I was able to absorb his lecture from a business standpoint. He talked about his successes and was somewhat forthcoming about his failures too. But there was a glimpse of the real Macalister near the end. Defensiveness crept over him when he brought up the Troubled Asset Relief Program money HBHC had accepted to bail them out and was quick to remind us that over five hundred banks in America had needed taxpayer dollars to keep from collapsing.

He took a few questions at the end, but they were softball ones. Unsophisticated questions meant to flatter, but he saw through the bullshit and was irritated.

I raised my hand, and when he nodded, "Do you think the bailout created a moral hazard for big banks?"

"I can't answer for every bank," he said, "but I believe the answer is no. There are protections in place like Dodd-Frank—"

"But you created the problem with your greed, were deemed too big to fail, and then given billions of dollars to get out of it. Without having to suffer the consequences, was there a lesson learned?"

If a pin had dropped in the room, everyone would have heard it, except perhaps him. His anger moved almost as slowly as a glacier as it rose up over his face, but I could see in his eyes it burned hotter than the sun. It was so rare he lost control.

"First of all," his speech was crisp and deadly, "I have been credited with a great many things, but personally causing the subprime mortgage crisis is a new one. Second, there *were* consequences—some of which my bank is still grappling with." The walls in the classroom closed in so it was just the two of us. Macalister speaking only to me in his sharp tone. "And third, I don't use the term 'too big to fail,' because failure isn't a word I allow in my vocabulary, *Marist*."

He'd scolded me like a child in front of the whole room, and I wanted to melt under the table and disappear. As he said his goodbye, I sensed the rest of the class wanted that as well. I'd meant to embarrass him, but I'd done it to myself instead.

I stayed up later than Royce did on the weeknights. I was a night-owl, and my earliest class wasn't until nine thirty, and there were some mornings where he'd gone into the office and was seated at his desk before I'd even gotten out of bed.

He told me to enjoy it while I could. After graduation and the wedding, Macalister had informed me I'd start as a credit analyst at HBHC and work on my master's in my spare time. It was an entry-level position, and I could probably land a better one on my own somewhere else, but he'd never allow a Hale to work outside the company. If I put in my dues and proved qualified, there would be fewer cries of nepotism when I moved into higher positions.

The past few weeks, I'd been staying up even later, studying or reading or just lying in bed unable to quiet the thoughts in my head. The wedding was in less than two months.

My wedding.

The one where I'd marry the man currently snoring

softly beside me, who still hadn't told me he loved me. He showed it, though. He was caring and attentive and devoted, and he couldn't keep his hands off me either. But Alice's words haunted me. Once I was Royce's wife, the chase was over. Would he lose interest in me? Be on to the next thing?

I threw off the covers. If I wasn't going to sleep, I'd go downstairs and grab something to drink, then retreat to my own room with a book and read until Hypnos, the god of sleep, came for a visit.

Lucifer meowed softly when I walked past the library. He was curled up in his favorite spot on the back of the chair and tried to entice me to come pet him, but his single meow wasn't a strong effort, and a half second later he put his head back down.

It had snowed this afternoon, hopefully the last of the season since it would be April next week. There was just enough to be a dusting of white blanketing the ground, and since it was a full moon and cloudless night, it was unnaturally bright outside.

I didn't bother turning on the lights in the kitchen. Instead, I used the light coming from the screen of my phone to help illuminate my path. I always carried it with me now as I moved from room to room in the Hale house, paranoid to be without the ability to call for help, even when Alice continued to live in the converted stables.

I poured myself a glass of water and padded over to the back window, looking out at the grounds while I drank. The evergreens of the hedge maze looked beautiful and deceptively enticing. It was bitterly cold outside, and I could feel it seeping through the glass pane, trying to get at me.

I shivered and turned away.

After I refilled my glass, I started for the door and was halfway out of the room when footsteps pounded loudly, approaching the kitchen from the back staircase. I turned in place and was silent as the door was thrown open and Macalister burst in.

He was shirtless and drenched in sweat, and he stormed over to the fridge like a guided missile. The door was yanked open, a bottle of the fancy sports drink he preferred was snatched up, and he didn't bother closing the door before he started drinking. The interior light of the fridge lit him up and made his sweaty chest gleam.

How many miles had he run tonight? It had to have been a lot because he drained the entire bottle and then reached for another.

It was interesting to learn Macalister Hale was not his meticulous self when he was tired. He haphazardly tossed the black cap onto the counter and gulped his drink straight from the bottle, rather than pour it in a glass and sip it calmly like the refined gentleman he pretended to be.

For the first time since Aspen, I saw him as something other than the Minotaur. He was just a man, running himself to the point of exhaustion so he could find sleep. His grace and elegance were missing, and I had to take advantage of his weakened state. It was exactly what he would have done to me.

"Any word from Ascension?" I asked, puncturing the silence.

I'd meant to startle him, and it worked. He jolted, the red liquid inside his bottle sloshed around, and his head snapped toward me, his eyes narrowed like he'd been ambushed. But the defenses came down when he spied me across the way. The fridge was shut, and he turned to fully face me, resting one hand on the counter and the other on the island on the other side. It gave me a view of the rapid rise and fall of his chest, faintly darkened with hair.

"Royce hasn't told you?"

"No. We don't talk about it," I lied.

His face was in shadow and the smile didn't materialize, but he knew I wasn't telling the truth. "Ascension's board voted to enact a shareholder rights plan."

Meaning anyone who already owned shares in the company would be allowed to buy new shares at half price. It was meant to dilute HBHC's ownership and prevent the takeover, and it even came with its own term. "A poison pill."

"Yes."

"So, they've decided to fight."

This time, his cold smile did materialize, and excitement lit his eyes. "Yes." He tilted his head. "But you already knew that."

I tossed a hand out, giving up the charade. "You're right. Royce tells me everything."

The excitement in him died. "No, Marist. I don't believe he has."

Alarm went through me like a spike, but I tried to recover quickly. This was another attempt to come between us, and his manipulation wasn't going to work this time. "We don't keep secrets from each other."

The trap he'd laid for me was so deep, I had time to feel the fall and watch the doors closed around me.

"Ah," Macalister said. "You've told him about the morning of Alice's apology, then. How did he take it?"

My voice was a ghost, not wanting to confront the memory. "That's . . . different."

He asked it simply, like it didn't carry enormous weight. "Why?"

"Because it'd hurt him." I swallowed a breath. "And because I'm ashamed."

There was a fleeting emotion that flickered through his expression, but it was gone too fast to put a label on it. Concern? Remorse?

"No," he said. "You'll give that to me, Marist. I was the one who forced that upon you, so it's my shame now, you understand me?"

His hands came down off the counters, and he took a cautious step toward me, like he was worried I might dart away if he got too close. A fawn in the woods, not aware of the wolf's approach.

"You may have learned I'm a decisive man." He sounded firm and powerful. "Once a decision has been made, it's final." As he drew in his next breath, his voice faltered. "But I have questioned myself every day since that morning, worrying the damage I did to us will be too much to overcome."

"There is no *us*," I said.

"Which is why I've stayed away all these months."

So, he *had* been avoiding me. "Except when you showed

up as a guest professor in my class."

He blinked slowly. "I'll admit I wanted to see you. I decided that was the safest way. What could I possibly do to you in a room full of people?"

"Embarrass me?"

He lifted a sharp eyebrow. "You did that to yourself. You behaved like a child, so I treated you as such."

He had a point, but I didn't want to concede to it. I shifted on my feet and put my hands on my hips, assuming a confident posture. "What I meant is, Royce and I love each other. We don't lie to—"

"Has he said that?"

"That he loves me?" I narrowed my gaze. "Better. He *shows* me."

Macalister wasn't fooled, and he used the opportunity to take another step my direction. "He hasn't, then. How exactly does he show he loves you?"

"I don't have to explain it to you."

"With his fancy gifts?"

"No," I snapped.

It was a demand. "Then indulge me."

He asked for it. "For starters, we fuck all the time."

His expression shuttered. "Everyone in this house is aware. It's yet another reason I've made myself scarce." He sighed almost dramatically and leaned in like he wanted to impart his wisdom. "I know you're young and inexperienced, but surely you're intelligent enough to know that sex does not equate love. I imagine for Royce, sex is meaningless."

I wanted to laugh. "It's not."

"For you, I'm sure it isn't. But he will tire of it and eventually lose interest."

My ears burned hot. "He won't, and I know it."

His blue eyes sharpened on me. "Oh?"

"If sex was meaningless to him, he would have slept with other people the year before we got engaged."

He had the same reaction when I moved a chess piece he wasn't expecting. "What?"

"I waited for him, Macalister. And for a year, he waited for me."

It was like he couldn't reconcile the idea in his head. "He told you this?"

"Yes." My lips turned up in a smug smile.

There was a level of dread in his voice that made my blood run cold. It sounded as if he was outraged for me. "And you . . . you *believed* him?"

Macalister was a splinter trapped in my skin, working deeper and more painfully each time I tried to get him out. He infected my mind and planted seeds of distrust.

When I didn't dignify his question with a response, he stepped back, maybe worried my delusions would rub off on him.

"Don't be a fool," he lectured. "Lying is the only thing my son truly excels at."

I didn't sound as convinced as I would have liked. "We don't lie to each other."

He shot me an incredulous look. "No? You already confessed to me that you do." It felt like he'd struck me in the center of my chest, and my heart slowed. "How easy do you think it is for him to do the same?"

That was the thought Macalister left me with as he exit-ed the kitchen, abandoning me in the darkness.

TWELVE

THE MORNING OF MY COLLEGE GRADUATION CEREMONY, I HAD a nightmare. It was the worst possible kind, where nothing seemed wrong during the dream—not until I woke up, and horror descended on me.

I'd dreamt about Macalister.

My subconscious had placed us in the candlelit dining room the night of the initiation, where I was naked, and he was in his tuxedo . . . only it was just the two of us. I was flat on my back at the end of the long, elegant table. His cold hands were splayed on my spread thighs, and his tongue slipped inside me. My hands threaded into his hair, holding on while he tasted and feasted, dragging a moan from my lips.

When I woke, I was hot and uncomfortable all over, but the ache between my legs throbbed the worst.

Wrong.

Not that I had any control over my dreams, but I felt the shame regardless, and anger toward Macalister, like he'd put the thoughts in my brain.

I brushed my hair back off my heated face, rolled over in

the bed, and my sleepy gaze found my fiancé who was already awake. Royce stared at the screen of his iPad, his blue eyes following intently whatever it was he was watching.

How did he always look so good? His brown hair was wild and his jaw dark with stubble, and it made the shadows of his high cheekbones more pronounced. The covers were mushed down around his waist, exposing the curves and ridges of his defined, bare chest. I licked my lips like he was a meal I wanted to devour.

It was then I noticed the rhythmic movement of his right hand under the sheets, centered between his legs. Oh, my God. Was he masturbating? My focus flew to his iPad and confirmed it. The couple on screen was seated on a gray couch, her tight black dress pulled up to her waist, showing off the gorgeous black thigh-high stockings she wore. The man had two fingers inside her, pulsing in and out as she squirmed.

My breath hitched.

Part of me was fascinated and enjoyed being a voyeur to this intimate act. But a much larger part of me, the insecure and inexperienced side, filled with worry. Had it begun to happen? Alice's warning that he'd lose interest persisted in my mind.

Was Royce already bored with me?

It was like he could hear my thoughts because he turned his head and caught me watching him, but rather than stop or look embarrassed, he simply smiled. His eyes were warm, matching his word. "Hey."

My mouth went dry. "Are you jerking off?"

"Yeah, I wanted to be ready to go when you woke up." He

gave himself another stroke beneath the covers. "You were moaning in your sleep."

Oh, my God.

I swallowed so hard, it had to be audible, and I scrambled to deflect. "What are you watching?"

He turned on the volume and tilted the screen so I could better see.

The pretty brunette had pulled her dress up over her breasts and shifted onto her knees on the couch cushions. It was so she could pull open the man's suit pants and slide his impressive cock into her mouth. There was something about the way she looked at him as she did it, and the way the handsome man gazed back at her . . . it felt authentic. As if they both were enjoying each other, rather than merely performing.

I clenched at such a sexy image and tried not to sound breathless. "They have good chemistry."

"They're married in real life."

"Really?" My pulse pounded in my throat as the man held the girl's long bangs out of her face and watched her take every inch of him between her rosy lips. Up and down she went in slow strokes, and when his eyes closed, he tipped his head back. Like the pleasure was too great.

Royce's hand matched the girl's steady tempo, and his voice was heavy with enjoyment. "I've probably seen every video they've shot together, which is a lot. They bring in friends sometimes."

It was difficult to know where to focus. The video on screen was hot, but the sheets had shifted, and now I could watch the glide of my fiancé's hand down his hard length. It was mesmerizing. I meant to tease and not accuse. "Watch a lot of porn, do you?"

"I'm a guy, so, yeah." He laughed softly. "Plus, there was a while where this was all I had."

I sucked in a breath. "The year you waited for me."

"Yeah." There was no hesitation from him, and the tightness in my chest dissipated.

Royce had a 'tell' when he lied. I'd discovered it after months of fundraising parties and social events where we'd played our roles of prince and soon-to-be princess of Cape Hill. He paused before saying something untrue. It was only a microsecond long—just the length of a single heartbeat, but I'd caught on. If there was a lag, he was going to tell a lie.

I wanted so badly for Royce to say he loved me, I'd made a point of telling him I loved him when other people were around, forcing him to deliver the same line back to me. That goddamn pause every time before he uttered what I longed to hear was a knife in my heart. But I told myself to keep doing it. If he said it enough, maybe the lie would become real, and one day there'd be no hesitation.

He wasn't lying about waiting a year for me, though. Not only were we alone right now, but he hadn't paused. He'd answered me quickly and convincingly.

On screen, the couple moved. As the man stood, she stretched out on the couch, lying down on her stomach, and clutched her hands on the cushion beneath her. Her husband sat beside her long, silk-wrapped legs, and let his hands wander appreciatively over her perfect body, before he placed one on her ass and slid two fingers of the other deep inside her pussy.

I sank my teeth into my bottom lip and reached for Royce. When I clasped my hand over the base of his cock, he sighed with satisfaction and eagerly made room for me to work.

The girl arched and bowed as the man drove his fingers, and her hips lifted when she rose to meet him, adjusting the angle of his thrusts. My pulse kicked when the man leaned forward and buried his mouth between the cheeks of her ass.

"Dirty," I whispered with excitement.

Royce jerked in my hand. "Yeah? You want me to do that to you?"

Yes.

The girl gasped and moaned. One hand flew back to her husband's head, but not to push him away. It seemed reactive, like she was overwhelmed by the sensation. Her mouth rounded into a silent 'oh' of bliss.

"Maybe," I said in a hush.

Royce chuckled sinfully and tossed the iPad aside, scooping a hand into my hair. "That's a fucking yes if I ever heard one."

His kiss was blistering. Addictive. His tongue pressed to the seam of my lips and demanded entry, and I gladly gave it. While he kissed me, he curled his fingers around the waistband of my shorts and began to stretch them down.

"You should know, this is my favorite part of the day," he said. "Waking up next to you." He grabbed my hip and pulled me toward himself, encouraging me to lie on my stomach. When I did, he got on his knees and pushed a finger inside me from behind. "I get to do it for the rest of my life, don't I, Marist?"

"Yes," I said mindlessly to both his question and his possession.

His voice was rich, like decadent chocolate. "Because you're mine."

"*Yes*," I whispered.

Because I was so very his.

My bridal bouquet was a hand-tied collection of white and blush pink roses, set against silvery green sprigs of eucalyptus. It perfectly matched the soft pink bridesmaid dresses Sophia and Emily wore, along with the crystal embellished Manolo Blahnik heels on my feet.

I'd told the florists I didn't want to see a single stem of lily of the valley. I would have had the groundskeepers dig up Alice's plants from the garden too, but Royce had beat me to it last October. It was one of the first things he'd done after I'd come home from the hospital.

For appearances' sake, Alice had spent the last two nights in the main house, back in her old room. The staff was discreet, but people were coming and going as the wedding machine geared up. I'd forbidden her from entering my room as I got ready, but her hair and makeup team was here, texting her pictures and making adjustments based off her feedback.

"I can't believe Sophia is a bridesmaid," my sister whispered. "Why is that again?"

"She's useful." I used my thumb to turn the enormous engagement ring on my finger like a screw being tightened to hold down my anxiety. "I mean, look at how good she is with Selene."

My sister turned her gaze across the room to Sophia, who sat on the floor with her pink dress flounced around her, cooing endlessly to my niece in her bouncy chair. In Sophia's defense, six-month-old Selene was the most adorable flower girl ever. She'd charmed everyone, including the pair of photographers in the room who were furiously snapping pictures.

My parents sat on the couch nearby. My dad looked handsome but uncomfortable in his tuxedo, although I wondered if it were his surroundings that really bothered him. Did he feel like he was losing his little girl to the Hales?

A quiet but persistent stream of tears had been leaking from my mother's eyes since I'd put on my great-grandmother's Harry Winston necklace. It was my "something old" to satisfy the tradition. My "something new" was my dress.

The borrowed item was one of the cufflinks from the pair I'd given Royce for his twenty-sixth birthday last month. Ares, cast in white gold, that I hoped he'd wear the day he usurped his father. He rested in the tiny pocket I'd had Donna sew into my dress.

My sister had given me an ice blue handkerchief with the words *keep your shit together* embroidered on it, which tucked around my bouquet to serve as my "something blue." So, I had all of the tradition satisfied, my dress and veil on, and my half of the bridal party at the ready. And while I didn't have cold feet, I had nerves in spades. I was quaking inside the bodice of my dress. The world was spinning too fast.

Selene began to fuss, no longer satisfied with Sophia's baby talk or the light-up stars dangling from the arch over her chair, and both my sister and my mother made a move for her.

"No, I've got her," my mother said to Emily. "What if she spits up? You don't have time to rinse it out before we head outside."

"That means you won't either," my dad quipped. "Give her here." He held out his hands enthusiastically.

"Oh, my God, Dad." Emily laughed. "You are such a baby hog."

He scowled. "I am not."

But he successfully maneuvered his granddaughter out of his wife's arms and into his own. My sister was right; he hogged the baby every chance he got. I didn't think it was possible for my parents to love anyone more than my sister and me, but my niece was giving us a run for our money.

A short set of knocks came from the door, causing our conversation and my heart to stop. Was it time already? When the door opened, I expected it to be one of the wedding coordinators, dressed elegantly in black and wearing an earpiece, but it wasn't.

A chill swept into the room with him.

"I need a minute alone with the bride," Macalister said.

His voice had an edge of strain, like he'd held back the desire to demand everyone leave the room immediately. They got the message loud and clear, though. My mother exchanged a furtive glance with me, unsure if she should go, but I nodded. There was no point in fighting this. It was his house, and he was paying the entire astronomical bill for this wedding, so they needed to honor his simple request.

He kept his head turned away, watching the photographers, my family, and Sophia file out of the room, and didn't look at me until the door was shut and we were alone. As if he didn't want anyone else around while he looked upon me for the first time.

His gaze began at the hem of my white satin dress, trimmed delicately with lace and beading, and ever so slowly climbed upward. Donna Willow had given me elaborate, showstopping pieces to wear in the past, but my wedding dress showed off her more restrained side. I'd given her three requirements, and she'd nailed each one.

The first was that the dress be sophisticated. It was classically elegant with a long train and a simple neckline, which played into the second requirement. I wanted to wear my great-grandmother's wreath necklace, and not have it compete with the garment.

My final requirement was that it show off Royce's favorite place on my body.

So, it was backless. My dark hair had been twisted up and pinned away, and my cathedral-length veil unembellished, so as I walked down the aisle, our guests would catch a glimpse of my bare back, obscured only by a thin layer of tulle.

Macalister hadn't seen that yet, though, since I was facing him, and I was glad. Him seeing me alone like this, before any other Hale, was a power move. It should have been Royce, standing at the end of the aisle, and I was angry his father had stolen that from him.

I also didn't like how he was looking at me. It was the same way Royce had looked at me the first time I'd tried on the red dress nearly a year ago. The longing in Macalister's eyes was downright terrifying and made my insides bubble.

"What is it?" I asked.

"Each time I think you couldn't possibly look more beautiful, you prove me wrong."

I swallowed painfully, struggling to get out my response. "Thank you."

There wasn't a wrinkle or speck of anything marring his black tux, and his white shirt was as pristine as his eyes. Everything was perfectly in place, from his dark brown hair to the white square peeking out of his pocket, and the white rose pinned to his lapel. Of course, it was. Today he was Zeus, the god all the other gods and goddesses looked up to.

My nerves obliterated whatever tiny filter I had on my mouth. "Every time I see you in a tuxedo, something bad happens."

"Nothing bad is going to happen to you. Today, you take my name and fully become a Hale."

"Royce's name," I corrected.

"Which I gave to him." As if a thought had just occurred to him, he reached inside his tuxedo jacket and strode toward me. "I have something to give you."

My heart lurched up into my throat. Whatever it was, I didn't want it. Gifts from Macalister came with strings, and I'd only felt free the last few months. "No, thank you."

He ignored me and produced a tiny black box, only big enough to hold something outrageously expensive. I shook my head, making my veil swish across my back. When I refused to accept the box, he opened it and thrust it forward.

The oval sapphire at the center of the ring was massive, and diamonds flanked it on either side, and it was so beautiful it stole my breath. My gaze fluttered from the ring up to his in disbelief. This ring was way, *way* too much. That size of it alone made me nervous, but for him to give me a ring—one that could have stood in as an engagement ring—it was wildly inappropriate.

"It's beautiful, but I couldn't." I took a step back, retreating.

He pulled the ring from the box, and his face was full of determination. "It's yours. You will wear this."

"No, I won't. Take it back."

Confusion was something I rarely saw in him, and it played out on his face, creasing his forehead. His voice went uneven. "I can't. I believe she would have wanted you to have it."

I froze, allowing the meaning to sink in. He wasn't talking about Alice because he'd used the past tense. "This was Royce's mother's?"

"It was an early wedding gift from me. She'd said she wanted something blue to wear." His chest expanded on a heavy breath. "Now it will be my gift to you. I'm sure it comes as little surprise that I'm not a sentimental person, but . . . I don't give this ring lightly. It's one of the few things of hers I'd kept just for myself." He glanced down, examining the stunning piece of jewelry in the light streaming from the nearby window, making it throw rainbows around. "But then

I thought if I did this, perhaps a part of her could be with Royce today."

This was the man I'd seen in the library, clutching a tumbler of scotch as he mourned the death of the woman he'd loved. I was all sorts of emotional today, and unexpected tears leapt into my eyes, but I blinked them back.

"I need you to wear this ring." And then he said the word he'd probably only used genuinely a few times in his life. "Please."

It came from me in a rush. "Yes, of course."

When I took it from him, our fingers brushed and—had he just let out a sigh? I slipped the ring onto the third finger of my right hand, where it fit perfectly, although it was heavier than I had expected.

We admired it together for a long, quiet moment, and I found the courage to speak.

"You did a nice thing," I whispered. He was at war with his son, but this felt like an overture toward a truce. It was encouraging to see him care about someone other than himself.

"Your influence, I'm sure." His gaze locked onto me and refused to let go. "When I brought you into my home, the plan was to mold you into how I thought you should be. Instead, you've changed me."

My heartbeat went into double-time, and trepidation inched up my spine. I sensed it before it happened but was unable to stop him. Macalister clamped a cold hand around mine and stepped into my space, taking all the air with it. His head was tipped down so he could peer into my eyes, searching them like a missing figure was hidden inside and he just had to look hard enough.

"I have tried harder than anything else in my life to keep my distance from you. I've told myself I don't care, nor do I want to change the way you feel about me, but no amount of lies will drown out the truth."

I tried to shake off his hold, but he responded by threading a hand between my back and the veil, and when his fingertips skimmed across my bare skin, lightning sparked, and his eyes clouded with dangerous, reckless desire.

"Macalister," I whined in a sharp, low voice so no one in the hall would overhear and come in.

"At first, my attraction was purely sexual in nature. I was consumed by the desire to get what I was owed and what you had denied me."

His hand on my back was a tool of torture. If I tried to move away, it forced me closer to him, putting us chest to chest. The full skirt of my wedding dress crushed between us.

"Say what you mean," I hissed. "You just wanted to win."

There wasn't a drop of shame in him. "Yes. But as time went by, the way I longed for you shifted and grew deeper. We have a connection, Marist. You cannot deny it. Perhaps you think I'm not good enough for you, but I know with absolute certainty Royce isn't."

His thumb swept across the ridge of my spine, causing me to tremble. His lips hovered so close, it'd take no effort for him to close the space and press his mouth over mine. "I understand you think you love him, but I'm only trying to protect you."

It was my wedding day, and I was only minutes from

walking down the aisle. Anger erupted inside me and spilled out, making me spit each word as a bullet. "*How dare you?*"

My castigation glanced off him and fell harmlessly to our feet. He was immortal and impervious.

"You'll marry him," he decreed. "We've come too far for any other outcome, but you don't have to love him. Behind closed doors, you can be with whomever you choose, such as a man who strives for perfection, who never gives up trying to be better." His expression was resolute. "My persistence means you and I are inevitable. We are inevitable, because I love you."

THIRTEEN

SHOCK MADE ME GO BONELESS. MY KNEES SOFTENED INTO nothing, and as I sagged, Macalister was there to keep me upright, his hands cold and splayed across my back.

"No," I cried in a horrified whisper. "You can't."

"And yet, I do." He looked confident as ever, saying it the same way he'd tell me money was green and his last name was Hale.

My hands were balled into fists with my forearms pressed to his shirt, and my muscles ached to move and beat my fists against his chest. It was so exceptionally cruel, I couldn't breathe. I'd longed to hear one Hale tell me those words and mean it, and instead the universe had sent me another.

A tear spilled out and rolled down my cheek, but I was too shaky to do anything about it. Macalister moved to cup my face and hold me steady, and to my horror, he leaned in until there was no space left. He kissed my cheek, tasting my tear.

I finally found my strength and shoved him away, tripping over my long skirt and nearly falling over. I didn't give a fuck who heard me now, and the sharp, angry word burst from my lips. "No. Get out."

Beneath my skin, his kiss burned and stung, and I wiped at my cheek, trying to soothe the invisible mark away.

He straightened, and something like hurt flitted over his expression, but then it hardened. "He doesn't love you. You're nothing more than a cog in his master plan."

"Get the fuck out."

Oh, Macalister didn't like that at all. His face soured, and aggression flared in his eyes. "If you don't believe me, I suggest you ask him about his relationship with Dr. Galliat."

I flashed back to the awkward reaction Selene's father had when Royce appeared in Emily's hospital room. The coincidence was hard to ignore. Was there a kernel of truth to what Macalister was saying? I shook my head, shutting down and trying to prevent an even worse overload. This was calculation. A strategic move he'd made to try to win the game of my heart, and I wasn't going to allow it. Instead, I exacted a dark, cold demeanor and spoke in a language he understood.

"If you don't leave this room right now, there will be serious and devastating consequences."

It was subtle, the way he flinched and began his retreat. "I am sorry if hearing the truth upset you." He gave me a final look, noting how I was shaking with adrenaline and a wide range of emotions, the strongest one being rage, and tipped his head to me in farewell. "I'm leaving this room, but you are smart enough to know I'm not going anywhere."

I stood like a statue as he opened the door, walked out, and pulled it closed behind him. My blood was thundering in my ears, but I heard him tell my waiting family I needed a minute to compose myself. At least he'd done me that favor. It gave me time to drag air painfully into my lungs and press my shanking hand to my throat and the diamond necklace there.

They said the fall from heaven was painful, but I didn't know going up to join the gods was going to be as well. Was I even going to survive it?

At some point, the door creaked open, and Emily peeked her head in. She gave me a once-over, her eyes widened, and she pushed into the room, announcing to everyone in the hall that I'd be out in a minute.

Seeing me in whatever state I was in made my sister go white. "What's wrong? Is it something with Royce?"

I was still struggling to catch my breath. "No."

"What did Macalister say to you?"

"He . . ." I couldn't tell her. There was too much, and my shame was too great. I closed my eyes and set my fingertips to my forehead.

She gasped. "What is that?"

When she seized my right hand, I understood what she was asking about. Her stunned gaze traced the huge blue stone and the half-moon diamonds on either side.

"It was Royce's mother's."

"Oh," she said wistfully. "That's wonderful." She looked at me with an understanding look, like she believed this was why I was so emotional.

And like a coward, I let her.

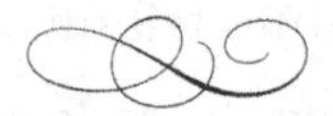

My father and I stood in the sunroom at the back of the Hale house, sweating despite the air conditioning. It would only get hotter when we stepped out onto the patio and began the long walk down the stone stairs into the garden, and then up the aisle to where my groom waited. And there'd be five hundred pairs of eyes on us as we did it, which was likely why my father looked ill.

At least I'd had some practice. Not only had I broken in my Manolos going up and down the steps numerous times the last week, but I'd been at the top of that same staircase nearly a year ago with Royce and withstood the scrutiny of Cape Hill's high society when I was a *nobody*.

In theory, today would be easier.

The photographers circling us made me feel like my performance had already begun, and I pulled my lips back into a bright, nervous smile. For the next ten hours or so, I'd be on stage, reprising my role of Marist Northcott the brand, not Marist Northcott the person. Hopefully, the smiles would come easier once my stage partner was at my side. Royce was an experienced actor, who'd cover up any forgotten lines and guide me through the scenes.

When the event coordinator opened the door and announced it was time, my heart clogged my throat. I clutched my bouquet tighter in my left hand and looped my right arm through my father's, and he set his hand on top of mine in reassurance.

"Your mother and I love you very much," my father said.

"We're so happy you're happy."

When his chin began to quiver, my eyes went wide. "Oh, God, Dad. Please. If you start, I'll start."

He nodded, blew out a long breath that seemed to even him out, and then we were off.

The music of the orchestra wafted up over the balcony as the processional concluded, and as my father and I made our way toward the top of the steps, the garden below came into view.

It'd taken a team of contractors five days to transform the space. Elegant white folding chairs were set in endless rows, twelve seats on each side of the wide center aisle, which was a boardwalk covered in flawless white. It led to a white, three-tiered platform at the front like a stage, and at the back of it rose an arbor, draped in gauzy curtains and decadent flower arrangements. It'd serve as the backdrop for the ceremony, and microphones had been hidden inside so everyone could hear us as we exchanged our vows.

The bridal party was already assembled. Emily and Sophia looked stunning in their pink dresses, and Vance and Tate were handsome as they stood on the platform steps in their tuxedos, sweating under the bright sun.

As my father and I appeared at the top of the steps, the guests' conversations abruptly stopped, and they rose to stand. I was Medusa once more, turning the entire crowd into stone.

During the rehearsal last night, my father and I had been instructed to pause here for a minimum of fifteen seconds. My father had been told not to start us moving again until he received a wave from the head coordinator at the base of the stairs. I was supposed to use this time to get my first look at my groom—that way I wouldn't be distracted while I descended the stone steps. It was precarious in four-inch heels, a full skirt, and a heavy train.

Fifteen seconds wasn't nearly enough time.

Royce was so far away from me, but it didn't matter. I could see his enormous grin from where I stood. I'd seen him in tuxedos before, but rather than the standard bowtie, he'd opted for a black silk necktie, tucked into a black vest, and covered with a classic matching jacket. It left only a V of his white shirt showing and drew my eyes up to his gorgeous face.

He made my heart stop, but as my father's arm gently pulled me along, it started anew.

I smiled as we slowly descended the stairs, my teeth clenched with concentration and my long train and veil trailing behind us. When we reached the bottom, I felt the full intensity of everyone's stares, but I had tunnel vision.

I only saw Royce.

And I wanted my father to move faster so I could get to my groom quicker. I couldn't wait for the moment when my father would put my hand in Royce's because I felt like I hadn't touched my fiancé in a lifetime, and I was desperate to have the connection back.

After the rehearsal dinner last night, we'd said goodnight and slept in separate bedrooms in the same house for the first time in months. He'd texted me in the morning to say he hadn't slept well, but only because he'd been missing me.

So, while he still hadn't said the words, I believed in my

heart he felt them. As I marched up the aisle toward him, he gazed at me with so much emotion in his eyes, it couldn't be anything other than love.

He came down the three steps of the platform to meet us, waited for my father to give me a kiss on the cheek, then accepted my father's hearty handshake. When my hand was finally set in his, electricity poured through me. I sighed in relief, feeling as long as Royce and I were together, there wasn't anything that could stop us.

Not even Macalister Hale.

We walked together up the steps toward the officiant waiting for us, and when we reached our places, Emily and Sophia hurried to spread out my train and make it picture perfect as it cascaded down the platform's steps. Royce stole a glance down at the unfamiliar ring on my right hand—and did a double-take. He gazed at the ring like he couldn't believe what he was seeing. He lifted his confused, rapidly blinking eyes to mine, and whispered, "My mother's?"

I nodded.

His incredulous smile nearly broke my heart, it was that full of love.

The ceremony was a blur, and it was a small mercy for our guests. Even though it was just the first week of June, it was hot and humid and there weren't any clouds in the blue sky, so we were all baking in the sun. I was sweating through my makeup, and there were undoubtably artists waiting to dab powder at me in the shade of the gazebo at the back of the garden, before Royce and I would pose for pictures.

Once we'd said our vows and exchanged rings, I couldn't

stop staring at the silver band across his finger. It was easily the sexiest thing I'd ever seen. It played a big part in how excited I was when it came time for Royce to kiss me.

"Ladies and gentlemen," the officiant said, his voice raised proudly, "I present to you Mr. and Mrs. Royce Hale."

We turned to face the crowd and their thunderous applause, and a thrilled smile broke on my face. Perhaps the sea of happy people before us were all sycophants and didn't really care, but they looked up at us with such excitement and joy I decided to accept it exactly as it appeared.

It was unavoidable how my gaze drifted to the couple in the front row on Royce's side. Alice's champagne colored dress had beads cascading down the front, like someone had tossed handfuls of glitter at her and they scattered over the fabric. She wore a perfectly manufactured smile as she stood beside her husband.

Macalister wasn't smiling or clapping; his expression was fixed. To others, he might look mildly irritated or bored, but I saw the scowl aching to bow on his lips and the seethe locked in his eyes.

I tangled my hand tighter with my husband's and gave him the biggest smile in my arsenal.

Royce was so exhausted by the end of the night, he fell asleep in the limo as it carried us toward the Four Seasons hotel. We'd spend our wedding night there, and tomorrow evening the Hale jet would take us to Nice, then we were on to Cannes where the yacht and her crew waited for us.

His hand was clasped in mine and nestled in the folds of my skirt, and I grinned at the ring gleaming on his finger. Would I ever get used to that? My smile grew wider, but it could also have been the three glasses of champagne I'd consumed on a mostly empty stomach. They'd been for medicinal purposes—my feet were *killing* me.

I'd expected the day to be long, but nowhere near as enjoyable as it had been—minus my visit from Macalister. Once I fully committed to my role as Marist Hale and treated the endless mingling as a game, it was . . . kind of fun. We'd put on a show and completed all the tasks required of us, cutting the cake and the first dance. We'd done our best to greet each guest and thank them for coming. We'd laughed at the toasts our siblings gave and kissed when people clinked their silverware against their glasses.

But we hadn't gotten a moment to ourselves until the limo, and he'd faded fast. I decided to let him rest, not wanting to bring up what his father had said and mar an otherwise perfect day.

I took a picture of him asleep in his tux, me snuggled beside him, and posted it to Instagram, tagging it with all the hashtags I would have hated or called cheesy a year ago. But now I believed them. It'd been a hard road to get here, but maybe we were a fairytale romance. We'd earned our happily ever after.

When the car pulled up to the front of the Four Seasons and the doorman opened the back door, I nudged Royce. "Power nap is over, husband."

He blinked his sleepy blue eyes and quickly became more alert, sitting up straight and flashing a lazy smile. "Okay, wife."

The elevator ride up to the presidential suite was quick, and I carried my excruciating pink shoes in my hands as I strolled toward the bedroom and flopped down on the mattress, my dress and bustled train billowing around me. Royce shed his jacket and unbuttoned his vest, and he leaned against the doorframe, watching me as he loosened his tie.

"You hungry?" he asked. "Want me to order something?"

"I'll be asleep before it arrives." I rose onto my elbows, half sitting up so I could look at him directly. "I can't believe I married you."

He understood exactly how I meant it, and the corner of his mouth quirked upward. "I can. I had you the minute I said you looked like Medusa."

I pressed my lips together. He was right, but it had taken me a while to figure it out. "And when did I have you?"

His eyes deepened. "I told you, long before that. That night you went to the club with Emily."

"Oh, right." I pretended I'd just remembered. "The night you called me a nobody."

He straightened from the door and stalked toward me, seduction flooding every inch of his face. "You're not a nobody anymore. You're my wife. Marist fucking Hale."

I loved the sound of it, and I grinned darkly. "Should I put that on my business cards?"

"Do it." He chuckled and climbed on top of me, straddling my hips and the wedding dress I wore. I lay back down as he delivered a slow, thorough kiss, like he'd been storing it up all day for me. His tongue dipped into my mouth, creating an achy desire that filled my body.

"I have to warn you," I said, my voice rasping, "I've had a lot of champagne, and I might fall asleep on you."

A short laugh was buried in the side of my neck. He echoed the same thing I'd said after I'd been released from the hospital. "I'll do most of the work. You can just lie there and take it."

I laughed. "Okay."

But once he started, there was no danger of sleep.

The plane had just leveled off when Royce asked, like he'd been waiting for the 'all-clear,' "When did he give you the ring?"

I was still wearing it, and instinctively tensed. I wasn't sure I was ready to have this conversation now. Maybe it was better to wait until we were too far across the Atlantic for Royce to order the pilots to turn around.

"Oh, uh, right before the ceremony."

I'd been anything but normal with my answer, and he latched on instantly. "What happened?"

I wasn't going to lie to him, but I stalled on telling the truth. "He said he thought your mother would have wanted me to have it, and that he hoped part of her could be with you on your wedding day."

It was like I'd just told him Vance had been elected

president. "He said that specifically? Or did he make you think that's what he meant?"

He didn't believe his father could do anything heartfelt because his father didn't have a heart. My breath caught as I considered the two possibilities. Either Macalister's gesture was genuine, and he was capable of feelings—meaning it was possible he was truly in love with me—or he was an emotional void, and the gift was just a calculated move to draw me in.

I wasn't sure which possibility was worse.

I cleared the lump from my throat. "No, he said it specifically. He said it was hard for him to give it away because it means a lot to him."

It was unavoidable, the way both of our gazes fell to the ring, and Royce's voice lost some of its power. "I asked him if he'd let me have it so I could give it to you. He told me no."

The urge to deflate was fierce, but I forced out a smile to stay strong for him. "When I look at this ring, I'm only thinking about her. All that matters is she was there with us, okay?"

He took in a deep breath and stared at me with his intense eyes, which saw all the way to the bottom of my soul. "Yeah."

When the conversation fell quiet, the only sound was the hum of the plane's powerful engines, carrying us away from Boston. I tried to let it go, but the truth itched under my skin. "Your dad said some . . . other things."

Royce's gaze had been out the window, but it turned back to me, and he looked wary. Like he knew whatever I was about to say would be bad, and he wasn't going to like it. "Like what?"

My pulse was whirring as fast as we were hurtling

through the sky. "He told me he loved me."

He turned to stone for a long moment, before a sneer curled on his lips. His tone was patronizing. "As a daughter-in-law?"

It was doubly cruel for him, as his father hadn't told Royce he loved him in at least sixteen years. Maybe his whole life he'd gone without hearing it.

I could barely choke the words out. "As in, he's in love with me."

"You believe him?" My husband's expression was measured and cautious.

"No." The word came quickly. "I don't know," I amended, staring at my hands in my lap. "It doesn't matter either way. I love you, and you love me."

My gaze flicked to his in a challenge, and he accepted it with a resounding word. "Yes."

It was the closest he'd come to saying it, which made warmth spread through my chest, but it was also the ultimate tease. He could be so strong and assertive when he wanted. Why was it so hard for him to say what we both knew was true?

"When we land," he said, "I'm going to get someone to find a place for us in Boston."

"It'll be midnight Eastern time when we land."

Determination pushed his mouth into a frown. "In the morning, then, but we're moving out."

Of course, I wanted to leave. The patriarch of the Hales was in love with me, and another wanted to kill me. But my practical side gave a humorless laugh. "He won't let us. You know he'll find a way to force us to stay, either with your job or your inheritance—"

"He'll throw us out as soon as I take his seat."

"But that could be months away." Ascension had fought tooth and nail while they looked for a white knight company to save them. It'd forced up HBHC's offer.

Royce shook his head. "No, they caved. Their board is voting by the end of the week." He adjusted the unfamiliar wedding band on his finger. "I bet the news breaks while we're still on our honeymoon."

"How long will you wait before you—"

"*I* won't do anything. I left the 'when' up to Tate, but I think he'll wait a few weeks before he blows the whistle." Arrogance threaded through his expression. "Just long enough for my dad to congratulate himself on his *big* win."

"And after, what happens to Ascension? To Tate?"

He shrugged like he wasn't talking about a company worth billions of dollars. "Obviously, we'll need to clean house, and Tate knows where the dirtiest people are."

Meaning he'd take care of his friend and put him in a high-level position to manage the restructure.

"Your father said something else." I watched him closely to gauge his reaction. "Had you ever met Dr. Galliat before that day in Emily's hospital room?"

There was only confusion in his face. "No."

"So, you'd never spoken to him before." I used the same word Macalister had. "You don't have any kind of relationship with him."

"Relationship?" he repeated. He paused to draw in a breath. "No, of course not."

My heart ground to a halt, and the rest of me went on autopilot. "Then why would your father say you did?"

Royce lifted a hand casually. "Because he wants to get between us."

And he'd been successful, because I was certain my husband had just lied to me.

FOURTEEN

SUN BOUNCED OFF THE RIPPLES OF BLUE WATER, AND EVEN though I had on sunglasses, the glare was so bright, I still had to shield my eyes. I lay next to Royce on the lounging bed beside the small in-deck pool and tried to focus on the novel I was reading. It was a modern retelling of the story of Ares and Aphrodite, and the book was so hot, it would have made me sweat if I wasn't already.

But I couldn't focus on my book, because as he'd done that first night in the library, he was staring at me. More specifically, he was staring at the white string bikini with gold accents I was wearing, and each pass of his lust filled gaze forced me to re-read the last line.

"I'm trying to read," I said, adjusting the way I was propped up by the pillows.

"Then read." I wasn't looking at him, but I could hear the devilish smile in his words. "I didn't tell you to stop."

He was distracting in every way. First, he was the poster child for a billionaire playboy right now, lying on the deck of his private yacht in only his aviator sunglasses and black swim trunks, three days' worth of suntanning making his skin golden brown. Second, I felt his relentless eyes all over me, touching every crevice, stroking each sensitive spot.

And third, when I didn't give him the attention he desired, he used his fingertips to trace the Medusa tattooed over my ribs. It was pleasurable lightning across my skin, and even more exciting when he leaned over and kissed the ink. It was enough of a distraction for him to grab one of the gold ends of my bikini top and start tugging at the string.

"Just what do you think you're doing?" I tried to fake a scowl, but it came out as a lopsided grin.

His kiss moved over the fabric cups of my top while he continued to slowly pull at the string, giving me ample time to stop him.

"We're in France."

I threaded my hands through his hair, holding his head to my chest as his mouth traced the edges of my suit. "Technically, we're in the Principality of Monaco."

We'd sailed down from Cannes yesterday afternoon and dropped anchor outside the port. The coast of the ultra-rich city-state loomed in the distance.

"*Technically*, we're in the territorial waters of the Principality of Monaco."

"Someone might see," I whispered, pretending to be reluctant.

His lips fluttered against the skin in the valley between my breasts as he spoke. "Then they'd be really fucking lucky because your tits are amazing. Come on, Marist. Go European for your husband."

I laughed and arched my back, reaching behind myself to undo the knot. I'd never been shy about my body, and they were just boobs. I wasn't going to be embarrassed if someone from the crew got an eyeful. They'd probably seen topless clients dozens of times.

Royce pulled the top away, the strings trailing over my body, and dropped it to the deck. "See? Better this way. No tan lines."

He sucked on my neck while his fingers drew slow circles around my breast, each circuit tighter than the last, closing in on my nipple. My eyes fell shut, and I surrendered to the sensations.

I didn't know what to do about how he'd lied to me. I had no evidence, only Macalister's word, which came with an agenda for sure. And I wasn't exactly being honest with my new husband either. I still hadn't told him what had happened during Thanksgiving in Aspen.

So, I didn't bring it up. Instead, I let his hand wander south and inch below the waist of my bikini bottom. My voice was husky. "Are you going to try to fuck me out here?"

"No. I *am* going to fuck you out here."

The multilevel yacht wasn't anchored near anything else, and it bobbed gently in the calm waters. The ship was huge. We were out on the lowest deck of the stern, and although we felt completely alone, there was a crew of six aboard.

His tone was sinful. "You don't want to?" His fingers worked deeper inside my bikini and strummed my clit, making pleasure sizzle across my nerves. "We've never had sex outdoors before."

But we had with other people watching, hadn't we? I pushed the thought away and refocused on what he was doing to me. When a soft sigh drifted from my lips, victory flashed through him.

He knew he had me.

Although our cabin was spacious, the bed was soft, and the waves served to rock us to sleep, it wouldn't come for me. This afternoon, we'd taken the dinghy into Monaco. We had dinner at one of the finest restaurants in town and played blackjack at the Casino Monte Carlo. We'd been up by twenty thousand euros at one point, but then our luck ran out and we managed to leave only a few hundred in the hole.

We'd had drinks and danced at a nightclub, full of loud, pumping music, a gorgeous atmosphere, and rich people. Heiresses, royals, and celebrities. At one point, we ran into one of the guys Royce had gone to Harvard with. Royce invited him to join us for a drink, but the guy declined, and I was relieved. He'd seemed like a dick, and right as we were leaving, I saw him snorting coke with two women I could only assume were models.

It was late when we'd climbed into bed, and Royce had fallen right to sleep, and although I was tired, there was a nagging at the back of my mind that would not be quiet. It told me if I didn't draw the line now, I'd be setting myself up for more lies in the future.

The disappointment that he hadn't stayed truthful was

hard to swallow, but what could I do? I wasn't going to ask my sister to talk to Selene's father about it. Emily wasn't ready to reach out.

That meant the only person who knew about it was Macalister. It was only eight-thirty at night in Cape Hill. I debated it for a long while, until the decision was made. I sat up, grabbed my phone off the nightstand, and went out through the sliding door onto the balcony.

My feet were cold against the deck as I paced back and forth, trying to figure out how to word it. Once I'd finished typing, my finger hovered over the 'send' arrow. Was I opening Pandora's Box by doing this? The need to know what Macalister knew was eating me from the inside.

Me: Royce says he doesn't know Dr. Galliat.

I pictured Macalister on the other side of the ocean, checking his phone and the message bringing an evil smile to his face. This was my honeymoon, and here I was, secretly texting my father-in-law in the middle of the night.

It was only seconds later that the gray bubble with the three dots popped up, and when the message came through, my blood ran cold.

Macalister: He's lying to you.

Me: How do you know?

There was no response.

Not even a bubble, so he wasn't typing.

I sighed and leaned my forearms against the top of the balcony railing, looking out at the lights dotting the coast of Monaco while the ocean wind whipped through my hair. My gaze went to the now dark screen of the phone in my hands, and the two rings glinted back. One from Royce and one from Macalister. Which one was the liar?

When the phone vibrated, I nearly dropped it to the deck below but managed to hang on. I unlocked the screen and blinked in confusion. What was I looking at? I rotated the phone to landscape and zoomed in. It was a $100,000 check issued to Dr. Brandon Galliat from RMH Industries, LLC—for consulting work, according to the memo field.

I started typing a response to ask what I was looking at, but Macalister's next reply rolled in.

Macalister: RMH is one of the shell corporations Royce uses to buy stock.

My stomach twisted in knots. Even before I read the next line, I knew he was telling the truth.

Macalister: It's his initials.

It was fresh in my memory, since four days ago I had become Mrs. Royce Macalister Hale.

I peered at the screen capture for a long time, willing the letters to change and make it untrue. I tried to make sense of it. What kind of consulting would Royce's sham company need from a psychology professor from an all-women's college?

I threw open the sliding door so hard, it slammed against the track stop, and Royce stirred. He blinked his bleary eyes at me when I clicked on the overhead lights.

"Wake up," I snapped.

He could tell by my tone something was seriously wrong, and he bolted upright, coming fully awake in an instant. The covers were gathered around his waist, and he pushed them down so he could stand, wearing just a pair of underwear. He gazed at me from the other side of the bed, taking in the short silk nightgown I wore and the cold fury burning on my face.

"What's wrong?" He couldn't have sounded more worried if he'd tried.

"Tell me again about Dr. Galliat and how you don't have a relationship with him."

His shoulders pulled back, and his shields went up. "Marist, what on earth?"

"Why did RMH Industries cut him a check for a hundred grand?"

It took a moment for the gravity of my question to sink in, and it was like I'd shot him. Royce's knees folded, and he sat at the edge of the bed, no longer able to look at me. He let out an enormous sigh. "I lied to you."

"No, fucking, shit. Tell me what the money was for." I prayed I was wrong, that it was just a terrible coincidence.

Royce leaned forward, putting his elbows on his knees and his face in his hands. "I had to be sure. My dad had such a hard-on for me marrying Emily." He scrubbed his face, turned his head, and gave me a devastating look. "I didn't want her. I wanted you."

He wasn't going to say it, so I did it for him. "You paid him to get her pregnant."

His guilty expression confirmed it. "Sophia found out who she was dating, and it wasn't hard to convince him. If it worked, I promised him I'd look after her."

For a split second, I considered telling him his money

had been wasted. Emily had confessed to me the night of the initiation she'd wanted to avoid the Hales so badly, she'd tried to get pregnant herself.

But if I told Royce that, it would be like letting him off the hook, and he'd done a terrible thing. He was a true Olympian god now, meddling with the mortal world and not caring what havoc it caused.

"You fucked with her life," I cried. "Do you get that? You changed the course of it forever. And she *almost fucking died*. For what?"

He rose and faced me directly, and his eyes were two cauldrons over the fires of war. "So you could be my wife!"

I stared at him with total disbelief.

His swift, deliberate footsteps brought him closer until we were chest to chest. "Everything I have done—every fucking move I made—was to bring us together. I'm sorry I lied to you. It's not an excuse, but I was ashamed, and I knew if I told you, you'd look at me exactly the way you are right now."

He jammed a hand in his messy hair and stared off into the distance, trying to organize the thoughts in his head. "I warned you before this was all over, you might think I was worse than my father."

"Don't you dare try to—"

He was determined to finish. "I'm sorry your sister was part of my contingency plan, but I was desperate by then and out of options. I'm not proud of what I did, but—shit—I *had* to do it. It was win at all costs." His hands were rough around my waist, hauling me up against him. "And I'd do it again in a heartbeat if I had to, Marist. As long as I got you in the end."

My heart split in two. One half swelled at hearing his declaration, and the other wanted to stomp all over it. I pushed against his bare chest, but he didn't move, and it made me stumble back a step.

Was this why he'd been so attentive to Emily? He'd confessed to me once he didn't care about my family. Had everything he'd done for my sister been out of guilt?

My emotions made my throat raw and sapped the strength from my voice. "Stop telling me what you think I want to hear."

"I'm not. It's the truth."

"How can I believe that? You said we wouldn't lie to each other—but you did."

His frame hardened, and the muscle along his jaw ticked. It restrained his biting tone. "Because you've been nothing but honest with me, right?"

Oh, no. My gaze plummeted to my toes like it was made of lead.

"Yeah, I thought so." He sighed. "He's been dropping comments for months, hinting there was something you weren't telling me. So, what is it?"

I hugged my arms around myself. Part of me was relieved to finally get the truth out, but I dreaded it too. "Our first night in Aspen," I said slowly, "when you went down on me. Your dad walked in on us, and . . . he watched."

I raised my tentative gaze back to Royce, not wanting to see his reaction but knowing I deserved whatever was waiting for me.

His expression was blank. Too guarded for anything to

leak out, but his stare was piercing. "He watched us have sex?"

"No, it was only for a minute." I shifted uncomfortably on my feet and frowned. "I'd been telling him for weeks I only wanted you, but he wouldn't stop. So, when he came in, I foolishly thought I'd show him."

Displeasure smeared across my husband's face, but he didn't appear that angry with me. Perhaps he was thinking unfortunately it wasn't the first time his father had witnessed us together, or maybe the basic, competitive male drive inside him responded to it. He'd shown his father which Hale I'd chosen, who had won.

"But it backfired." My voice was empty. "He held it over my head and forced me into another deal."

That stopped Royce cold. "What'd you do?"

"He made me watch Alice's punishment and listen to her apology." There was no soft or elegant way to say it. "And to punish her, she had to go down on him and then he came on her face."

"What?" It took forever for the words to sink it.

"I didn't want to be there, but he threatened everything would go back to how it was before. You know, after you'd sold me to him."

"You watched my dad get a blowjob?" He grimaced. "That's fucked up, Marist."

It was, but he wasn't being fair. I'd done it *and worse* so we could be together. My eyes went so wide with fury, they nearly burst from my head. "Not nearly as much as your family's fucked up initiation, *Royce*."

Anger tightened his eyes to slits. "I've told you that's the first thing I'm going to change when I'm chairman."

There was a meanness growing in me that was frightening, but I was powerless to stop it. Opening Macalister's text message had been Pandora's Box, and all the evils spilled out.

"But why?" I mocked. "Is it because when Vance joins the board, you'll already know what Jillian's pussy tastes like?"

He flinched. "Okay, first, that was years ago. And second, if you think I'd put anyone else through what we had to do, you're out of your fucking mind."

I was, though. My seams tore open as I unraveled. Everything was falling apart.

"You know what's the worst part?" Tears welled in my eyes. "*He* told me he loved me, and you haven't. I'm your wife, and you *still* haven't." He opened his mouth to say something, but I lifted my hand to stop him. "And if you said it now? How could I believe you?"

His eyes trapped mine, refusing to let go. "You may not believe me, but paying off Emily's professor is the only lie I've ever told you when it was just us. I swear."

He sounded so sincere, and I longed to believe him, but my mind refused. We'd begun as fiction and become real, but he'd let this lie live between us since the start. All the trust he'd built back up after the awful night he'd sold me to his father was shattered.

Oh, God. What if everything Macalister had been telling me from the beginning was true, and everything from his son was a lie?

"Where are you going?" he called, chasing after me as I hurried from the room and down the narrow hallway.

"I'll sleep on one of the couches in the living room."

"Fuck, no, you won't. Come back to bed, and let's talk about it."

I gave him a death glare. "I need to be alone right now."

He gave a sigh of frustration, and when he pinched the bridge of his nose, my focus landed on the wedding band. It hurt. That ring was the prize he'd wanted and gotten at my sister's expense.

"Fine. I'll sleep out here," he said. "You take the room."

I gave a short nod and headed back the way we'd just come, while he stood statue still. But I paused in the hallway with my back turned when he abruptly spoke.

"This is what he wants," he said. "Don't let him do this to us."

My memory drifted back to the night he'd sold me and how I'd pleaded with him as he'd walked away. It had wounded me deeply how he hadn't given me a response then, or even turned to look back at me, but now I had cruel insight as the roles were reversed.

If I said anything or so much as looked at him, I'd break down completely. The only way to survive was to get the hell out of the room.

So, I did.

FIFTEEN

Breakfast was served outside under the shade of the top deck, and although the view was spectacular, all I could see was Royce in his white polo shirt and jeans, picking at the fruit salad on his plate.

I was sure the crew had noticed he'd slept on the couch last night and they had picked up on the tension running between us. Maybe they'd overheard some of our argument and were gossiping to each other. But they were professional and discreet, and because they were so good at their jobs, most of the time I forgot they were there.

"I didn't sleep last night," I announced.

Royce's gaze turned to me, his voice going soft. "Yeah, me neither."

"The upside is it gave me some perspective. You're right, I don't want your father to come between us. We're stronger together." I put my elbows on the table and leaned forward. "I'm sorry I didn't tell you about Aspen. I'd stupidly thought if he just saw us, maybe he'd leave us alone. The thing with Alice . . . he manipulated me into staying, and I'm ashamed

I let him." I pulled my eyebrows together, struggling to put the words together. "What I'm trying to say is, I'm sorry I lied to you."

The way he looked at me was heartbreaking. "God, Marist. Me too. I'm sorry I lied, and I'm sorry for what I did to disrupt Emily's life."

"You have to tell her," I said. "She needs to know before she lets him back into her life. I mean, when he found out she was pregnant, he offered her five thousand dollars to get rid of the baby."

After Royce had paid him a *hundred thousand* dollars.

A scowl swept over him. "I'd told him I'd take care of her, but Jesus." He blinked and refocused. "Yeah. First thing when we get back, I'll tell her."

"Good." Anxiety tensed the muscles of my back, making my posture stiff. "I have another request, and you're probably not going to like it."

"What is it?"

"I'd like to go home, and when we get back to the house, I need to stay in my old room for a while."

I'd spent a lot of time last night thinking about this, and my anger had given me clarity, sharp and focused. Like an economist, I identified the problem, forecast scenarios with different variables, and considered the pros and cons of each outcome. I'd been dealing with each obstacle as Macalister had thrown them at me, never thinking two moves ahead like he did.

That was going to change, starting now.

Royce held my gaze for an impossibly long moment.

"You're right, I don't like it. You want to leave our honeymoon? How are we supposed to be together if we—"

"I love you, Royce, but I'm not very happy with you right now. You put yourself first in everything. You fucked with Emily's life *and* my life, so you could get whatever you wanted. You're even doing it now to Tate."

"What?" he scoffed. "Tate's a big boy. He makes his own decisions."

"Right. So, if he suddenly decided he was happy at Ascension and didn't want to blow the whistle, you wouldn't do anything that would impact his life?"

Frustration dragged a sigh from his lungs. "It's not that simple."

"I'm asking for some time away from the orchestration of it all, so I can figure out how to move forward."

It was like every bone in his body hated this idea, and the spoiled rich boy who lay dormant in him slipped out. "You know how that's going to look to him? Canceling our honeymoon and staying in separate rooms?"

"It'll look like he won," I said. "But he hasn't. I'm still your wife and your partner, and if you care about me, you'll put my needs above your wants."

Both of our phones vibrated in a short burst on the tabletop, and when he flipped his over, we each saw the breaking alert. The Ascension board had voted unanimously to accept HBHC's offer.

It should have been a happy moment for him. He'd made a mountain's worth of money and passed another checkpoint in his plan, which meant he had almost everything he wanted—but it wasn't good enough.

Resignation flagged in his eyes. "Fine. Let's go home."

Macalister was out of the country when we slipped back into Cape Hill and returned to the house. We told people we'd cut our trip short due to the Ascension takeover, and everyone believed it except for my father-in-law. Adding to his delight, he discovered I'd moved a black pawn on the mythology chess set in the library, answering the opening move he'd made months ago.

I want to play, Macalister.

The next morning, I found he'd moved a second piece.

The first few days back, Royce didn't know what to do. His hands longed to reach for me, and I craved his touch, but I denied it. It was painfully awkward with my husband, but I reminded myself it was necessary. I had to stick to the plan I'd laid out. One wrong move would make the board change, and my chances of winning would dwindle.

He made good on his promise. We took Emily out for lunch, and he confessed what he'd done to my sister, her eyes going wide while I bounced Selene on my knee. He'd been anxious about telling her, but she was quick to forgive like I thought she would be. He looked enormously relieved and yet stunned when she announced she'd gotten pregnant on purpose to avoid him.

"You were such a dick," she said with a flat smile.

"Only because I didn't want you to get attached. I was

totally into your sister."

Emily's gaze dropped to Royce's hand covering mine on the table. "Well, you got her, and I got Selene, so it worked itself out, didn't it?"

We were newlyweds and out in public, which meant we had to keep up appearances. It was hard on me, but brutal for him. He didn't like it or understand why I was keeping myself at such a distance, and I couldn't tell him. If he knew what I was planning, he'd try to intervene or worse– put a stop to it.

On Monday, after I'd secured a new driver's license, I drove myself to an appointment with my attorney in Boston. There was paperwork that needed to be signed off on with my new legal name, Royce had told me. He'd already done his part and had work to do, so he wouldn't be meeting me or our attorneys.

It was there at the prestigious law firm I got my first true taste of what life was like when your last name was Hale. The receptionist nearly tripped over herself as my attorney and I were led back to the conference room. It was full of walnut furniture, expensive artwork, and what looked to be the entire team of partners at the firm.

"Can I get you anything, Mrs. Hale? Coffee, or a soft drink, or water?" the woman asked, pulling out the chair at the end of the table.

It took a moment to realize she was talking to me. "No, thank you."

I lowered into the seat and set my gaze on the people at the other end. Typically, facing an entire legal team staring at you would make you want to sweat, but rather than look intimidating, they looked . . . excited? I glanced sideways at my lawyer, but he looked just as perplexed.

The woman set a leather portfolio in front of me and a fancy black fountain pen beside it. It felt like I'd been shoved onstage during a play and had no idea what role I was playing or lines I was supposed to say.

I opened the portfolio and stared at the dense text in front of me. Royce had been vague about what I needed to do, but there'd been so much with the prenup, the merging of assets, and my name change, I'd expected today to be about one of those things.

But the document before me was a transfer of ownership. I slid it over to my lawyer.

"Uh," I said, "can you explain what we're looking at?"

"I'd be happy to," said one of the older gentlemen across the room who wore a silver patterned tie. "Your husband has initiated a transfer of one of his corporations. He has elected you as the chairman of its board. This is RMH Industries, which holds assets of approximately twelve million shares in Ascension."

Everything ceased working inside me—my mind, my heart, my lungs.

My voice was a ghost. "I'm sorry, what? Did you say twelve million?"

He grinned. "I did."

I swallowed thickly. "What's Ascension trading at?"

One of the partners seated to my right had his phone out on the table, probably in anticipation of this question.

"Fifty-four dollars and twenty cents."

I couldn't imagine what I looked like to them. A pale faced twenty-two-year-old girl who was so shocked, her usually intelligent math brain wasn't working properly. How much money was that?

The silver tie man took pity on me. "The assets are valued at approximately six hundred fifty million dollars. RMH Industries has a four percent controlling interest in Ascension."

My lawyer made a sound like he'd been kicked in the chest.

When presented with that much money, it triggered my fight or flight defense, and my desire was to bolt screaming for the door. It was more than *half a billion* dollars.

"Oh, dear," the woman said, who hovered to my right. "How about some water?"

She didn't wait for me to respond, not that I could. I sat stupefied while a tall, slender glass appeared next to the portfolio and ice water from a pitcher was poured inside. I had no idea if I was thirsty, but the water was there now, and it was an action I understood. I took the glass and drank while everyone studied me.

I set the glass down, leaving my hand wrapped around it, staring vacantly at the polished tabletop. "I don't understand."

"RMH Industries doesn't manufacture anything. The business is set up solely to hold the assets. Doing it this way prevents you from incurring an enormous gift tax."

"No, I meant I don't understand why he did this." I wanted to know what the condition was. Nobody just fucking gave someone a half a billion dollars without expecting something in return.

The man brightened. "Oh, I see. This is a wedding gift from your husband. Mr. Hale had us organize the paperwork so the deal could be executed once you were married and your name had been legally changed."

Meaning Royce hadn't done this incredibly insane thing to try to get back in my good graces . . . he'd set it up weeks or months ago.

"I imagine," the man continued, "this is quite a happy shock."

"Yes," I breathed.

"We're here to help, and we'll take as much time as you need to go through everything."

It was a conditioned response and I didn't know what else to say. "Thank you."

The rest of the afternoon was spent in the conference room. I was still in shock and absorbed only fifty percent of everything they said, but when the time came and with my attorney's blessing, I picked up the pen and began to sign in the places they told me to, across from the signature my husband had already scrawled on the pages.

The first time I signed, I started to use my maiden name and had to adjust it. I wasn't a Northcott, I was a filthy rich Hale now.

I didn't remember the drive home. I blinked, and then I was sitting on the bench beneath the fountain at the center of the hedge maze. When I'd moved into the house, this had been my favorite spot. I could still remember the way the fireflies had winked among the hedges when Royce had gotten down on one knee and asked me to be his wife.

I was determined not to let Macalister take my love of this place away. He'd already taken so much.

You have enough money now you can build your own maze.

It was true. As chairman of the board of RMH Industries, which had exactly one member, I could vote to pay myself whatever salary I wanted.

Royce emerged from the hedges, his gray suit coat off and hung over an arm and his navy tie askew. He scanned his surroundings, and when he saw me, I stood. It allowed him to look at me in my plum colored sleeveless dress and nude heels.

His gaze was magnetic. It sucked me in, drugging me as he tried to extract all my secrets.

It was clear he expected me to say something, but when I didn't, he went first. "I got your text."

"Why didn't you tell me?"

His expression was guarded as we felt each other out. "It was a surprise."

"It . . . was very surprising."

A smile hinted at his lips. "That's what Frank said. He was worried you were going to pass out, but you held it together."

"Why? Why'd you do it?"

His eyes glittered, trying to lure me in. "Come here, and

I'll tell you."

Oh, my God. The realization washed through me, warming me all the way to my toes. He was going to finally say what I'd longed to hear. My heart soared, but my mind sent it crashing back down to earth. "No."

My refusal derailed him, and rightfully so. He'd given me nearly everything he had, and I wouldn't fulfill the simplest of his requests.

"No?" he repeated, stunned.

"We said we aren't going to lie anymore, right? Well, there's something I have to do, but . . . I can't tell you what it is."

His chin pulled back. "Why not?"

The biggest reason was because he'd try to stop me, but I went with an easier one. I mirrored the words he'd told me while we'd stood in the maze in the rain. "That way you can't tell him what you don't know."

His face was a mixture of concern and disappointment. "Marist."

"I'm asking you to trust me."

"I do trust you, but you're making me nervous."

My heart ached as unease twisted in his expression, but I had to stay strong. "I know, and I'm sorry."

It wasn't the answer he expected, and he when he didn't get a better explanation, irritation simmered below his surface. "That's it? That's all you're going to say?"

I swallowed a breath. "That's as much as you gave me after you sold me to your father."

Oh, he really didn't like that. His jaw clenched as he probably bit back the words he wanted to say and took a long moment to assemble the words in his head. His voice was cool. "We're not at that same place. You weren't my wife back then."

"You made difficult decisions to get what you wanted. Win at all costs, right?" I squeezed my hands into fists to prevent myself from reaching out to him. "I have to do that now, for us."

He stood so still, he could have been another beautiful statue in this garden. The moment hung, each second more agonizing than the last.

"Fine," he said quietly. "If you can't tell me your plan, then I can't tell you why I gave you the shares." His eyes dulled with resignation and disappointment. "Let me know when you're ready to trust me again."

His posture was stiff as he turned and disappeared into the hedges.

The party to celebrate the acquisition of Ascension was a relatively modest affair by HBHC's standards, but the management employees and their spouses seemed to be having a good time.

The event space was a cozy ballroom in a hotel not far from HBHC headquarters, and by the time Royce and I arrived, the place was already loud with conversations. Open bars were set up around the room, and fancy appetizers circulated on silver trays carried by event staff.

I stayed close to Royce as we mingled, flashing vacant

smiles and making small talk. The game of it wasn't as enjoyable as it had been at our wedding, but that was probably because I was distracted by what I'd have to do. My gaze found Macalister across the room, standing with Mr. Shaunessy and Mr. Powell, and the three board members seemed to be congratulating themselves on their latest conquest.

He must have sensed my gaze on him, because his head turned my direction, and his eyes zeroed in on me. Caught, I quickly darted my gaze away and stared at the ice sculpture with the HBHC logo carved in it.

As dinner drew to a close, I kept my phone in my lap and hidden beneath the table, checking the notification I'd received a new Instagram message.

> Sophia: I heard something about Alice today. Call me when you get a chance.

My breath caught. Sophia was like the CIA. Very little happened in Cape Hill without her knowing about it, and concern grew in me with each passing second. Had she found out that Alice had poisoned me? My gaze flicked to her across the table. She looked on as her husband talked to Mr. Lynch about the last time he'd gone skeet shooting.

If word got out, I had no idea what it would do.

I put my hand on Royce's knee and gave him an overly bright smile for the benefit of the people we were sharing a table with. "Excuse me. I'll be right back."

The ladies' restroom was thankfully empty, and I hurried into the last stall while punching the button for Sophia.

"Hi," she said. "That was fast."

"Hey." I forced casualness into my voice. "What's up?"

"I didn't want to put this in a text. I don't know if Royce reads your stuff, or if he might accidentally see, but it sounds like Alice is having an affair."

My pulse skittered. It wasn't the poisoning, but this was equally bad, so the surprise in my voice was genuine. "What?"

"You know how I'm friends with Penelope Marino?"

I didn't even know who that was. "Sure."

"Her parents are being complete dicks to her right now because she still hasn't found a job. They say she's being too picky, so to motivate her, they made her get a shitty job over at Cheveux as the receptionist."

Cheveux was the salon Alice took me to when she'd had my green hair dyed back to its original shade of brown and the crazy painful wax job. But where the fuck was Sophia going with this? "Okay . . ."

"Well, she comes in yesterday after her lunch break, and one of the stylists says their client left their phone. It's sitting behind the desk, and for the next hour while Penelope waits for the girl to return and get it, all these dirty text messages are rolling through." She paused, probably for dramatic effect. "Alice was the one who came to pick it up."

"Those could have been from Macalister," I lied. That wasn't his style, but it absolutely sounded like something Vance would do. He'd seemed genuinely into Jillian, but had he started hooking up with Alice again on the side?

"No. They were from—get this—Richard's dad."

The bathroom was empty, but still I dropped my voice to a hush. "Liam Shaunessy?"

"Yup. Someone needs to show that girl how to hide her

text messages, and also—what a step down. I mean, Macalister to Mr. Shaunessy? He's barely decent looking, and Macalister's so hot, I need a shower after looking at him."

Ugh. I pushed aside my disdain and focused. Alice wasn't with Mr. Shaunessy for his looks, she was with him to get her husband's attention. "Who else has Penelope told about this?"

"No one, as far as I know."

I was playing the long game, and the last thing I needed right now was for the board to suddenly change. "Then I need to ask a really big favor," I said. Sophia would likely think this was just concern for my new in-laws. "Don't let this get out. If the rumor has already started, you think you could kill it?"

I pictured her on the other side of the phone looking proud and powerful. "Yeah, probably."

"God, thank you, Sophia. If Macalister were to find out, I don't know what he'd do." Truer words had never been spoken. "Hey, let's get together this weekend on Vance's boat. I'll have Royce invite Tate."

She wanted Tate badly, and I could practically hear the thought in her head. Vance's sailboat was big, but it wasn't big enough for Tate to escape from her like he'd managed to do in Aspen.

Her voice was loaded with excitement. "Definitely."

When I was finished with the call, I left the restroom and only made it a few steps before Macalister emerged from the shadows. "Marist."

My mouth went dry, but I matched the innocent tone of

his greeting. "Macalister."

The party was going on in the next room over, but the hallway was empty, and it felt like the rest of the world had abandoned me to this man, who the last time we'd been alone had professed his love.

"How was the honeymoon?" His eyes glittered with arrogance.

I kept my voice perfectly level. "It was great."

He was amused. "But you cut it short. Why was that?"

I pressed my lips together for a moment, not wanting to be too obvious. "You know why."

Genuine surprise rolled through him. He hadn't expected me to reveal the truth, and excitement worked its way into his eyes.

"Besides," I added, "Royce wanted to be back for the acquisition. This is a big deal for HBHC." I squeezed out a smile. "Congratulations."

"Thank you." His excitement thickened. I held my ground as he shifted his weight, subtly leaning closer to me. "Perhaps you'll help me celebrate by joining me tonight after the party is over. We could finish our round of chess."

My stomach bottomed out and breath caught painfully in my lungs, but I pushed forward. I had to do this. "Of course." My anxiety shot through the ceiling, causing my voice to go weak. "Should I bring the board to your room?"

SIXTEEN

CARRYING THE CHESSBOARD WAS AN INSURMOUNTABLE TASK. Not because it was heavy, but because I shook violently and worried the pieces would shift off their squares. There were miles between the library and Macalister's bedroom.

I'd never been in his room before. At most, I'd glanced through his open doorway, but I was rarely down at this end of the hall, and his room was typically closed to keep Lucifer from going inside.

Not that the cat would. He craved attention, and since Royce and I were the only ones who gave it, Lucifer largely ignored the other humans in the house.

Tonight, the door was ajar and soft light curled around its edges, beckoning me to see Macalister's lair. I gingerly used the edge of the chessboard to inch the door open, my breath held tight in my body.

The master bedroom of the house wasn't much larger than Royce's. Like his, it had tall ceilings and oversized windows. However, instead of a view of the hedge maze, the room looked out over the shore. The bright edges of Cape

Hill gave way to the ocean, and I wondered if Macalister liked how his castle looked down over his kingdom.

Despite the fancy, ornate chandelier hanging over the bed, the room was deeply masculine with its slate gray walls and moss green chairs in the sitting area. I lingered in the doorway, unable to cross the threshold.

Macalister must have thought I was waiting for an invitation. It was more of an order than a request. "Come in."

My legs barely worked, and I tottered a few steps into the room before willing myself to get it together. I'd asked for this, I reminded myself. He gauged me critically, perhaps cataloguing every nervous bone I had, before gesturing toward the sitting area and the low table he intended me to set the board on.

A huge mirror hung on the wall behind the chairs, and when I caught my reflection, I saw what he saw. My flushed face and wide eyes, looking very out of place in my father-in-law's bedroom. I tore my gaze away and set the board down, sliding it to the center of the table while he closed the door.

"Have a seat. Would you like something to drink?"

"Uh, sure." I ran my hands under my skirt as I sat and crossed my legs at the ankles. Tension kept my back straight and my body at the edge of my seat.

He didn't give me options to see what I would like. Instead, he went to the far side of the room and opened a paneled cabinet, revealing a small fridge. He pulled out the green bottle with a golden label, retrieved a glass and a small towel from the counter, and stalked toward me.

My pulse tumbled and raced faster. He was carrying a

bottle of Dom Perignon. "Champagne?"

He leaned over me to set the flute on the table, straightened, and went to work peeling off the foil and cage. "The occasion calls for it." He put the towel over the cork and began to twist. "I'm happy we're playing chess again."

When the loud *pop* of the cork rang out, I flinched.

"You seem nervous." He folded the towel, set it and the cork on the table, and picked up the glass.

"I am nervous."

As he poured, his gaze was on the bubbles, but his focus was on me. "Why? We've played many times before."

"I'm not nervous about the game. It's what happens after."

He handed the glass to me but paused and didn't release it. Even the god Zeus was a slave to his male desires, and lust coiled in his eyes. "Is something going to happen after I defeat you?"

"You've already defeated me."

I'm here, aren't I? I hoped I said with a look.

He let go of the glass, and I held his stare for a beat too long, letting my double meaning settle on him before casting a hand toward the board. "You'll take my queen in two moves, and then I'm just running after that."

His pleased expression was insidious. As he set the bottle down, I turned toward the mirror and watched his reflection as he unbuttoned his suit coat and sat in the chair opposite mine.

"I'd like to know," he said, "why you wanted to play here tonight rather than the library." Macalister was smart. He didn't trust me and knew I had an agenda.

My chest was uncomfortably tight. I had to be careful and loaded my statement with as much truth as possible. "Royce wouldn't like it if he saw us playing together."

The smile on his lips was faint, but an evil grin threatened the edges of his mouth. "I see," he said. "In that case, it's your move."

I took a sip of the chilled champagne. It was manipulative on every level. Not just the obvious, where the alcohol would lower my inhibitions, but it was seductive. This felt distinctly different from any other time we'd played. His gaze zeroed in on my lips as they were pressed to the glass, and my throat when it dipped in a swallow.

Had the staff found it strange when Macalister asked for champagne? He only drank once a year, and preferred scotch.

For the first time ever, I didn't care if I won or lost the match. The outcome was irrelevant. We were playing a more intricate game with higher stakes, and that was where my focus lay. As we moved our dwindling pieces around the board, anticipation drifted in the air as an invisible fog.

"Your tattoo is Medusa," he said when we entered the endgame, "but I see you more as Nyx."

That gave me pause. Nyx was the goddess of night and wasn't mentioned much in mythology, which I found interesting given how she was one of the most powerful gods. She had spawned the dark things in life—strife, pain, sleep, and death.

"Why is that?" I asked.

His eyes teemed with carnal desire. "She's the only one Zeus feared."

The best myth featuring Nyx was the one where Hera convinced Hypnos to put Zeus to sleep so she could scheme behind his back. When her husband woke, he was furious and chased after Hypnos. But the sleep god darted into his mother Nyx's cave, and Zeus wouldn't dare step inside. He was terrified of her wrath.

Was Macalister saying he feared me? I didn't believe him for a second. I finished my glass of champagne and moved my knight, knowing this farce of a game was about to be over and we'd move into the middlegame of the one that mattered.

His gaze lingered on my right hand. "You're wearing the ring I gave you. It looks nice." Finally, he moved his bishop. "Checkmate." He leaned back in his seat, rested his elbows on the armrests, and steepled his fingers together. "Do you want to play again?"

"No. I'm interested in something else."

He looked at me with cautious eyes, like what I was saying was too good to be true. "Which is?"

"I'd like to negotiate." Hopefully, the last negotiations I'd ever have to do with him. "I want you to be honest with me."

He was offended. "I've always been honest with you."

My hands craved to tighten into fists, but I settled for tightening my smile. "Forthcoming is a better word. I'll ask you questions, and you'll give me the truth. The *full* truth."

The offended look evaporated. "In exchange for?"

"That's what we'll negotiate." I sat back in my chair, crossed my legs, and settled in, trying to match his body language. "Make me an offer."

He considered it thoughtfully. "Spend the night with me."

I'd expected his opening bid to be high. At least he'd found a somewhat classy way to ask for the sleezy, amoral thing he most wanted. I steeled my reaction, hoping not to anger him and blow the negotiations.

"No. I love my husband and I'm a married woman." When he looked like he was going to push that line, I added, "With a clause about cheating in her prenup."

"We will be discreet."

I blinked slowly to signal I wasn't impressed with his proposal. "No. Make me a reasonable offer."

He exhaled lightly and stared at the chessboard as if it were the drawing board.

For Royce's sake, I needed to know what his father knew, but my blood pressure spiked as excitement worked across Macalister's expression. Whatever idea he'd latched on to, he liked it a *lot*.

"You let me give you an orgasm."

This was one of the variables I'd plugged into my forecast, and my voice was strained as I admitted it. "I charged the vibrator this afternoon."

He let out a half of a laugh, and it was downright evil. "You misunderstand. You won't just give me control—you'll allow me to give it to you *physically*."

Microscopic threads tugged at my skin in a thousand different directions. "No."

"How about this?" The soft, moody lighting in his elegant bedroom exaggerated his Cheshire Cat smile. "I won't even touch you." He had an afterthought. "Your hands. You'll allow me to touch those."

For a split second, I wondered if he'd laced the champagne with something, because the idea of him bringing me to orgasm by holding my hands made me want to giggle. But my drink hadn't been poisoned—I'd watched him open the bottle and pour my glass—and besides that, I was smart enough to know better.

He had a plan to win.

"That's it?" I asked pointedly. "You'll only touch my hands?"

He said it plainly as if he were talking about the minutiae of a financial disclosure. "You'll be naked, and I'll be allowed to kiss you."

I pictured me on my back on his bed, his hands pinning mine at my sides, while his kiss wandered down across my naked flesh. He wanted his two minutes, and the word came out in a rush. "No."

"I don't see why this is an issue. You've let me kiss you before."

"*No.*" It came out more honestly and aggressively than I wanted it to. I had to make him believe there was a chance I was starting to fall for his seduction. "Not tonight."

Liquid heat pooled in his eyes at my implied opportunity. *Not tonight, but maybe some other time . . .*

"If I'm naked," I squeezed the armrests, digging my nails into the upholstery, "every stitch of your clothing stays on."

When I took that and kissing off the table, I expected him to have to rethink his plan, but he didn't. He gave a nod, picked up the bottle of champagne, and poured me another glass as he spoke.

"Here is my offer. You will do what I say and allow me to bring you to orgasm. I can touch your hands but nowhere else, and I cannot kiss you. During this time, I'll answer any questions you ask truthfully and to the best of my ability." His gaze sharpened like a knife right before it plunged in. "You also agree to accompany me to the office on a day of my choosing."

Wait, what?

My confusion played out on my face.

He lifted the champagne glass, extending it toward me like it was part of his offer. "I enjoy your company, Marist. It's as simple as that."

Nothing with him was simple. I peered at the flute in his hand, watching the tiny bubbles break free of their hold at the bottom of the glass and float upward to their escape. I was jealous of their short trip. The gauntlet I had to run to break free was going to be much longer and harder.

I accepted both the champagne and his offer, sealing the deal when I pressed my lips to the glass and drank. Dark satisfaction twisted through his eyes like a sea of ice blue snakes coiling together.

My blood rushed in my body as he stood from his chair, grabbed the back of it, and lifted. The heavy green armchair was set down facing the decorative mirror that leaned against the wall. Once that was done, he focused on dragging the table out of the way, and the chess pieces rattled as the legs chattered across the hardwood floor. It meant there was nothing to obstruct the mirror's view of the chair.

"Stand," he said.

I was rooted in place, the half-empty glass of champagne cold in my hand. All he'd done was rearrange some furniture, but there was something terribly sinister about it, and second thoughts kept me immobile.

He sensed my hesitation. "What's your first question?"

When he reminded me of my goal, focus released my body. I stood, took a final gulp of the champagne, and sauntered over to set it on the table, my heels clicking quietly on the floor. "The image of the check to Dr. Galliat. How'd you get it?"

He pointed to a spot on the floor in front of the chair. "Here. Face the mirror."

My breath came and went in shallow pulls, but I did as ordered. When I faced the mirror and lifted my gaze to the reflection, I saw the two of us. Me in my black cocktail dress, my dark hair spilling around my flushed face, and him in his finest suit standing behind my shoulder, looking down at me. He was Zeus, eager to make the mortal he'd captured submit to his desires.

I silently repeated the Hale family motto in my head, which kept me in place.

"I have several people in my employ," he said, "whose sole job is to keep me informed. It's a necessary part of my business. I've invested hundreds of thousands of dollars cultivating the best management team. I deserve to know if other companies are intending to poach them."

"You mean you have spies." I fixed my gaze on his through the mirror.

"They do more than just spy. For example, they may

persuade someone to pass along documents I'll find interesting or useful." His attention went to my back. "Pull your hair to the side so it's not in my way."

There was the slightest tremor in my hands as I scooped up my hair, pulled it to the front and draped it over my shoulder, revealing the back of my dress. He liked his effect on me. Power curved his lips into a wicked smile.

My hands may have wavered, but my voice didn't. "Do you have access to everything Royce does?"

"Access? No. Hold still. I'm not responsible for inadvertently touching you if you move." His fingers found the zipper pull at the top of my dress, and he took care not to let them brush against any part of me. "I don't know every detail. I only hear about the more interesting moves he makes."

"Such as?"

The zipper was quiet, but there was the tug of the dress on my shoulders, and the cool air seeping in announced he'd unzipped me all the way to the small of my back. The sides of the open zipper peeled apart, and one pull from him sent the top of the dress falling to my waist, trapping my elbows at my sides.

"How he'd amassed a considerable stake in Ascension." His gaze trailed over the cups of the black bra I wore. He leaned over, and although he wasn't using his hands, his desire to do so was so fierce, I felt them anyway. They traced my shoulders, caressed my spine. They wandered and explored and relished, causing my mouth to go dry.

"What do you think he intended to do," I swallowed hard, "with that stake?"

"He planned to buy them, but I beat him to it." His gaze landed on the black line of elastic on my shoulder. "Lift that strap up."

I didn't understand his intent until I picked it up and he plucked it from my fingers. He'd had me lift the strap away from my skin so he would avoid violating our agreement. My heart pumped furiously in my body. I wasn't just going to be naked—he was going to undress me first.

Royce had done terrible things to bring us together. Hopefully he'd understand when I did the same to keep us together.

Down Macalister pulled the strap as he walked around me, causing the bra cup to peel away and expose my breast to him, like seeing it through the reflection wasn't good enough. He wanted his gaze to touch me with nothing in the way.

His voice was thick with lust. "Now the other side."

I repeated my action, as did he, and the bra joined the dress that hung around my waist. He was distracted, so I used it to my advantage. Even though he'd promised not to lie, he'd changed the rules on me enough times that there was no trust between us.

"You bought Ascension just to stop Royce." I refused to give an inch and let him see the nerves swirling inside me. "Are you happy with it as a business decision?"

"I was at first." His shoulders lifted on a deep breath as he stared at the topless girl before him. His high cheekbones were razor sharp when he licked his lips.

Goosebumps flooded down my arms as he leaned over me, bringing the tip of his nose so close to my skin it nearly grazed me. His parted lips hovered, and he moved from one breast to the other, caressing me with only his warm breath. I didn't want it to, but my skin sensitized at his almost-touch.

Even though I wasn't trapped, the clothes halfway off my body felt like restraints, holding me under his magnetic power.

"I'm a man who finds it difficult to admit when I've taken a misstep." He bent onto a knee before me, bringing his gaze level with the hard points of my nipples, and my pulse climbed higher still. "Royce knew if he made a play for Ascension, I'd go after it, and I'm embarrassed at how easily I fell for his ploy." His words hadn't sunk in before he hooked a finger at the front of my pulled-down bra and jerked it toward him, making me stumble forward and almost into his hands. "This and your dress come off."

My muscles were rigid, but somehow, I found a way to undo the clasp of my bra and push the dress over my hips. They both cascaded down to a pile at my feet, leaving me clad only in a scrap of black lace and the heels I wore.

It was strange how my power grew as I shed my clothes. It helped that Macalister was on his knees, and the wanton desire dripping off his face made me feel like I was the one better in control of myself.

I didn't want to tip Royce's hand, but I had to know if his father had figured out the plan, which I feared he had. "Why aren't you happy with Ascension now?"

It took Macalister's slow-moving gaze eons to travel the length of my body before it reached my eyes. There'd been a lingering pause on Medusa. Had he been counting her snakes, or admiring the beautiful artwork?

"I despise your tattoo," he said, "and how you marred such a beautiful body. If I had my way, you'd start the removal process tomorrow."

A sinful grin burned across my lips as I stared down into his frosty eyes, wordlessly reminding him he didn't have that kind of control over me anymore. Of course, he hated my tattoo. It wasn't the design that offended him, it was the visual reminder of what he'd lost.

The power I felt flagged, though, when he motioned toward one side of my panties. "Lift."

I slipped my fingers beneath the edge and stretched the fabric away from my hip, only for him to fist it, holding it away from me like a rubber band he wanted to release and snap against my skin.

His expression broke, turning dark and resentful as he spoke. "The level of fraud happening at that company is staggering."

He drew the panties down my legs at an angle, which made the lace dig in and scrape over my skin as it went. As if that company's actions were somehow my fault and he was punishing me.

Maybe he was. I'd denied him so many times, his enormous ego couldn't handle it.

My hands hung awkwardly at my sides. "When did you find out?"

"May."

May? How could that be?

I stared down the slope of my body. I watched him as he

studied my nakedness, and I tried to disconnect from what was happening. It was infinitely harder when he bent and leaned into the cradle of my lap, his lips only a breath away from the delta of my thighs.

"Look in the mirror," he ordered.

I didn't want to, dreading what I'd see, but I obeyed.

As my gaze struck the glass, he inhaled and exhaled deeply, causing an unstoppable shudder in me. In some other life, I might have found the image erotic. I would have thought it was sexy to see a man in an expensive suit on his knees in front of a naked woman and how it looked like he was going down on her. It would have turned me on to watch her chest rise and fall dramatically as she struggled not to pant, or how her eyes were wild, and her pupils dilated to black holes.

I hated what he did to me.

"That is what we could be," he said.

No.

This wasn't some other life. I was Marist Hale, and he was my father-in-law, not to mention I was in love with someone else. Plus, there were no myths of Medusa and Zeus being lovers, only Zeus's son who'd slain her. And that was what Royce had done, wasn't it? Slayed me?

I ignored what Macalister had said and refocused. The tremble crept into my voice, but only a little. "I don't understand. The takeover didn't happen until June. You had time to—"

Macalister abruptly came to his feet, towering over me. "No. I would have looked weak."

I was stunned. "You put yourself over your company."

He abandoned me, not agreeing or denying. His feet fell heavily on the wood floor as he strode to the chair he'd placed in front of the mirror and sat down in it. I turned, stepping out of the heap of clothes at my ankles, and faced him.

What was supposed to happen next? With him in the wide chair, his legs spread, and his hands curled over the upholstered armrests, he looked like a king on his throne. Was he going to ask me to entertain him?

Or was he going to continue to stare at me like art and contemplate his existence?

His command was wrapped in velvet, trying to coax me. "Sit down."

Relief poured through my system. If he'd told me to dance, it would have been awkward for both of us because I didn't have the vaguest idea of how to do that and make it remotely appealing. I walked toward my chair and—

"No. In *this* chair."

My heart crashed through my body, lurching to a stop. "You want me to sit on your lap?"

His expression was corrupt. "I would like a great many things from you, Marist, but we will start here tonight."

"No, that's touching."

He looked at me like I was being ridiculous, and his tone was sharp. "No, it isn't. I have my clothes on, so there's not skin contact."

Even though I'd made a deal with the devil, I hesitated when he came to collect.

He raised an eyebrow. "I suspect there's more you want to ask me, and this is what you agreed to."

I crossed an arm over my stomach, subtly brushing the side of my thumb over my Medusa tattoo. She wasn't afraid of men. They feared her, and I drew from her strength.

One foot in front of the other, I walked on unsteady legs toward him, and he watched the sway of my hips and the undulation of my bare breasts. When I'd made it to the chair, I turned and reached behind me for the now-empty armrests, and ever-so-slowly lowered myself.

I wasn't actually in his lap. He'd made room for me between his legs, and I sat perched on the edge of the chair. With the mirror in front of us, he could see both my nakedness in the reflection and his favorite part of me up close—the long line of my back.

I'd kept my knees together, and once I had my balance, I rested my hands there. With the armrests no longer in use, he took them back, and the way his fingers curled around the edges, it made me wonder if he'd done it to remind himself he could look, but not touch.

"Lean back." His voice was a whispered sin. "Spread your legs and let me tell you a secret."

There was a thick taste of debauchery in the air, and no amount of dry swallowing could remove it from my mouth. My eyes fluttered closed. Maybe he'd think it was me falling under his spell, but the truth was I didn't want to see the desire etching his expression while I made myself totally vulnerable. All I wanted to think about was Royce.

Macalister's chest was firm, his suit coat soft, and the silk of his tie was cool against my back. The worst part of this position was how it put his lips right beside my ear, and his steady, quick breathing filled it. The proximity made it so much easier for his commands to invade my mind, but hopefully his secrets too.

"I didn't stop pursuing Ascension," his voice was low, "when I learned what I was truly buying, because I know what his next step will be."

My eyes burst open, and I was treated to the full, shocking image of us slumped back together on the green chair, my legs spread and his parted wider around mine. We were fitted together like puzzle pieces, and although I told myself this image was perverse, my body had a different reaction. A bolt of interest reverberated through me.

That wasn't allowed. I was only playing a part, following the advice Royce had given me the night of our first date. I was simply being the version Macalister wanted me to be.

Win, no matter what.

In ancient Greece, I was in my perfect form like this, unadorned of clothes. The pinnacle of strength and beauty, and in the mirror, Macalister viewed me this way. His heavy gaze swept along the tips of my breasts, down the curve of my waist, and skated over my legs.

"Show me how you touch yourself."

Static played in my mind. "What?"

He was irritated he had to repeat himself. "When you masturbate. Show me how you do it."

In one of the models I'd forecast, this was a variable. I'd weighed the pros and the cons and decided it was a viable action if he asked for it. My right hand slowly curled inward, and as I brushed my fingers across the insides of my thighs, my gaze slipped down to the bottom of the mirror.

So, I didn't watch his reaction when I set two fingers on my clit and rubbed a sluggish circle, but it didn't matter. He inhaled with satisfaction, which was a sound I couldn't block out, and with my back against him, I rode the swell of his chest.

The way I was touching myself was devoid of pleasure, but it still made it hard to organize my thoughts. "What do you think his next step will be?"

"Word will break about Ascension's greed. Either he'll leak it or someone else will at his direction." His pause forced me to stir another circle, and only then did he continue. "It will shake the HBHC shareholders' confidence, and they'll be looking for someone to blame."

"Which would be you."

I jerked to a stop when his right hand grabbed mine. The words were on the tip of my tongue to tell him he wasn't allowed to touch, but I caught myself just in time. He hadn't violated the rules. My hands were fair game. He dragged it upward, and my gaze with it, until my fingers were in front of my mouth.

"Open."

In this position, he felt the shudder rattle my body. Did he think it was with disgust? Anxiety? Or excitement? It was terrifying that, at least to some degree, I felt all three emotions. My lips parted, and he pushed my first two fingers deep into my mouth, damp with my own taste.

He pulsed them in and out as he spoke. "The moment everything is at its worst, Royce will strike." His lips were so close, they moved the air beside my ear. “He’ll call an emergency board meeting and demand a vote of no-confidence in my leadership.”

Oh, my God.

Macalister knew everything.

SEVENTEEN

IRONICALLY, I WAS GLAD MACALISTER HAD FORCED MY FINGERS into my mouth because it muffled the gasp I made. I stared at my reflection, whose eyes were so wide they were practically white, and willed myself to remain calm.

I wanted to ask how he'd figured it out, but he made that impossible. The image in the mirror was of a scared girl sucking on her fingers while her disapproving daddy loomed large behind her.

His voice was villainous. "Are you wondering how I discovered his attempt to usurp me?"

With no other way to communicate, I nodded.

"It's what I would do if I were him, and he learned everything he knows from me." His grasp on my hand tightened, and he guided me to withdraw the wet fingers from my mouth. "My son is smart, but he'll never rise to my level. He thinks he knows me well—and it's likely he does—but as he studied me, I studied him."

Down my hand went under his direction. I swallowed a breath as he placed it between my legs and urged me to move.

This time, it was harder to ignore the sensation, and a faint tendril of enjoyment curled its horrifying, beckoning finger, asking me to follow it.

I squeezed my eyes shut and pictured Royce.

If Macalister knew about the no-confidence vote, why hadn't he done anything to stop it? "I don't understand." As his hand encouraged mine, it swirled the thoughts in my head. "You're going to allow it?"

"Of course. I've already informed the board of what I suspect is coming. Royce stayed silent about the trap we were walking into with the takeover, and his deception did not sit well with the directors. I've secured assurances of their loyalty, and they won't vote against me when the time comes."

My eyes cracked open. Now there wasn't anything to hold back the sharp exhale from me. It burst from my lungs, taking all my hope with it. Macalister wasn't just two moves ahead of Royce—*he'd already won.*

"When he loses the vote," Macalister said, "hopefully he learns a valuable lesson, and it should dissuade him from any further attempts." His voice swelled with absolute power. This was Zeus speaking. "I am the chairman of the board, and chief executive officer of HBHC, and will remain so until I choose to step down."

His left hand closed on top of mine, and then he was forcing me to move that one too. His fingers threaded through mine, curling around my palm as if it were his now, and together he made me cup my breast.

Because I was leaning back against him, I could feel him rapidly harden, and his erection dug into the small of my back.

It was dangerous and made the air in the room evaporate.

He issued his order in a warm and pleased voice. "Look."

I already was looking at us in the mirror, and on a basic level, I responded to it. The physical sensations paired with the visual were too much to stay immune to. Uncomfortable heat bloomed inside me, pooling in my limbs and flickering in my center. He pushed my right wrist to stroke faster, bringing more pleasure into my body physically with my own hand, but really his.

The look in his eyes was lecherous. "*Look* at us, Nyx."

When he referred to me as the most powerful goddess of them all, I detached from myself for a moment. We weren't mortals, but two gods of Olympus, above reproach or consequences. My head fell back on his shoulder, my cheek grazing the faint stubble on his, and I sighed.

Wait. I wasn't Nyx.

There were other questions to ask him, but his presence was gathered around me like smoke filling a room. It made me heavy, weighing me down. His grip on me was oppressive and dominating. As he slid my hand from one breast to the other, his warm breath cascaded down my neck and rolled over my chest. He was closing in, surrounding me, waging war on multiple fronts.

I boiled the question down to its simplest form and said it between two enormous gulps of air. "Why do you hate him?"

"Royce?" His hands slowed, and mine followed suit. Something like hurt filled his eyes, but it was fleeting. "I don't. I'm only hard on him because he's spoiled. You asked me once if I have a moral hazard, but it's him you should worry about. He's had anything he's ever wanted, and it's made him soft. He'll need to be much stronger if he's going to succeed me someday."

Except Macalister was wrong. What did it matter if you got everything you wanted . . . if you didn't get to *keep* it?

Like his mother.

Or his father's love.

It was clear Macalister didn't want me thinking about anyone other than him. His hands started up again, and determination painted his face in dark shadows.

"I'm not soft," he said, and for added effect, he pushed his pelvis forward, and the hard bulge ground against me. A noise of satisfaction rent from his lips. "I'm going to bring you to orgasm with my hands essentially tied behind my back. Imagine what I could do to you if you allowed me the full use of my body."

I wasn't sure which was more terrifying. Him, or the reaction he provoked. My bottom lip quivered, and I bit down to stop it.

He noticed, because of course he did. Nothing seemed to escape him, least of all me. "Don't you want that?"

"No," I said.

His smile was all-knowing. "You were right. You're not very good at lying."

But I was tonight. At least, I hoped.

His right hand made me go faster still, and my heartbeat banged in my chest. My ragged breathing rang out, masking a quiet moan that seeped from me, and I fought myself not to like it. Beneath his hands, I tried to stay at his direction and not adjust to the perfect spot that would maximize my pleasure.

My body had other ideas.

When my hips moved, it rubbed against his erection, and he hissed his pleasure through tight teeth. Both of his hands came off me, and I froze, my fingers still pressed to my needy clit.

"Up. In my lap, so you can feel what you do to me."

Oh, God.

Win at all costs.

I reluctantly set my hands on the armrests, lifted myself up, and pushed back so my ass pressed against the hard length of him beneath his suit pants. He groaned under his breath, and before I could take my hands off the chair, he snatched them up. He shoved them right back where they'd been, one on my breast and one between my thighs.

"Does the idea of me frighten or excite you, or both? That's how I know when to pursue something—when the thought of having it is thrilling."

His controlling hand pushed mine down from my breast, making it glide over the flat of my stomach and down to my hip. He urged me to rock, to slide my ass back and forth over the fly of his pants.

What the fuck was wrong with me? Every sigh and heavy breath from him seduced the terrible part of me that didn't mind it so much. It had no problem being pulled deeper under his power. But the rest of my brain was screaming in protest, beyond angry.

"You're a dangerous creature, Nyx." His words invaded.

They destroyed like thunderbolts hurled from above. "And someday you will let me possess you completely."

No, this was too much. The defiance built inside me, but he guided my left hand down farther. His cold fingers were much longer as he curled them over mine, tucking them in—all except for our index fingers, his stacked on top of mine.

And then he pushed them *both* inside my body.

My mouth rounded into a silent cry, too stunned to find words. The sudden stretch was painful, but he kept advancing, sliding our fingers deeper. It made my brain fracture. Words like *no*, and *wrong*, and *rules* all tried to come out at the same instant, producing only a choked off noise of surprise.

As Macalister crossed the hard line I'd drawn, the only thought in my head was Royce and what a mistake I'd made. I'd come into this room and done a terrible thing for us, but the cost was too high. I jerked and bucked, but that made me shift harder in Macalister's lap, and his groan was louder and more satisfied this time.

I finally found my voice as I tried to pull our hands away. "*No.*"

"The only places I'm touching you are your hands and fingers. One of them just happens to be inside your body."

Was he insane? "You're fucking touching me."

His right hand was still moving, making my fingers rub across my clit and right above where he'd slipped our fingers inside, but if it felt pleasurable, my mind refused to acknowledge it. It was blank with shock and rage.

"Macalister," I cried, "*stop.*"

When he broke one rule, he broke them all. His damp

lips grazed my neck. “Surrender, and I’ll set you free.”

I panicked when the darkest part of me whispered to do it, just let him have me. He was never going to stop until he had what he wanted. Alice had said as soon as I gave in, he’d leave me alone.

But a fire ignited in my belly and seared across my limbs, burning away the fog of unwanted desire and screamed at me to fight. I wasn’t Nyx.

I was fucking Medusa.

And I would brandish my full power. “Do you love me?”

He solidified, turning into stone, and sensed the trap I’d laid for him, but there was no going back. He gazed at me in the mirror and how I was lying against him, his suit-covered arms circled around my nude body and our hands pressed between my spread legs. As the truth climbed across his face, it was the first time I ever saw him look tragically beautiful.

“Yes,” he whispered.

I was unmoored, floating in the ocean at night, too far away to see the lighthouse, and I swallowed so hard, it was audible. “Then you’ll stop.”

The strength went out of his muscles. His retreat was quick, and instantly I was up out of the chair, whirling to face him. He looked devastated, realizing he’d gone much too far, and I wasn’t prepared for the uneven words that came out of him.

“I’m . . . sorry.”

The force of his apology knocked me back a step.

Macalister Hale didn’t apologize. He didn’t make mistakes or have a heart, but presented with all this evidence to the contrary, I didn't know what to believe anymore. He looked as off-balance as I felt.

"It's not enough," I said. I wasn't just angry with what he'd done to me, but with what he'd done to Royce.

My chest heaved breath into my lungs as he hesitantly came to his feet, and I stepped out of his path when he walked toward the mirror. No—wait. His destination wasn't the mirror, it was my clothes heaped on the floor. He bent, scooped them up, and moved toward me with them in his hands like a peace offering.

"But we're not finished," I snapped.

He blinked, suspicion clouding his expression. What I'd said sounded too good to be true to him, but the truth was simpler. If I didn't see this through, he'd twist it around. He'd find ways to use it to his advantage, and next time if I was dumb enough to be caught in his trap, he might not stop when I told him to.

I had all the power now, and we'd finish this on my terms.

I marched to his bed and sat at the foot of it with my heart in my throat, and kept my gaze pinned on him while I moved backward. My naked body slid across the smooth, satiny cover, which felt luxurious and soft and nothing like the ruthless man I'd been pressed against moments ago.

Macalister's expression was fixed, but his body language gave him away. He shifted on his feet, unsure.

"You come any closer," I said in the firmest voice I possessed, "and I'll stop."

He was still uncertain until I drew my knees up, set my heeled feet on the mattress, and lay my head down. I snaked my hand down my body, pressing my fingers to my clit, and began to stir. I stared up at the ceiling and heard his ragged breath, but otherwise he was quiet. He'd asked me to show him how I masturbated, and so I did, but this wasn't a reward—it was punishment. I was showing him what he couldn't have.

"I'm thinking about Royce," I declared. My eyes drifted closed, and I pictured my husband.

It was like my pleasure was on a switch, and it took no effort to turn it on. I thought of the afternoon on our honeymoon when he'd pulled at the strings of my bikini bottom and pushed down his swim trunks, and we'd lain on our sides while he fucked me senseless from behind. Or months before that, when he'd picked me up and carried me into the shower with our clothes still on. How he'd torn my shirt and pushed me up against the glass, so desperate to have me he was incensed.

I moaned, as low and deeply as I had then. The heat building inside me intensified.

What about the memory of what I considered our first time? In the wine cellar, he'd pulled me down into his lap, and I'd ridden him to a blistering orgasm. I could still remember how he'd kissed me afterward on the couch, our sweaty, naked bodies still connected.

Tingling pinpricks scurried over my skin as the orgasm approached, and I squirmed on top of Macalister's bed, my left hand balling the bedcover into a fist.

After all the times Royce and I had been together, still no memory compared to that first night in the library. When he'd pushed me against that bookcase, shoved his hand up my dress, and said I was his now.

I'd never stop being his.

The orgasm crashed into me. It broke like waves over a reef, the pleasure hitting me so hard it drove me into the mattress. The ecstasy made me contract and writhe like a wild, untamed thing, who fought against the heat ripping through her body.

When it finally diminished, I inhaled slowly and pushed to sit up.

Macalister's mouth hung open, looking like he'd just uttered the word *fuck* and been frozen like that. My clothes were on the floor by his feet. Perhaps he'd dropped them in surprise. Beneath his suit coat, his upper body was tense, his hands fisted at his sides. He'd had to stand perfectly still to maintain control over himself.

The power had flipped between us, as had everything else. His gaze put out heat, but mine was icy cold. I was deliberate in my movements while he stood awkwardly. As I dressed, I stared him down, defiance dripping from my expression.

"I was in your bed," I told him after I finished tugging up the zipper on the back of my dress. "I hope you enjoyed it, because that will never, *ever* happen again."

EIGHTEEN

I DIDN'T SLEEP THAT NIGHT. INSTEAD, I SPENT IT PLANNING, unable to go to Royce until I had something to soften the blow that his father had figured out his master plan, and how I'd come by that information.

Years of effort were just . . . gone.

It was the weekend, so for once I was showered and dressed before he was even awake. I stood at the edge of his bed and looked at him sleeping peacefully, not wanting to shatter it. After today, I doubted he'd sleep much for a while. And he looked so good with his tan skin against the white sheets.

He stirred when I sat beside him and his eyes blinked open, hazy with sleep. They gazed at me, and it only took a moment for them to sharpen with recognition. He slid back, propping himself up on his pillow.

"Hey," he said, looking happy to see me.

I did it like ripping off a bandage. "Your father knows."

Resignation washed down his face. "That I signed my shares over to you? I figured he'd find out."

"No." The lump in my throat made it difficult to talk. "He knows about the fraud at Ascension and your plan to call for a vote of no-confidence. He's already told the board."

"What?" Royce sat upright and stared at me with disbelief, his chest moving rapidly to keep up with his furious heart. As the words soaked in, his gaze drifted away from me. He was distracted, deep in thought and working the problem. "He told you this?"

"Yes."

"Why? Why would he do that?"

I'd thought about that quite a bit last night and come up with two reasons. "Because he's either hoping to scare you out of calling the vote, or because he thinks he's already won, and it doesn't matter."

He considered both for a long moment, then abruptly threw off the covers and climbed out of the bed.

"What are you going to do?" I asked.

His expression was as hard as stone and fire burned in his eyes. "Fight," Ares answered.

My heart picked up, matching the rhythm of his war drums. This was what I'd expected he'd say. "He told them you knew about Ascension and stayed quiet. He's been campaigning against you for weeks already."

"Yeah? It won't fucking matter when the stock is in freefall. There's only one person responsible for that, and the shareholders won't accept anything other than his removal."

Excitement made me rise from the bed and join him. "You only need four votes, and I think I can get you Scoffield."

He paused. "What?"

"You wanted to know how Emily found out about the initiation. It was Mrs. Scoffield." The rules were strict about this. Just like I'd signed an agreement to never talk about it, so had she. "If you tell him you have proof she violated her NDA, he'll side with you." I crossed my arms over my chest. "Who else? Burrows? Geffen?"

"Burrows, maybe. Geffen will be . . . tough. I don't know him like my dad does."

"We won't be able to get Lynch." He was Macalister's right hand and would follow his boss to the ends of the earth. "What about Powell?"

Royce made a face as he considered HBHC's chief operating officer. "Doubtful."

"That leaves Shaunessy and Vanderburgh," I said. "You can get them."

It wasn't lost on me I'd spent weeks learning about the men, so I could prove my loyalty and respect for the board, and now I was using it to try to topple it from the inside.

If Royce was unsure, none of it showed. He looked confident and ready for battle.

But a thought leapt into his mind, making him wrap an arm around my waist and draw me in. "Marist." His eyes searched mine, and he turned serious. "What did you have to do to get him to tell you this?"

"I was worried he'd figured your plan out, but I had to be sure, so I did what I had to." I sucked in a preparatory breath. "It was win at all costs, so I made a deal."

Royce's nostrils flared with alarm. "What?"

"I'm sorry," I said on a broken voice, "but I can't tell you what it was—not today. I love you, and I promise I will tell you everything, but you need to trust me. If you're going to beat him, right now you can't worry about me. You have to focus."

Royce's eyes went wider than the Wall Street bell. "Marist, what did he do?"

"Did you hear what I just said?" I gripped his face in my hands. "Please. We have to make him think he's won. You want to destroy him? This is how we do it."

"Jesus, just tell me."

But I couldn't. It was Pandora's Box. "It's over. Done. All knowing would do is distract you, which is exactly what he wants."

His hands abandoned me so they could ball into fists, and he stomped toward the door, growling it with pure malice. "Fine. I'll go ask him."

"Stop," I cried. "First off, you're not even dressed. And second, you can't."

He turned in place, giving me a defiant look, and since he was only wearing a tight pair of gray underwear, I saw him in all his glory. Anger corded his muscular chest and twisted the tendons of his arms. He was more beautiful and perfect than a statue of Adonis.

But he wasn't Adonis, he was Ares, and his tone was loaded with aggression and indignation. "What do you mean, I *can't*?"

"He won't tell you. And if you go after him, he'll say he has cause to pull you off the board."

And it would be impossible to call for a vote then.

There was rage flowing through his blood, but as the

cold realization fell on him, I watched that fury become caged inside his stiff body. He yearned for reckless battle, but the strategic side of him was stronger.

"I know you want war," I said, "and I *promise* you it's coming, but we have to strike when it's right."

"So, I'm not supposed to do anything? Just sit around in the fucking dark?"

"I know all too well that it's not easy," I said. "You put me through that once. But believe me, I will tell you when it's all over and this is for the best. *Trust* me." Could he see how important this was? "And know that I'm yours, completely. I didn't give him what he wanted, Royce."

Anxiety twisted on his face. The desire to know was fierce, but I was determined to blot it out with a different desire.

I grabbed the hem of my dress and lifted, stretched it up over my head, and tossed it away. "I have some ideas on what to do while we wait."

With the dress gone, I stood before him in the most expensive French lingerie I'd ever owned, purchased for our honeymoon. The mesh and lace were a creamy beige color and the exact shade of my skin tone. It hid nothing, not the dusty color of my nipples or the bare slit between my legs. It was like an optical illusion. Only the faint outlines and the pattern of the lace showed on the bra and panties. I looked naked otherwise.

Yearning flooded through me, and I hoped at least a fraction of it showed on my face. "I need you to do all the things to me only my husband can."

My request gave his anger a place to go, and it channeled

eagerly toward release. Royce's swift approach was accompanied by a dark, intense look that announced he'd vanquish anyone who stood in the way of what he wanted—and the thing he wanted most right now was me.

He crushed his lips to mine in a kiss that didn't care if I liked it or not. He licked into my mouth with a harsh, dominating tongue and filled his rough hands with my flesh. God, there wasn't anything else like it. He treated me as an opponent. One who he'd show no mercy.

All the frustration he had at not being able to strike back at his father funneled into the way he picked me up and hurled me onto the bed. I landed on the mattress with a hard bounce, but I didn't scramble out of the way when he threw himself on top of me. He bit a path down the side of my neck, creating a line of fire, and the stubble across his jaw burned as it abraded my skin.

I moaned my satisfaction darkly.

As his mouth continued to carve a trail along the edge of my bra, he shifted and moved to one side of me, giving himself room so he could shove a hand between my thighs. With the whisper-thin panties, his touch felt like there was nothing between us, and each caress of his hand sharpened my need like the stroke of a whetstone on a blade.

I wanted him to feel the same painful need I did. When his mouth closed around my nipple and sucked at me through the lace, I jammed a hand beneath the waistband of his underwear and closed a fist around the hot, hard length of him.

"*Oh*," I groaned, my body bowing off the mattress as he clamped his teeth down and pulled the distended nipple away from my body. It hurt, but in a good way. Pleasure tugged deep in my belly as his tongue fluttered over the pinched skin.

I was only able to pump my fist on him a few times before he released my nipple and rolled away onto his back, hooking his thumbs under his underwear and yanking it down his strong legs. When I tried to follow his lead and take off my bra, he grunted his disapproval. He climbed on top of me, straddling my hips and pinning my wrists to the bed.

Being trapped beneath him was exciting. His cock was hard and heavy on my stomach, and I squirmed, trying to wriggle upward so he could rub it lower between my thighs. The ache for him was relentless, the craving for him to be inside me brutal.

But I wasn't just caught under Royce's hands. His powerful gaze held me down like gravity. He leaned in, tracing the tip of his nose at the corner of my mouth and brushing his open lips over mine. It mercilessly teased his kiss. When I chased him, he was ready for it. His bottom lip swept over my top lip. Contact, but not connection.

It only made me more insatiable.

"Why'd you do it?" Accusation hinted his tone. He was angry with the situation I'd put him in and struggling hard not to show it. "Why'd you go to him?"

"Because I want you to win." I tried to kiss him, but he held himself back, just beyond my range. "This is what you've wanted all of your life. You said everything you did was to get to this point, and I love you. I want you to have it."

Gone was his anger. The heat in his eyes morphed into something deeper as he stilled. "Ask me again why I gave you my shares."

My heart stumbled, running faster than the rest of me, making me go breathless. "Why'd you do it?"

"Because I love you." He declared it without hesitation. His voice wasn't loud, but it was powerful. "Whatever you want, it's yours, Marist. I'd give up everything I have just to be with you, and that includes my name." His expression was devastatingly beautiful, full of love and adoration. "You don't have to stay with me out of obligation. You can walk away from all of this . . . I just ask that—fuck—you take me with you."

"Oh, my God," I whispered. I couldn't manage anything else. Tears sprung into my eyes and blurred my vision, but I blinked them back, determined not to miss the moment he gave me his heart.

I never would have believed the prince of Cape Hill knew how to plead, or that he'd be willing to renounce his throne for me, but it was the most honest and real I'd ever seen him.

I was going to tell him I loved him, and he didn't have to give anything up. When he'd proposed, he'd told me he was an ambitious man, and eventually he was going to want it all. We could have it, I wanted to say. But I didn't get a chance because he let go of my wrists, cased my head in his hands, and delivered a kiss that flipped my world upside-down.

Which made sense.

He wasn't Ares now, this was Hades, the king of the underworld. I was Persephone, the mortal girl he'd stolen and dragged into his world. He'd made her fall in love with him, and now she was happy to rule at his side.

Everything else faded away until it was just us. The anger, the shame, the lies we'd had to tell each other were obliterated in the heat of this kiss. Our lips only broke long enough for us both to yank at my underwear and get it out of our way, the threads ripping.

It felt like I was going to die if we didn't connect in every way possible, and I sighed with relief as he pushed inside my body. He was trembling, or I was shaking badly enough for both of us, and I wrapped my arms around his shoulders, holding on so nothing could ever take him away now that I had him completely.

If someone had said to me a year ago Royce Hale would be the love of my life, I would have told them to go to hell. But it was true. We were each other's first and only loves.

That morning, he told me he loved me with not only his words, but with his beautiful body. He held my face in his hands as he claimed me over and over, stealing my breath and making my legs go boneless.

And when the pleasure became too much, I gave a soft cry, and he chased me over the edge, because wherever I went, he wanted to follow.

Royce and I continued to sleep in separate bedrooms, to keep up the lie Macalister had divided us. It was a Tuesday morning, so I wasn't with him when the story broke that the SEC had opened an investigation into Ascension. I sat cross-legged on my bed in my room, the mythology book in my lap ignored, my eyes glued to the television as I watched the stock ticker scroll.

Every time HALE rolled past, it was down another half point.

I could feel the rumbling dissent of the HBHC shareholders like an approaching storm and pictured the churning chaos their headquarters must be right now. The Hale men would be in conference rooms with the heads of each department, mapping out a strategy to calm fears.

When the markets closed, HBHC stock was the lowest it had been in five years, and the commentators used words like *disaster* and *catastrophe.* It pivoted immediately to an interview with the chairman and CEO of Hale Banking and Holding.

He must have taken the helicopter to the city and done damage control at the New York branch of his bank, before going to the studio. I blinked as Macalister appeared on screen. He looked calm and collected as he sat in a red chair opposite the female broadcaster and answered her questions, even as she needled him. He was cold, indifferent, and untouchable. Maybe it would inspire confidence in the shareholders, but it might also spark irritation. With his enormous ego, he came off flippant.

Which was good for Royce.

When the interview concluded, I expected Royce to text me. We hadn't spoken all day. I didn't want to bother him, and he was clearly busy, but when my phone rang, I nearly dropped it. This wasn't the Hale I was expecting. He'd only been off the air for five minutes, and now he was calling me?

"Hello?"

Macalister didn't give me a greeting, he just barked out his order. "Tomorrow, you'll accompany me to the office."

In the background, side conversations went in and out around him. He was on the move, and I pictured him striding toward the studio exit and the car likely waiting for him. Would he have more interviews to give, or head back to the helipad?

"Why is that?" I asked, although it was rhetorical. I knew exactly why he wanted me to go with him. It was to strip Royce of my support and rub salt in the wound after he lost the vote. I faked innocence. "Is something happening tomorrow?"

"Royce called for an emergency meeting of the board." Wind whipped through the phone, then died away as a car door slammed shut. "I'm rather surprised. I'd heard he was having difficulty finding time to speak with the directors. Their schedules have been quite full."

Once Royce started his campaign, Macalister had done everything in his power to hinder it. It was another game for him to play, and one he enjoyed immensely.

I said nothing, not wanting to give my position away or make a mistake.

His tone was harsh and impatient. "Are you there?"

"Yes," I answered. "I'll go with you tomorrow."

"Excellent." He paused, as if he were reluctant to say anything else, but it felt calculated. "He doesn't have the votes, Marist. I know he thinks he does, but anyone who promised him their vote was doing what he does best—lying."

I bit my tongue from telling him we'd find out who was lying tomorrow.

"He's walking into a slaughter," Macalister added. Was he nervous? Overcompensating with bravado? "You'll wait for me in my office until it's done, and then we can discuss arrangements on what happens next."

I let out a tight breath. After he returned to his office victorious, he'd have all the leverage and would expect me to want to cut a deal to save Royce's job. I swallowed down my emotions and my desire to fight, and instead I kept my tone even.

"All right," I said coolly.

This time, his pause wasn't manufactured— He'd anticipated pushback, and I'd genuinely caught him off guard. "Excellent. I will meet you in the foyer at seven thirty tomorrow."

He didn't say goodbye; only the abrupt silence on the other end told me he was gone.

Macalister was wrong, though. He couldn't be meeting with me, because . . . tomorrow?

I'd become Medusa.

NINETEEN

Now

Disappointment had etched Royce's face when he asked me to go with him into the office this morning and I'd turned him down, claiming I was too nervous. I told him I loved him, wished him luck, and kissed him goodbye.

I hoped he'd forgive my deception when it was all over.

He turned and went down the front steps to the car that was waiting, a pair of headphones in his hand, and I expected he'd spend the entire ride to Boston using them to shut the world out and focus. Maybe he'd listen to Beastie Boys' "Sabotage" as he visualized the meeting and ran through his notes.

Macalister must have been skulking in the shadows watching us, because as soon as Royce's car drove away, he appeared at the top of the grand staircase. Every cell in him seemed to be inflated with his pure arrogance as he descended the steps and walked toward me.

"Good morning," he said.

He probably thought it was.

His appreciative gaze ran over me, taking in the fitted red

sheath dress I wore. It was the most powerful color I owned and the same shade as the red, hissing mouths of Medusa's snakes. I stared back at him in his black three-piece suit and pale gray dress shirt. His tie was rich black and pin-dotted with silver, and the silk of his pocket square matched.

I didn't acknowledge him with words. I simply lifted an eyebrow, turned, and strode out the front door. The heavy clops of his shoes announced he was following as I walked down the stone steps, heading toward the sleek black Range Rover as it pulled to a stop.

Macalister's hand was on the door handle before I could reach it, but I didn't offer any gratitude as I ducked inside the back seat. I slid over the leather bench as far away from him as possible.

He asked it when the door was shut behind him and the car crawled down the driveway, heading for the main road. "How was he this morning?"

"Don't," I said. "I agreed to come along, but I didn't say shit about talking to you."

He didn't like what I'd said, but rather than sour his good mood, it made desire flare in his eyes. He loved to be challenged, and he was excited for the impending showdown. He peered at me now as if I could be the amuse-bouche to his main course.

"It's a long ride to Boston." He shifted in his seat, angling his knees subtly toward me.

I narrowed my eyes. "If you wanted someone to chat with, you should have invited your wife."

He let my statement deflect right off him. "Have you

considered what he will be like after today? My son doesn't handle disappointment well."

"Neither do you. Have you considered how you'll react if this doesn't go the way you want it to?"

He smiled like I was being ridiculous. "That's not possible. I have personal assurances from at least four members, and I've made it perfectly clear to the board that voting against me is the fastest way to lose their seat."

My pulse throbbed and banged. I had to hope at least one of those four had lied to Macalister and told Royce the truth, or he was screwed. I tamped down my fear and let it fill my voice with strength. "I think you're going to look back on today and be filled with regret, Macalister."

His laugh was cruel. "Perhaps you're thinking of Royce."

I didn't say another word the rest of the way. He was riding a prebattle high, and it made him more cocky and talkative than ever. He filled the silence with the speech he was preparing to give at the meeting and then revealed who he was confident would vote in his favor.

At least it was the four names I suspected.

It wasn't until we were alone in the glass elevator and he'd grabbed my hand that I spoke and told him he was nervous. I fought the urge to shake off his hold or remind him he might lose his hand. But either the meeting played out like I hoped it would and this was the last time he ever touched me . . .

Or I'd be in his office afterward, hoping to negotiate my way out of the corner I'd painted myself into. I figured it was best not to react in the moment. Besides, I was holding it together on the outside, but beneath my mortal surface, the gorgon inside hissed and slithered, desperate to break free of her cage. I couldn't spring her too early, though.

The timing had to be just right.

Oddly, it seemed the closer we got to the battlefield, the more unsure Macalister became. His cold hand was clammy as it clung to mine in the elevator, and we watched the numbers tick up as we climbed into the sky. The trip to Mount Olympus didn't take long, and when we reached the top, he dropped my hand, and his cold, confident persona snapped back into place.

He was impervious Zeus again as the doors opened and he gestured for me to exit first. He couldn't have timed it better. Ares stepped out of his office and glanced down the hall, his gaze catching mine.

"Marist?" Royce said. His questioning look froze as he noticed the man at my side, and then my husband turned to stone.

Macalister's smile was sinister. "I asked her to ride in with me this morning, and she graciously accepted."

Royce pinned me with a look of hurt, and I felt the stab of it deeply, but I'd prepared myself for this. Yes, it looked like I had chosen Macalister over him, but I hoped my husband could trust me. I grabbed my wedding rings, pulling them off to the first knuckle and then reseated them on my finger. It might have looked like a nervous tick, but did he understand the meaning behind my action? We'd said as long as I wore his ring, I was with him, no matter what lies we told while other people were around.

He came back to life and set a murderous gaze on his father. "How nice for you."

The hallway was wide and long, but the animosity between father and son filled every square inch. What would it be like when it was confined to the boardroom?

Macalister's focus didn't leave Royce, but it was clear he was speaking to me. "My office is one floor up. I'll have someone show you where it is." His statement was patronizing. "This shouldn't take long."

Royce's expression was a loud *fuck you* to his father.

"All right," I said softly.

When Macalister marched toward the boardroom, I followed. My heart banged so noisily in my chest, I wondered if anyone else could hear it. Royce walked behind me, bringing up the rear of the parade of Hales, and I sensed how badly he wanted to ask me what the fuck was going on.

Macalister hadn't yet reached the open doorway when he sensed I lingered in his shadow. He stopped and turned, confusion hinting at the corners of his eyes. "You misunderstood. Wait here, and someone will be by to collect you."

Collect me? Like I was some lost little girl? A short laugh welled up and bubbled out, masking the snarl Medusa gave as she emerged from her shell.

"Oh, no," I said, my voice dripping with rich satisfaction, "you misunderstand." I pointed to the boardroom. "I'll be joining you in there."

Irritation coursed through Macalister. "No, Marist. This meeting is closed to anyone not seated on the board. You'll have to—"

"I'm a voting board member today, chairman."

He would have looked less shocked if I'd slapped him. "Excuse me?"

"Mr. Shaunessy has decided to step aside and make me his proxy." My gaze went from the older Hale to the younger one, and Royce had a similar look of disbelief. He was so handsome in his black suit and red tie, even when he was frozen in place. I smiled reassuringly at him. "I'll see you in there, gentlemen."

They were too stunned to stop me; not that they could, anyway.

It'd been a year since I'd been in this room, and physically it hadn't changed. There was still the sweeping view of Boston beyond the panoramic window wall, and the long, glossy conference table in the center with tall-backed chairs gathered around it. It was cold and over air-conditioned, despite the summer heat outside, and the men seated at the table were all the same from before.

But the boardroom felt wildly different. Last time I'd stepped in here, I'd been seeking Macalister's approval, and now he'd need mine. All the anxiety I'd had when I'd sat for the interview had been replaced with power and determination.

The board members stopped their conversations at my entrance and lifted their heads, treating me to puzzled looks. Mr. Shaunessy's gaze quickly sank to the tabletop, heavy with dread.

"Liam," Macalister snapped as he strode into the room behind me, followed by Royce. "What have you fucking done?"

It was like the men were seated in electric chairs and

all received the jolt simultaneously. It took me a second to understand their reaction. They'd never heard Macalister curse before. Mr. Shaunessy was up out of his chair so fast, it made it spin. He couldn't bring himself to look at his boss and stared at Macalister's tie like it was fascinating.

His meek voice barely reached to the end of the table. "I've elected Marist as my proxy for any voting that takes place today."

A red flush bloomed up Macalister's neck and peeked out over the top of his collar, but the color didn't reach his face. It was too full of a dark, ugly look, and there wasn't room for anything else. He didn't have to use words to threaten him because his piercing glare was more than enough, and Liam Shaunessy physically withered under it.

But Macalister abruptly straightened, and a calm washed over him. "You're terminated, effective immediately." His focus swung to me. "As you are no longer a proxy for a board member, I'll ask you to leave."

I stood there in my nude pumps and powerful red dress, grinning darkly. *I am two moves ahead of you.* "You can fire him from his job, but you can't remove a director during a board meeting unless you have cause. Isn't that right, Royce?"

Excitement flashed in my husband's eyes. "It's in our by-laws."

It was there specifically for situations like these. It protected members from retribution if they needed to vote against the chairman.

Macalister's stare tried to burn a hole into me as he realized how he'd been trapped. He couldn't cancel the meeting, stop or delay the vote. I'd put him in check, and now we'd find out if he could survive the endgame Royce and I had created, or if he was going to lose, once and for all.

"Do you have cause to remove Liam?" Mr. Burrows asked. He had a soft spot for Royce and been the easiest to sway to our side.

Macalister grabbed the back of his chair at the head of the table and pulled it out, his usually graceful movements jerky with frustration. "Not at this time, although I strongly oppose that he's willing to risk the future of this great company and pass his power off to someone who has no experience."

I strode to Mr. Shaunessy's seat, which was now mine. "I promise I have what's best for this company in my mind. And you're aware, more than anyone, how far I'm willing to go to protect it." My gaze swept over the rest of the table. "Don't forget, I've already proven my loyalty to every person in this room."

A few of the men shifted uncomfortably in their seats. What they did to me was safe in the darkness of the dining room, but out here, under the bright lights of the boardroom, there was nowhere to hide.

Mr. Shaunessy took one of the empty seats at the far side of the table because he'd have to stay and observe. I smoothed my hands under my skirt and sat in the chair, keeping my posture straight and my chin up. Alice would be so proud of how I looked as I attempted to destroy her husband. I thought of her in her office right now, probably unaware of what was happening in the boardroom just down the hall.

And once the two Hale men were seated, Royce directly

across from me, all nine men in the room set their gazes on me and promptly turned to stone, realizing how dramatic the shift in power had just become.

To say the room was tense was an understatement.

It wasn't welcoming at the table I'd had to buy, negotiate, and blackmail my way to get on, and I stood out in my red dress from the group of men in dark suits, most of whom were twice my age. But I didn't fucking care if they liked it or not. A year ago, they hadn't cared whether I liked being on the table, had they?

Medusa impatiently tapped her polished nails on the tabletop, wanting to get started, hungry to vanquish her foe.

Mr. Burrows was the oldest member of the board, but he was a marathon runner and in excellent shape, making him look like he was still in his fifties. His bright eyes blinked as he was the first to break.

"Right." He glanced down at the iPad before him. "I hereby call to order this emergency session of the board of directors of Hale Banking and Holding and note that all current members are present for the proceedings. Marist Hale is also present, representing Liam Shaunessy's interests today as his appointed proxy."

Macalister dropped his arm on the table with an angry thump and ran the tips of his fingers over the pad of his thumb as he spoke. "Yes, let's get on with it. Royce, you have something you'd like to say?"

If my husband were nervous, I couldn't tell. All I saw were the beautifully violent eyes of Ares as he drew in a preparing breath and readied his weapons to strike.

"I was against the purchase of Ascension from the beginning. It wasn't the right time, or the right company, but my father wouldn't see reason. I had concerns about the numbers over there and that we were taking on a huge risk, but . . . no, I didn't speak up about it. I should have, but, frankly, it wouldn't have fucking mattered anyway. My father is obsessed with winning, whether it's good for the company or not."

Royce took a moment to look at each member, driving the point home.

"When he discovered the truth about Ascension, he didn't back down. He just kept pushing for the acquisition, even as he knew what a terrible buy it was going to be. He didn't care. To him, all that mattered was closing. He carelessly put us into debt to buy Ascension, even as he knew it wasn't going to bring a return, and the result is millions of dollars lost for our shareholders. You want to know why?"

His expression demanded attention and his words were full of conviction.

"Because the great and powerful Macalister Hale doesn't believe he's capable of making mistakes. He's unfit to continue as the chairman of this board, and I call for a vote of no-confidence in his leadership."

Cold slithered along the table from Macalister, blanketing the room, and his tone was just as frosty. "Are you finished?"

When Royce nodded, Macalister turned his attention to the rest of the board. It was his turn now to plead his case.

"My son is young, inexperienced, and too impatient to

see the long-term gains that are to be had with Ascension. I admit their issues are great, but they're not systemic. I can and will turn the bow of the ship, but only *I* have the expertise to do so."

It was clear he had more to say, but Mr. Lynch looked squirrely sitting beside his boss. "I agree," he interrupted. "Macalister has my full confidence, and voting any other way would be unwise."

Spoken like a true lackey.

Mr. Burrows wasn't fazed by the threat. "I have the same concerns as Royce and, regrettably, must vote no-confidence."

And just like that, we were off. The rest of Macalister's prepared argument was pocketed, and it was for the best. I'd heard it in the car this morning and doubted it would change anyone's mind.

I wasn't sure who would vote next, but Macalister's gaze fell on Mr. Powell. His eyebrows pulled together as he contemplated his vote. "While I'm incredibly disappointed in the lack of care Macalister exercised, a change in leadership is the last thing HBHC needs right now. I believe it's best we weather the storm under his direction."

"A storm he knowingly steered us into," Royce pointed out.

Mr. Scoffield looked pained. His turn was next, although he very much didn't want it to be. His gaze darted to Macalister and then to Royce, and my heart missed a beat. Was he about to back out?

Macalister's patience cracked. "Well?"

"I vote no-confidence," Mr. Scoffield said, reluctance filling his expression.

His boss had expected an explanation and when it didn't come, irritation smeared across Macalister's face. "That's it?"

It was.

"Coward," Macalister growled.

All gazes turned to Mr. Vanderburgh. He was one of the outsiders—a pioneer in the tech industry who'd made his first billion when his company went public. He was young like Macalister, but he was a maverick. He was known more for being creative and lucky than smart and strategic. I'd thought we'd have been able to convince him, but the car ride in with Macalister had confirmed my suspicion.

Macalister liked the balance Mr. Vanderburgh brought to the table, and Mr. Vanderburgh liked the stability the chairman maintained.

"Transitions are messy and painful," the man said. "I'm with Powell. Trying to install a new CEO right now is a terrible idea."

Breath evaporated from my lungs, and my mouth went dry. Macalister had three votes, which meant if Mr. Geffen voted in his favor . . . this was all over. There'd be no point in me voting, and all of this would have been for *nothing*.

Mr. Geffen was a wild card. Royce hadn't been able to pin him down with any kind of commitment. My focus darted to my husband and my heart careened down to my stomach. What was I going to do if he lost?

You'll do whatever you have to.

Royce was the persona he'd spent a lifetime perfecting. Cool, calm, and indifferent. As if everything didn't hinge on the next words out of Mr. Geffen's mouth. It was a lie, of course. He had to be thinking the same things I was, about how his father would never let this go. Even if we ran away from the kingdom of HBHC, Macalister would haunt us for the rest of our professional lives. His reach was far. Inescapable.

Mr. Geffen placed his hands on the table and laced his fingers together. He too was from outside the company. A former president of Rosso Media Group, he didn't have a strong banking background, but he was a tough businessman. He was deep in thought as he stared at polished wood and the reflection of the Boston skyline.

A lifetime passed.

Finally, he lifted his head and rolled his shoulders back like a decision had been made, and every muscle in my body went rigid.

TWENTY

Everyone waited with bated breath for Mr. Geffen's vote. It was as if the boardroom were covered in mousetraps, and the tiniest move would set them off in a cascading flood of snapping jaws.

"It's Macalister's lack of remorse," he said, "I find the most troubling about this whole disaster." When Macalister looked ready to protest, Mr. Geffen lifted a hand to cut him off. "Our stock is down fourteen percent, which is a disaster if I've ever heard of one, and I'm sure the shareholders agree." His gaze zeroed in on the chairman. "In hindsight, I don't believe you'd do anything differently. You made an egregious mistake. Worse, you won't admit to it, or any failure, and that has me questioning your judgment. I've been in the business a long time. Not every decision I make is the right one, but I know there's a lesson in failure. I don't think you're willing to learn it."

I sensed what was coming before the words were out of his mouth, and my pulse fluttered. My heart soared in my chest.

Mr. Geffen turned his attention to the rest of the board. "I hold Macalister personally responsible for this, and removing him is the best way to appease the angry shareholders we all have to answer to."

Oh, my God.

I put my hands flat on the table to prevent myself from flying out of my chair. Three votes for, three votes against, and I would be the tiebreaker. Everyone realized it at the same instant.

"That's it, huh?" Mr. Lynch was pissed. "It all comes down to the whim of some twenty-two-year-old girl, who'd probably rather be out shopping than here, doing her husband's bidding."

"You've no fucking idea what you're talking about," Royce snapped.

"Don't be fooled." Macalister said it begrudgingly. "Marist is young, but she might be one of the smartest people at this table."

Did he think flattery would save him? Or was he thinking about how he'd been so confident he was going to win, he'd told me his plan and given away everything?

Mr. Lynch gave his boss a skeptical look. "Well, hopefully, she's smart enough to make the right decision, then."

Macalister's pale blue eyes were filled with alarm he tried to disguise. Was he coming to terms with what he'd thought was impossible? He sat in his chair looking tense, and I imagined he could feel his control over HBHC weakening as it began to slip from his grip.

"Marist." He said it the same way he'd command me to

be reasonable. "You don't want to do this."

My tone patronized. "I don't?"

"Abstain your vote. You shouldn't have to choose between family."

My laugh was devoid of warmth. Like that was even an issue, and he didn't care about that. It was a nice try, but I was aware if I didn't decide, a tie would be ruled in the chairman's favor.

Cracks of anxiety began to bleed out of him. He gripped the armrests of his chair and sat at the edge of it. "Or you could be brave and make the difficult, right decision—and *choose me.*"

I sucked in a breath. There it was, what Macalister had truly wanted from me since the night of the initiation when I'd made Royce his father's proxy. I'd picked his son over him, and Macalister had never recovered.

His chest began to heave. Inside him, chaos brewed and ate away at his self-control. His eyes were wild and unfocused, and his expression desperate. He looked so incredibly mortal as his world began to fall apart. "Pick me, Nyx."

Confusion splashed on the rest of the board's faces, but I wasn't deterred. Medusa wasn't just taking him down, she would destroy the perverse tradition that had drawn her into this world. Did he understand that? I'd thought Ascension was the Trojan Horse, but had it been me all along?

"I'm not Nyx," I spoke with a tone of absolution, in a way he would best understand, "but you were right to be afraid of me." My gaze turned back to my husband. I wanted to watch Ares' face when we claimed victory. "I vote no-confidence."

All the air went out of the boardroom, making it a vacuum, and for the second time this morning, I turned the men into stone. They became a garden of statues gathered in a semicircle around the table.

I stared into Royce's eyes. In the window behind him, the city of Boston loomed like it was resting on his shoulders. Was he ready for the weight of it? I thought so. He'd spent so much of his life preparing, plus he had me as his partner, and I was eager to rule alongside him.

It was obvious to me he felt a mixture of emotions, but he kept them contained. Hardly anything leaked out. There was only the hint of a smile twitching on his sexy lips before he spoke. "The board has voted to remove you from your seat. Vice-chair David Burrows will be our acting chairman and CEO until a new one can be elected."

The single word from Macalister fell like a frozen sledgehammer. "No."

Royce paused. "No?"

It was like no one else was in the room. Macalister's gaze trapped me, and his voice went as black as his suit. "I don't accept this. You'll change your vote."

Tension worked along my back, and nerves fluttered in my stomach. I flashed back to the night I'd beaten him at chess and how his malice-filled stare had stabbed into me. It was exactly the same now. He wasn't willing to accept losing any better than the last time.

"It's over," I said. "Checkmate."

"No." The volume of his voice rose right along with him out of his chair. "I do not accept this, Marist. I brought you into my home, into my family, and you will not take away everything I've built . . . and *give it to him*."

Violence whispered the hairs along the back of my neck and drew me from my seat. And when I stood, so did the rest of the men, although not out of polite courtesy—they felt the same threat I did. There was a pulse thrumming in the room, and it quickened when everyone was on their feet.

Macalister had brought me into his family. He'd taught me how to strategize with chess, and how to ruthlessly win at all costs. Did he not think I'd learn how to lie and deceive like the Hales could?

It wasn't wise, but I said it anyway. "I told you you'd regret this."

Macalister went wooden, his muscles taut beneath his suit. Something cracked inside his chest, and the panic of it filled his expression. It was frightening how his eyes darkened to black ice. No longer a god, he became a monster, and the Minotaur burst forth.

The horror of it locked me in place. It was why I couldn't run when he seized the rolling office chair by its armrests, lifted it high into the air, and then hurled it at the wall with all the force left in his body.

Board members gasped as the chair flew like a missile. I stumbled backward, putting my hands up to cover my mouth and the startled sound I made.

The chair crashed to the floor with a thunderous boom and tumbled noisily into the table of beverages and pastries that had been set out for the meeting. The impact knocked over the stainless-steel coffee server, and its lid came off, dumping a tidal wave of steaming coffee across the carpet.

When Macalister charged at me, everyone felt the danger— most of all my husband.

The fastest way for Royce to get to me was over the long conference table, and I blinked in shock as he took it. He scrambled as a blur across the glossy surface, his dress shoes squeaking against the veneer and his face full of determination. It announced there was nothing in the world that was going to stop him from getting to me.

His feet hit the floor, and a split second later I was spun around in his arms, his body a protective wall between me and his father. I was shaking with adrenaline, but Royce was warm and solid, and I clung to him with relief.

"Marist," Macalister roared as he struggled against the arms holding him back. Several of the men had stepped up to restrain him, and it looked like no easy task. "I love you," he cried. Betrayal etched his face. "How can you do this to me?"

When the day was over, which part would the board find the most shocking? That Macalister was out as CEO, that he'd lost control and hurled a chair across the room . . . or how he'd admitted he was in love with his daughter-in-law?

Royce squeezed me tight as he turned his head and lobbed his words over his shoulder toward his father. "If you're looking for someone to blame, why don't you try your-fucking-self? You had every opportunity to stop this, and you didn't, and I'm not just talking about this vote." His expression was pure contempt. "If you hadn't tried to take her away from me, we wouldn't have had to take everything away from you. I warned you this day was coming."

He had, the night in the hedge maze when he'd offered fifty million dollars to buy me back from his father and Macalister had refused.

"My biggest regret," Royce continued, "is that it didn't come sooner."

Macalister seemed to claw back a shred of control and quit struggling against the hands holding him back. He sneered at the men. "Release me."

They hesitantly did, but everyone stayed on alert, not trusting his calm demeanor would last. He grabbed the sides of his suit coat and straightened it, regaining some of his composure mere seconds before two men in gray suits poured into the room. The crash of the chair had drawn security, and they surveyed the tense scene quickly.

"This meeting is over," Mr. Burrows announced. "Please escort Mr. Hale to his office upstairs. He needs some time to cool off before we can discuss the next steps."

Rather than fight or look defeated, Macalister appeared how he always did. To the two security guards, he was composed and reserved. Only the hurried movement of his chest and the pulse pounding in his neck hinted that something was amiss.

None of the board moved as he strode to the doorway and disappeared through it, the two gray suits trailing behind like imperial guards.

"Jesus," Mr. Vanderburgh breathed. "What the fuck was that?"

Royce's tone was pointed. "Still happy with your vote?"

Mr. Burrows was all business and focused on Royce. "I'll

get Carolyn to work up a draft of the press release."

"Tell her to move fast," Royce said. "He wasn't exactly quiet, and it won't be long before the entire building knows what happened. Hopefully, we can get it out to the other branches before word hits Twitter."

The damage was done; now it was a race to control it from affecting the stock price further. I stood awkwardly beside Royce as the men began listing problems and offering solutions. The agenda for the day had been blown to hell. A meeting with the mergers and acquisitions team would be pushed an hour, and as soon as the announcement was made that Macalister was out, Mr. Geffen would start the media blitz.

My part was done, and I wasn't needed here any longer, but when I tried to inch away, Royce's hand wrapped around my wrist and stopped me. "Guys, I need ten minutes. We can get someone in here to clean up the mess and all take a few moments to regroup."

He didn't wait for them to respond, but most looked relieved at his suggestion.

"Where are we going?" I asked softly as Royce pulled me out into the hall.

He kept my wrist clasped in his hand, gently guiding me toward the end of the hallway. "I need some air."

The curious eyes of the employees were fixed on us as we went, making me feel horribly on display. It wasn't until we stepped into the elevator that I was able to catch my breath. I'd expected we would head down to the street, but Royce punched in his passcode and pressed the button for the top floor.

As soon as the doors shut, the full gravity of what had happened hit me. "You did it," I whispered.

He gave me a look like I was crazy. "No, Marist. You did." His hand slipped down until he could thread his fingers with mine. "How the hell did you get Liam Shaunessy to give you his vote? I couldn't convince him to break from my dad."

I swallowed hard. "My offer was ten million dollars . . . and that I wouldn't tell your father he was having an affair with Alice. I think it was the second part that convinced him."

"What?"

"Sophia told me."

Royce closed his eyes and shook his head. "First Vance, and then Liam. She sure knows how to pick the guys to get under my dad's skin."

The elevator came to a stop, and the doors peeled open to reveal a hallway similar to the one we'd just been in downstairs. I didn't get a good look because Royce slapped the *close door* button, sealing us back in together. The mood in the elevator shifted and thickened, aided when Royce's arms wrapped around me.

I set my forehead against the side of his neck and laid my cheek against the lapel of his coat. "I'm sorry I didn't tell you my plan, or that I was coming in with him today. You can read through his lies, but I think the same is true for him."

And I'd needed his hubris to keep him talking in the car this morning. If he'd told me he'd swayed one of the votes we were counting on, I'd have told Royce to cancel the meeting and delay until we had the numbers.

Or a new plan.

But my deception had worked, and Royce had dethroned his father.

My husband's chest lifted, and he stroked a hand over my hair. "You did what you had to, and it was nothing compared to what I put you through."

I closed my eyes, grateful to have both him and everything we wanted.

The elevator didn't move. We were trapped together in the glass box atop Mount Olympus, and even though we could see ships moving in the harbor and people on the sidewalks, it felt like we were all alone. I wanted the moment to last longer than it did, but Royce made a strange sound. His chest shuddered.

Oh, my God. Was he . . . crying?

I lifted my head, only to find an enormous grin on his face. He wasn't crying, he was *laughing*, with relief or simple emotional overwhelm, I couldn't tell.

"I can't believe he fucking threw a chair."

His laughter was kind of contagious. A much-needed release. "And you climbed over the table."

The arms around me tightened, and as he finally got his laughter under control, his eyes filled with love. "Because the thought of losing you scared the shit out of me."

The elevator doors slid open with a mechanical grind, interrupting what likely would have been a kiss. Instead, he took my hand again and pulled me out into the hall.

I'd never been on the top floor before. It was only the C-level executives and their assistants' offices, plus a private kitchen and meeting spaces. Royce knew exactly where we were going. Our first stop was the kitchen, where every day a chef prepared a full lunch for the executives. I rested a hand on the prep table while Royce pulled two bottles of Evian out of the fridge. He made a joke about needing something stronger, but it was nine in the morning.

We'd celebrate later.

Bottles in hand, we went farther down the hall. "My dad's office is there," he said, gesturing to the door at the end. The shades were down over the glass, making it impossible to see inside. What was Macalister doing in there right now? Sitting at his desk while the guards stood nearby? Was he already plotting how he was going to get control back?

Before we reached Macalister's office, Royce turned to the left and pushed open a heavy paned glass door. I blinked against the bright sunlight as I followed him outside. It was a garden balcony cut into the building with potted trees and surrounded by living walls of greenery. Like the house in Aspen, the railing was glass so it didn't obstruct the view.

The harbor and the city stretched out at our feet.

"This is beautiful," I said.

"It was Alice's idea. She thought my dad would like a space close by that didn't feel like he was trapped in the office."

I understood. Running a multibillion-dollar international company was not an easy job. We rarely saw Macalister, and when we did, he was usually on the phone. My gaze drifted from the morning traffic down below to the balcony door that connected straight to Macalister's office.

"What happens now?"

He followed my gaze. "With my dad?" Royce unscrewed the cap of his water and took a sip. "He'll keep his office and stay on as president. It's a figurehead position—no real power. An advisory role, if he accepts it."

Because Macalister was still a Hale and an integral part of the company.

"What about you?" I asked.

"I expect Allen will be CEO for the next few years, and I'll be the chief operating officer." He was talking about Mr. Burrows. "When I'm ready, I'll step in." When surprise flooded my eyes, he gave me an easy smile. "I've spent my whole life preparing for this, but I think everyone would be more comfortable if I had a little more experience. I'm twenty-six, and patient. I know my time will come."

A pang of relief warmed my chest. Being COO of HBHC was still a demanding job, but not as bad as the role at the very top, and this meant he might not spend every waking minute in the office for the next few years. It'd give us more time together.

Below us, rush hour was winding down, and as the streets grew quiet, the sun overhead became more intense. I took a long drink of my water and set my gaze on him.

"How does it feel?" I asked softly. "All your planning is over."

He set a hand on the glass railing, looked out over the city, and hesitated. "It feels . . . different than I expected. I dunno. Maybe it hasn't sunk in yet."

I heard exactly what he wasn't saying. As much as he disliked his father, he still cared about him and there wasn't joy in destroying him. "You know your dad's going to be okay," I said. Macalister wasn't the type to sit around and lick his wounds. "He can focus on the Federal Reserve now."

Royce turned toward me, crossed his arms over his chest, and leaned back against the railing. "True."

The door to the hallway swung open, and we tensed as the tall blonde strode toward us, her Jimmy Choos beating out a swift, urgent tempo. Her expression was stricken.

"Is it true?" Alice asked. "Macalister's out?"

"Alice." Royce straightened, and his shoulders lifted with a reluctant breath. He felt compelled to explain. "He knew how bad Ascension was, and he bought them anyway."

She didn't care about the why, only the outcome, and her head snapped toward me, full of anger and disgust. "I heard Liam made you his proxy, and you used it as the deciding vote against Macalister."

Was I supposed to feel guilty? Because I didn't. I lifted my chin and looked defiant. "Yes."

When she'd drugged me before, she hadn't looked at me with the kind of malice she did now. This was a whole new level. Pure, unfiltered hatred poured out of her. If she could have killed me with a glare, she would have, but even Hera didn't have that power.

Instead, Alice settled for a knife, and the morning sunlight gleamed off its sharp blade.

TWENTY-ONE

SOUND FADED OUT AS MY GAZE FOCUSED IN ON ALICE. IT wasn't clear where the knife had come from. I assumed she'd grabbed it from the block in the executive kitchen, but had she been hiding it in the folds of her skirt? Neither Royce nor I had noticed it until she raised it and pointed the tip menacingly at me.

Her eyes were wild with madness. "How could you?"

I sucked in a breath, and my whole body went tight, making the bottle of water crinkle in my hand.

When she took a step toward me, Royce tossed his bottle away with a loud thump against his father's office door, and he moved between us, his hands out in front, trying to keep her calm. "Alice." His tone was soft. "What are you doing?"

His nonconfrontational attitude made no difference to her. She was too far gone and determined to get to me. I realized it as he did, and Ares activated. He lunged for the knife the same moment she jabbed forward.

I gasped and backpedaled, slamming painfully into the railing. Fear had me immobile and my reaction slow, but not

Royce. He grabbed Alice's wrist and struggled with her. He was bigger and stronger, but her dark motivation made her match his strength. She tried to cut him, but his grasp prevented her from getting at him and made her slice awkwardly at the air.

It was a frantic battle I was powerless to stop, and I had to watch with my breath halted horribly in my lungs. He gave a grunt of pain, followed by hers, and the blade flashed between their hands before he was able to shake the knife from her grip.

It clattered loudly to the concrete, and Royce kicked it away as he clasped a hand over the sleeve covering his forearm. With the weapon gone, it left the two of them glaring at each other and breathing hard. She'd been disarmed, but danger continued to swirl on the balcony.

Adding to it was the cold wind of Macalister, who stepped through the side door of his office and took in the scene. His gaze went from the knife near his feet, then to Alice, before moving on to his son.

"Royce," Macalister's expression was . . . strange. Concern pulled his eyebrows together. After what had happened in the boardroom, worry was the last thing I would have expected.

"I'm okay," my husband said quickly.

Too quickly.

My heart thudded to a stop.

He stood to the side, so I couldn't understand what had put anxiety in Macalister's eyes, but his expression was enough to give me genuine fear. It was then I noticed the red drips on the concrete. It was so much worse when Royce turned to face me. His black suit sleeve was wet, and crimson blood slipped through his fingers. It poured down his wounded arm, dripping from his listless hand.

No. Oh, no.

I dropped my water bottle with a thud. He was the one who was hurt, but as he took in my ashen face and saw how I had an arm braced against the railing to hold myself upright, he only seemed to be worried about me. "Marist, it looks worse than it is."

"Oh, my God," I moaned.

I wanted to be strong, but my body wouldn't cooperate. My knees became gelatinous, my stomach rolled, and my vision narrowed. I was going to pass out again, and I fought the sensation with every fleeting ounce of strength I possessed. There was just enough to turn away from the gruesome sight and grip the railing with both hands, hard enough my fingers ached.

If I could catch my breath and get my legs back under me, I'd be all right, I told myself. It was fucking ridiculous I was so weak. Alice had cut him. What if she'd done worse? All while I stood there, paralyzed with—

A pair of hands hit my shoulders and shoved. The shocking force of it, combined with my weakened state, made me pitch forward.

"No!" The word was so horrified, I couldn't tell which one of the Hale men had yelled it. This was the thought that ran through my mind as I tipped over the ledge, the ground no longer beneath my feet.

The disorienting feeling of falling was the first to slam into me.

Then—utter terror.

I screamed as I tumbled over the side of the railing and clawed desperately for anything to hold on to. One hand found the thick, blunt edge of the smooth glass, and I jerked to a stop so hard, it wrenched my shoulder. If I'd had any left, the pain would have taken my breath away.

My shoes came off my dangling feet and fell, one after the other, plunging the sixty stories down to the sidewalk below. I didn't think about the building I was hanging off of, or the city surrounding me. Only the survival part of my brain was functioning, overruling everything else. It kept me clinging to the glass ledge, even as it felt like it was going to sever my fingers.

"Marist!" Royce yelled, and then he was leaning over the side, both of his bloody hands clasped on my wrist. "I've got you."

I'd never seen him look more determined or focused, and if I wasn't sure I was going to die, I might have thought his expression was beautiful. But the creepy-crawling sensation inched up my spine as his blood smeared brightly across my skin.

No. You cannot pass out.

Because if I did, I'd fall to my death. His hands were slippery and his arm weak from Alice's knife. He wouldn't be able to hold on to me if I let go.

"Just hang on," he pleaded. His grip on my forearm was ferocious, a vise of steel, but it didn't matter. I was slipping, inch by bloody inch from his grasp.

My whole body trembled, and I tried not to swing my legs, even though my feet were desperate to have something beneath them. I needed to get my other hand up, but I was terrified any movement would make me slip.

"Don't let me go!" I cried.

"No." His tone was absolute. "I've got you."

Macalister appeared at his son's side, matching Royce's determined expression. He latched a clean hand on my arm below Royce's, while stretching out his other. "Give me your hand."

It had never been easier to follow Macalister's urgent demand. I gulped in a shallow breath and reached up. He may have been crushing the bones in my hand as he grabbed me, but I was grateful.

And as soon as he had a good grip, the Hale men began to lift and pull, dragging me awkwardly up over the side of the railing.

"We've got you," Royce said. His intense gaze had the strongest hold on me, and I stared at his blue eyes as the men pulled me to safety.

The second my feet hit the ground, Macalister let go, and I wrapped both arms around Royce's shoulders. I couldn't feel the bones in my body or hear anything over the roaring rush of the blood in my head, but as long as I was pressed to him, I knew I was alive.

"It's okay," he whispered. "You're safe, I've got you, you're okay."

It sounded like he was talking to himself as much as

he was to me. I melted into him. I was trembling, and as I pressed to him, I could feel his heart pounding as frantically as mine. He was solid and warm and the love of my life.

"You could have killed her." Macalister's voice was arctic. The scariest I'd ever heard him sound, and perhaps it was for Royce too, because he tucked me in at his side and turned so we could both see how his father stared at Alice.

Macalister gazed at his wife as if she were vile. Like he could see all the ugliness hidden inside her.

"There's a security camera over the door," he said. "Even if I wanted to—which I don't—I can't save you this time."

Like me, she was trembling, but hers was with a different emotion. Her husband's look of disgust cleaved her in two, and all her panic and desperation poured out. Her eyes glistened with unshed tears. "But I did it for you."

He said it with pure disbelief. "For me?"

Alice's eyes flicked to me before returning to him. "Marist took everything from me. From *us*. She seduced you, Macalister. Can't you see that?" When she shook her head, her tears fell, but they went unnoticed. "She tricked you and everyone else, all so she could take your power and give it to Royce."

Macalister's posture was tense, and his hands curled into fists. When he moved toward her, she took a step backward and raised her hands, silently warning him to keep his distance.

Her tone was cautious as she gauged his reaction. "Everything can go back to the way it was before you knew she existed."

"No, it can't." He stood tall, unashamed as he admitted it. "I don't want it to."

Another round of tears sliced down Alice's face as her expression soured. "I gave you anything you wanted, and still you don't see me. She's fucking blinded you."

"You know that's not true. My issue with—"

Rage made her shake violently. "It is true! If you weren't so blinded by that stupid girl, you would have seen what I was doing with Liam Shaunessy right under your goddamn nose."

He stiffened, and his jaw set as the new information slapped him.

It looked like he was carefully selecting the words of his response for maximum impact. It was hot outside, and there wasn't a breeze, but Macalister's voice was so chilling, it made me shiver. "You're mistaken if you think I care at all what you do, or who you do it with. You lost that privilege the night I found Marist half-dead on the stairs."

Her chest heaved as she backed up against the railing, and her gaze frantically darted away. She hadn't expected his indifferent reaction, and since it wounded her deeply, she scrambled for a new weapon to strike back with.

"And Vance too," she spat out. "Do you know how many times your son happily climbed into my bed when you wouldn't?"

Royce and I froze in place. Everything around us decelerated to a stop, and the world focused in on Macalister.

The glaciers in his eyes flash boiled, but his voice was eerily calm and quiet. "What did you just say?"

Alice peered up at him with love and hatred twisting

together into one painful emotion. "He was just a substitute at first, but the truth is he was better than you."

Macalister had lost his seat and his company this morning, but it didn't compare to what she'd just revealed. This was the perfect thing to destroy him altogether. He was a glass hovering at the edge of a table. One tiny push and there'd be no going back. Catastrophe felt imminent.

He straightened his shoulders as he loomed over her, his shadow covering her face. "Perhaps you're right, and I did not give you the attention you so pathetically desired." He sneered as he seized her shoulders. "But my eyes are open now. You came after my son with a knife. You've nearly killed Marist twice now. You've hurt the people I love, and that is something I will never, *ever* forgive."

"Love?" Her laugh was incredulous. "You're not capable of love. You said it yourself, you're not even human anymore after Julia died."

He jerked her like he could shake sense into his wife. "Enough."

"No." Her smile was hollow and cruel. "You taught me to never give up, to win no matter what. You fucking made me this way." Her face was scary. "I'm just as tenacious as you, and I won't stop until I have what I want, you understand?"

She reached up and set a hand on his chin, squeezing her fingers on his cheeks.

"As long as she exists, that girl is in our way," Alice said. "You're a monster," each word carried its own gravity, "but you're *my* monster."

I believed what she'd said. It was win at all costs, and

Alice would never stop coming after me. It was obvious Macalister believed her too. When she tried to kiss him, his control burned away. The Minotaur broke free and reared back.

"*No,*" he roared and shoved her away with all his might.

Horrified surprise went through her face as she tipped backward. I knew the sensation all too well, how disorienting it was to go over the railing. Unlike me, Alice was too stunned to make a sound, and although her hands clawed at the air, she didn't find anything to grab on to. There was nothing to save her.

I stood paralyzed as her legs went up to the sky and her body spilled over the side, slipping toward the earth.

And then she was gone, vanished over the edge of the building.

I screamed beneath the hand I clasped to my mouth, which was wet with Royce's coppery blood.

Time suspended, dragging out each second until it was a century long.

I blinked desperately, trying to clear the image from my mind. I wanted to pretend I hadn't witnessed Macalister shove Alice off the sixtieth-story balcony, or that she had just plunged to her death.

He had his hands on the railing and leaned over it, his tie dangling in the wind and his face utterly white. No one moved. No one said a word, not even as the distant, panicked screams carried upward from the sidewalk below.

My heart wasn't working, and neither were my lungs as Royce and I watched the realization of what he'd done crush Macalister to his knees. He turned, collapsing to sit on the ground with his back against the glass, and dropped his heavy head into his hands.

He looked broken.

Defeated.

He'd killed her.

And I'd probably wonder the rest of my life if it was purely by accident or if he'd lost control and subconsciously done it to save me.

I wasn't sure which one of us pulled the other along, but I found myself on my knees beside Royce, huddled next to Macalister. My husband's voice was hushed and hurried. "She jumped. We'll make the video go away."

When Macalister lifted his weary gaze to his son, we all aged ten years. He looked like he appreciated the idea, but sadness consumed him. "You can't."

He gestured to the hallway door and the group of horrified faces that had gathered around it. There were at least a half dozen employees and far too many witnesses. Nothing could be taken back or undone.

"It was an accident," I whispered.

I didn't know what compelled me to do it, but I put my hand on Macalister's. Was it how he'd helped Royce pull me to safety? How he'd included his son in the list of people he loved? Or how he'd removed the threat of the woman hell-bent on destroying me? His hand was colder than ever, and I squeezed, trying to impart some warmth. It looked very much like Macalister was going into shock.

His eyes struggled to focus on the shredded cut in Royce's sleeve which was still bleeding. The sight of blood no longer had a debilitating effect on me. All I could worry about now were the two Hale men.

Macalister grabbed Royce's arm with his free hand and squeezed down on the cut. "Keep pressure on it. You'll need stitches."

He wasn't Zeus or the Minotaur. For the first time ever, I saw him as he was supposed to be—a father concerned about his son. With all of us stained with Hale blood, my hand on Macalister, and his on Royce, we had to look like a tightknit family unit . . . which ten minutes ago couldn't have been further from the truth.

Misfortune had brought me into the family, and now tragedy bound us together forever.

Macalister blinked, and his eyes cleared. He looked at Royce as if he were handing over his life to him, and perhaps he was. "You distance yourself as much as you can from me now. We're already vulnerable, and if the stock goes much lower, you'll be fending off takeover attempts. Lean on Allen and the rest of the board." He moved closer to his son, and his tone verged on a plea. "Don't let our company go."

Royce's eyes widened. "I won't."

Macalister's focus shifted to me, or more specifically, to my hand resting on top of his and the sapphire ring he'd given me. My heartbeat went erratic. My heart belonged to Royce, but I hurt for Macalister. He'd lost two wives, his company, his dream of sitting on the Federal Reserve . . . all he'd had or ever hoped to have, was gone. Not that he was blameless, but his fall into ruin was swift and harsh.

"I know it's irrelevant," he said, "but she was wrong." He

lifted his eyes to mine, and they were haunting. "Even monsters are capable of love, Medusa."

It added to the turmoil swirling inside me, but he'd said it with such a finality, it sounded like a goodbye.

The hallway door to the balcony swung open, and footsteps rang out. I glanced over my shoulder to see Macalister's assistant Nigel, who wore a somber expression as he took in the sight of us. "Paramedics and police just entered the building, sir."

Macalister nodded and reluctantly pulled away from me. When he let go of Royce, my husband set his right hand back on the wound to slow the bleeding and rose to his feet, towering over us. He extended his available hand out, offering to help his father up.

It was surreal to see these two men in bloody suits, who'd been sworn adversaries in the boardroom earlier, united now. I didn't know what the future held for any of us, but it gave me the tiniest glimmer of what could be.

TWENTY-TWO

Eighteen Months Later

LUCIFER WAS DETERMINED TO GET HIS BLACK HAIR ALL OVER my dress. It was more my fault than his. I'd finished getting ready early, and Royce was late as usual, so I'd lit a fire in the fireplace in the library and nestled into the cat's favorite chair to read while I waited.

At least the dress was dark. It was navy chiffon, with thin straps that held the top up and crisscrossed low on my back. There was a mini lint roller in my clutch too that I could use in the limo before we made our entrance to the HBHC Christmas party.

Lucifer's deep purr rumbled as I stroked his back, and he shifted in my lap, finding a more comfortable spot. He didn't bother lifting his head as footsteps came down the hall and Royce moved swiftly into the room.

"Hey, sorry." He already had his tie off and his fingers worked to undo the button at his collar. "I swear the L.A. branch loves to save their most important meetings for Friday afternoons."

I leaned forward, set my iPad on the side table beside the mythology chess set, and smiled. "How was your day?"

"Long." His intense gaze swept over me and heated as it lingered over my cleavage. "Better now."

Or perhaps it wasn't my cleavage he was staring at, but the deep emerald strands of my hair. I'd begun coloring it again a few months ago, but every time he looked at me, it was like he was seeing a long-lost love. It made breath hurry in and out of my lungs.

"How was yours?" he asked.

"It was . . . fine. I went to see him."

Royce's movements slowed. "Yeah? How is he?"

There wasn't an easy answer to my husband's simplistic question, but Macalister was tough. He was surviving.

There couldn't be a trial. He wouldn't allow any scandals to be aired in public, and no one needed to know how twisted and fucked up the Hales were. He took a plea deal to involuntary manslaughter and, given the circumstances of his emotional state following the contentious board meeting, the judge had been lenient in sentencing.

Two years.

It likely felt like a lifetime to Macalister. He was a man who craved control over all things, and he'd been forced to give it away. The state of Massachusetts now told him what to eat, what to wear, when to sleep. The first time I'd seen him in the shapeless khaki-colored uniform, I could barely speak.

He'd looked mortal, but even then, unbreakable. He was a man on the road to redemption, and he was determined to win.

I lifted a shoulder before answering Royce. "He's looking forward to coming home."

My husband nodded slowly. "What did you do?"

"We played chess and talked."

It was the same thing we'd done every time I'd gone to visit him over the last few months. He'd carried the prison's grimy chessboard over to our table, and we'd moved the pieces around the board, and I pretended like his life was all fine and normal.

I wasn't sure if it was a good idea. It made Royce uncomfortable, although he'd never said it outright. But Macalister had saved my life. He'd lost everything, and by giving him an hour with the illusion he had control, he told me I was saving his.

Royce picked the cat out of my lap and dropped him onto the window seat, encouraging Lucifer to find a new place to settle. "What'd you tell him?"

"I told him you were preparing for the annual shareholder meeting." A smile curled on my lips. "He had some thoughts on that."

Royce gave a dry chuckle. "I'm sure he did."

"And we talked about my job a little." I'd recently been promoted within HBHC and was on the fast track to become a benefits and compensation manager.

He leaned back against the edge of the desk. His tone was casual, as if he didn't really care, but I heard the interest beneath it. "Who won the chess match?"

"He did." I took in a breath as I remembered the moment Macalister had uttered *checkmate* and followed it up by telling me he suspected I'd let him win.

"I didn't," I'd lied. "I'll just have to come back next month and try again."

Macalister's blue eyes had flooded with relief.

I snapped out of the memory. "Oh, and my 'ridiculous' hair. He had some thoughts about that too."

Royce grinned as he straightened. He grabbed my hand, drew me to my feet, and twined his fingers in my hair, pulling firmly on the strands. "This hair isn't ridiculous. It's fucking perfect."

His mouth moved in, latching on to the side of my neck, and my eyes hooded at the sensation. I wanted to melt into him, and I tilted my head to give him better access, in direct opposition to the fake protest I gave. "We're already late."

"Whatever. I don't like parties." He echoed what he'd said to me the first time we'd been together in this room. "I'd rather stay here in the library with you."

He carved a path to my lips, and although his mouth was soft, his kiss wasn't. It was demanding and controlling. It didn't stay in one spot for long, though. His other hand curled into a ball on the skirt of my dress, ever-so-slowly dragging it up.

"If I put my hand up your skirt right now," he uttered against the shell of my ear, "would my fingers come away wet?"

Excitement coursed through me as we played the game, acting out the scene from years ago. "Find out," I challenged.

"Oh, don't worry." His gaze was arrogant and seductive. "I plan to."

I was nearly crushed to death under the weight of my

anticipation, but he drew it out. Once his hand was under the layers of my dress, he dragged his palm from one thigh to the other, sliding them over my legs but not touching me where I wanted him most.

A gasp punched from me as I was turned roughly and pushed against the nearby bookcase, so hard it rattled, and I had to brace my hands on a shelf. He sank his teeth into my bare back, not biting hard enough to leave a mark, only hard enough to make me weak with desire. This time he used both hands on my skirt, and it came up much faster.

"I'm going to fuck you under this dress."

I moaned my approval and pushed back against him, rubbing my ass over the erection building inside his pants. He reached around my body and slid his hand over the damp crotch of my panties.

His tone was wicked and triumphant. "What's this?"

He stroked again and again, provoking more moans from me, and my grip on the bookshelf was ferocious. I remembered all those desires from that night, and they swirled together with my need now. I wasn't the virgin I'd been back then, a lifetime ago. No one was going to come through the library door and disturb us, and even if they did, they wouldn't see Royce fooling around with *nobody* Marist Northcott. They'd find Royce with his wife and partner, who was Marist Hale on the outside and the fearsome Medusa inside.

Only he saw the real me, and I saw the real him, and I loved that about us.

"I want this," he growled as his fingers massaged and teased. "Give it to me."

"Yes," I cried.

And then we deviated from the script. His pants were undone in a rush, my panties yanked halfway down my legs, and he pushed inside me.

"Fuck," we groaned together.

His hand tangled in my seaweed colored hair and his other was on my hip, holding me steady as he began to thrust. It was rough and raw the way he fucked me, but it wasn't loveless. In fact, it was so full of love, it overflowed from us.

He gasped his love for me over the hissing fire and swore he'd never get enough. We'd be together until the end of time, a love of mythic proportions, that, despite all odds, had avoided a tragic end.

Ours was the only love story in the myths that I believed had a happy ending.

We were Persephone and Hades.

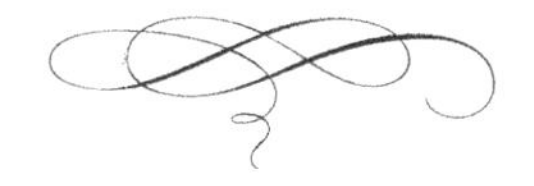

THANK YOU

First and foremost, thank you to my amazing husband, who should get story credit for this book. We spent many hours brainstorming the finale while we drove back and forth from the Nashville airport while traveling. I think we crafted 80% of this going to and from Book Bonanza 2019. When we returned from RARE London, I was only twenty thousand words into the book, which I suspected it would be eighty thousand (it was), and I was two weeks from deadline.

I am not a fast writer, y'all.

He was working a fulltime job, coming home and cooking dinner for the whole family, and let me disappear into the writer's cave for nearly three weeks to help me get it done. There is absolutely no way this book, or the series, would have been possible without him.

So, a huge THANK YOU to Nick. I love you so, so much!

Thank you to Andrea Lefkowitz, who was my story editor, beta reader, and cheerleader. Her invaluable notes and support kept me from throwing my hands up in the air and letting Macalister take over.

A big thanks to my writer support group of Nana Malone, Kennedy Ryan and Willow Winters for offering advice and laughs. ("I'm so behind on goals I offered Pacemaker a thousand words and a hand job.")

Thank you to Veronica Larsen for her supportive chats, brainstorming, and being a great friend.

Thanks for everything to Nisha Sharma ("I need hot daddy."), and Sierra Simone ("Hey, fuck you for the ending of THE OBSESSSION!").

Thank you to Lori Whitwam for editing the piecemeal, Frankenstein manuscript I sent her, which was also three days late, and somehow she made it work. I love you, don't ever leave me!

Thank you to my publicist, the priceless Nina Grinstead. She talked me out of bad titles and covers and into all the things that helped give this series the spark it needed.

THANK YOU to you, reader, for sticking with me through to the end. When I sat down to write the first book, I didn't know if anyone was going to like what I was crafting, but I have been blown away by the responses. Writing this series was . . . *magical.* I don't know another word to describe it, and it was the readers who made it happen. Your support and enthusiasm for these books has been nothing short of amazing, and I am so humbled and grateful. Thank you from the bottom of my black, twisted heart.

OTHER BOOKS BY NIKKI SLOANE

THE BLINDFOLD CLUB SERIES

It Takes Two

Three Simple Rules

Three Hard Lessons

Three Little Mistakes

Three Dirty Secrets

Three Sweet Nothings

Three Guilty Pleasures

One More Rule

THE SORDID SERIES

Sordid

Torrid

Destroy

SPORTS ROMANCE

The Rivalry

THE NASHVILLE NEIGHBORHOOD

The Doctor

The Pool Boy

The Architect

FILTHY RICH AMERICANS

The Initiation | The Obsession | The Deception

ABOUT THE AUTHOR

Nikki Sloane fell into graphic design after her careers as a waitress, a screenwriter, and a ballroom dance instructor fell through. For eight years she worked for a design firm in that extremely tall, black, and tiered building in Chicago that went through an unfortunate name change during her time there.

Now she lives in Kentucky, is married and has two sons. She is a three-time Romance Writers of America RITA© Finalist, also writes romantic suspense under the name Karyn Lawrence, and couldn't be any happier that people enjoy reading her sexy words.

Website: www.NikkiSloane.com

Made in United States
Orlando, FL
06 January 2025

56963962R00200